White Rose Witches

In Silence and Shadows

by

Georgie St-Claire

Cover design by Castenzio Cusumano
Cusumano Designs Ltd

Interior design by BAD PRESS iNK

ISBN: 978-1-0687203-0-7

published by www.badpress.ink

Dedicated to my husband for unfailing patience, kindness and having all our ducks in a row. Not forgetting my teenagers who are funny, amazing, infuriatingly stubborn, and know how to keep me in the real world.

To the book-filled childhood I shared with my sister. My memories are of libraries, reading, and believing in our dreams.

4500 BCE

Every good fairy tale starts with Once Upon a Time.

Once upon a time there was an island surrounded by smaller islands where an abundance of rainfall produced forests, fens, grasslands, crags, marshes, and moors. On this island the predator had turned prey, lured into the chalked circle at the top of the cliffs. Below, the sea viciously sprayed salt water on the rocks and lapped at a beach filled with wooden boats. Men and women of strong fighter strength came from their hiding places, swords in their hands, to view the slight woman. She had amber and tin beads around her upper arms that reflected the northern sunset behind them, a black stone necklace of properties they couldn't determine, and a dress woven of what they would later describe as shimmering spider threads. Surrounded and outnumbered, her chin tilted, her head held high, her hair was both brown and blonde, as if designed by the gods of these islands to camouflage her in the forests. It shimmered in the late daylight. She raised her hands, palms out, to show them she didn't intend to hurt.

'It doesn't need to be this way,' she told them, in their native language rather than her own.

'The Order of Vidar is committed to wiping out those who intend to hurt others.'

1

'Isn't that what you're doing to me? Hurting me?'

'You come from the Isles, the place of magic and monsters. You weld powers and traditions from all over into the very fabric of your green lands until it feeds you as food.'

'And yet, still you come here in your anger to conquer and oppress, and when you cannot, you vanquish us.'

'You can renounce your power and live.' A man with summer blue eyes stepped forward, his grip on his sword so tight his knuckles were white, a freshly inked symbolic axe visible on his arm.

'As a slave to you, Eric's son? Or worse, a gift to your father who tried to get me himself only this summer? I'd rather die. But I'll die knowing this; our descendants will be together and will raise a family, Anders, son of Eric. Your blood and mine will forever be mixed from that point forward. Your descendants will wield the magic of these lands as their fate.'

His jaw tightened and he raised a strong muscle-bound arm that held his sword as he lunged forward into the circle. Around them, on the wind, came the sound of childish, playful, ethereal laughter. His sword sliced through the air. The woman was gone.

Chapter 1

Creaking branches arched over old trees. A strong breeze rustled through her brown wavy hair causing Evie to look up, her thoughts centred around how long she had until the rain started to fall. The last thing she wanted was to turn up at her children's school drenched. She wasn't a child anymore, she had a carefully crafted image to maintain, one that her television studio constantly reminded her about, and insisted upon her continuing to present outside the studio. She had to look put together at all times in public. It had been a long learning process for Evie, raised without even the bare minimal guidance from her physically present-but-eternally-absent parents.

Through the woodland canopy of the still green early autumn leaves, warm grey clouds were starting to gather. She could still see blue patches in the sky. Evie scrambled down the bank with grace, the wildness of her childhood briefly surfacing through her polished veneer, and ended in a ditch that ran close to the entire length of the public footpath and brushed the dry, fallen, dusty skeletal remains of last winter's leaves aside. Underneath that natural compost damp soil met her hand.

Inky liquid warmed her hand, coiling around her bare skin like a futuristic fluid bracelet. She struggled to control it and shook her hand in the air, still focused entirely on the damp soil. Certain that she was alone, Evie cleared the topsoil away from the bank and placed her palm directly onto the soil underneath. It was cold, but not wet, not quite dry, but she definitely had a problem. She walked further, checking the ditch the same way at intervals. She was lost in her own thoughts about the soil as she examined the level of damp in it. The forested area used to be a wet woodland but someone, at some point, had messed it up. Liquid ink dripped from her fingertips at unnoticed intervals causing tiny green shoots to emerge behind her in the ditch as though it was a warm spring day.

Evie could feel the soft pulsing under her feet in a quiet relaxed welcome from the trees. She wished she could spend winter cosily resting instead of the relentless merry go round she was stuck on of filming, farming, and primary school demands. She edged her way further along the ditch, acutely aware that she might be a distance away from the public footpath that dog walkers used but it wasn't unknown for the villagers to stray from paths. She couldn't suddenly fix her problem with her gift, as much as she wanted the whole issue to be resolved. There would be paperwork to complete, people to talk to, footpaths to assess. If she could just use her gift and claim it happened naturally then only her brother would know the truth. The villagers would gossip, but they always had, and reality told the world that witches with power to flood the woods didn't exist. She would defend that false statement until her last breath.

She didn't dare use her gift though. If it had just been her brother and herself who had to endure the village gossip she would go ahead. For the sake of her children being able to have friends, she had to conform. The village was their home too, and unlike her own childhood, her children seemed to be accepted by their peers.

'Are you supposed to be in the ditch?' A male voice shook her from her own world back into the reality she lived in. The Australian accent surprised her. Yorkshire had tourists, but not as many international ones as London or the south, certainly never in the ancient woodland that was technically hers. She guiltily pushed her hands into the pockets of her quilted jacket in the hope that he hadn't noticed the liquid dancing around her hands and fingers. She looked up through lowered lashes.

His work boots were so scuffed she could see the steel toe caps. She liked that. The worn look. The little hole in the tracksuit bottoms, the washed out, well-worn hoody; she found the rebellious casual look sexy. She'd never been one for smart clothes or men in suits. A small black German Shepherd pup was wagging its tail at the end of the lead. He kept a tight hold of the lead and struggled as the puppy pulled forward. A weather worn face looked back at her, heavily tanned from the summer. His bright blue eyes reminded her of endless summer skies, her favourite time of year. Evie suppressed a smile as she watched him wrangle the stubborn puppy into a sitting position with the promise of a treat. He was gentle. Once he had his puppy under control he returned to his original question: 'Are you supposed to be in the ditch?'

'Yes.'

'Do you need a hand?'

'I can check my land alone, but thanks.' She turned away to end the conversation, startled by the fact that she had actually almost smiled spontaneously. That was not how Evie Hepburn behaved. She couldn't get a reputation for being nice.

'I meant getting out. Aren't these public woods?' He didn't let her off easily when he called out after her.

'Actually, they belong to my farm.'

'Ah, you're that farmer. The one that bought the McGregors out when they went bankrupt because one farm wasn't enough.'

The way he said it told her much more than she needed to know. The old villagers didn't let things go, grudges died hard in Yorkshire and they'd held one against her ever since she was born. They were the reason she learnt to pretend words were water off a duck's back with a smile and a casual attitude, just like she did now.

'Is the village still talking about that?' She fixed a mask in place and looked up with a smile that told the world she didn't care.

'Very much so.'

'And I'm the witch for buying them out?'

'From the way they talk I'd say so.'

'Would they rather a developer had the land for housing?'

'Maybe so.' He looked amused at her exasperated sigh. In frustration she flipped her carefully styled brown hair to the side. Recognition hit him with that gesture. His eyes widened as he exclaimed, 'You're Evie Hepburn!'

'I am.' She flipped her hair onscreen whenever she was annoyed. She knew that there was a drinking game around the gesture, and it was all her fault. She flipped her hair when right wing political comments were made because she had to keep a blank face.

'Why are you getting dirty in a ditch in the woods instead of, I don't know, drinking cocktails in the city?'

The reference to her other persona caused irritation

to rise up ready to lash out in a sarcastic remark. She bit it down with bitterness and took a deep breath, pulling forward a professional smile. It came easily now. She'd been practising hiding who she really was her whole life; a quick smile, dead eyes, an internal alarm reminder that she'd been foolish enough to sign a contract that demanded control of her image.

Evie replied, 'I do enjoy a cocktail. However, we're working to get the woods back to their original wetland habitat for wildlife. They were dried out by the McGregors or their predecessors years ago.'

'Aside from being on TV, you're a what? An ecology expert?'

'I'm a qualified ecologist,' she replied casually, as her eyes moved from him to the low sun, guessing the time from its position in the sky, 'I'm done for the day anyway. I have to pick my children up from school.'

'Here.' He held out his hand to help her. The cuff of his sleeve rode up slightly, enough for her to see the tiniest edge of bold tattoos around his wrist.

The sides of the bank came as high as her shoulders and were vertical. She didn't see even the slightest hint of a slope. Evie accepted his hand. His palm was sandpaper rough against her own. In a quick move he pulled her up with more strength than she had anticipated. She barely managed to stay upright, bracing herself with a hand on his chest to stop her from falling. A waft of freshly washed clothes hit her. Her favourite smell. She stopped herself from breathing in.

'Sorry,' she muttered, apologising for almost falling on top of him.

His eyes might have widened a tiny fraction and he

looked like he was fighting a smile. She took her hand from his chest and looked down. He released her other hand without hesitation. She pretended to dust her jeans down from specks of dirt to control the sudden rise in her pulse, and pull her bitch face back on instead of the crazy grin she wanted to give him.

'Thanks. You work outdoors.' It was supposed to be phrased as a question, but her brain and her mouth worked separately, and it came out as a statement. She kicked herself for that.

'I'm a builder. Construction.'

'What do you build?'

'Anything and everything. Houses, warehouses, offices.' He shrugged.

'So, if I was looking to get two houses and two small cabins built who would I get a recommendation from?' She turned to walk back to the farm, towards the edge of the woods. He walked with her. He kept the puppy at his side.

'You could try the rugby club. We did that four, almost five years ago now. I can give you a list of more recent customers.'

'I'll speak to the rugby club. If it's still standing despite their antics, then I guess you could keep a house upright.'

'You know the rugby club?' He sounded surprised that she did. Evie noticed that his left eyebrow raised a little in cynicism.

'A few went to my school.'

'Matt? Garrett? It's not hard to figure out the posh ones.'

'Do you know them?' She was surprised that he knew names if he'd only built the club.

'We played on the same local Sunday team for years.'

'Played?' she caught the past tense. The fact that he had played rugby explained his physique. She had noticed it. She needed to stop noticing it.

'Too old, too many injuries.' He shook his head as he spoke, a touch of regret in his voice. He offered a smile, a genuine one that made his whole face light up, his eyes crinkled with deep lines etched from hours outdoors, 'I'm Robbie Anderson. Of Anderson Builders.'

'Nice to meet you.'

'Where are you building these houses?'

'In the farmyard. You can demolish buildings too, right? The old farmhouse and outbuildings are going.'

'You're taking down the historic farmhouse? That's what—' He stopped himself from saying the last words.

Evie knew what he had been going to say. They left the sheltered canopy of the woodland. At the same time the last of the struggling sunlight disappeared, casting them out of the warmth and into the shade. Clouds started to gather thickly, growing in greyness as the wind picked up. Evie glanced up before she spoke, guessing how much longer she had before the onslaught of the rain, and balancing it against the distance left to walk. Far too much of her childhood and teenage years had been spent in damp clothing on the farm. She brushed the comment off as they walked down the narrow lane.

'That's the current talking point of the villagers and another reason why I'm the witch and the outcast. Yes. We have planning permission despite their prejudice, petitions, and endless objections.'

'We?' a hint of doubt lingered in his voice, a slight acknowledgement that she might have someone back at the farm.

'My brother. My brother and I own the farm.' Not that she needed to clarify her living situation to someone she had just met, but a small part of her wanted to.

'What do they have against you and your brother?'

'I never cared enough to ask.' Practised insouciance littered her tone.

She knew very well what the born and bred locals had against her and why. They lived in The Witch House, an aptly named house for someone with her gift. The nickname for the house had been around longer than she had lived in it. True locals spoke of it in hushed whispers and gave each word a capital letter, incomers picked up on the name but didn't give it the same reverence. To people like Robbie, it was simply the witch house.

'That's the farmhouse?' Robbie nodded over to the right as they reached a gated entrance off the narrow lane. There was nothing majestic or glamorous about her home.

Ancient dry stone walls lined the grass verges, separating the farm boundary from the lane that flowed down the gentle slope into the village below. Huge stone boulders weathered out of shape sat as gateposts, their tops flat, the vaguest suggestion that they might once have held more stone above. A worn out grit and dirt driveway that might have been impressive once led to her old and gloomy farmhouse which imposed itself upon its surroundings, foreboding and full of contempt. A crack in one pane of glass in the upper windows ran from one corner diagonally, its serrated edges throwing out an invitation to imagine the horrors that could lay beyond. Her muscles stiffened when she saw the house, the tightness coiled around her as it always did. It had never felt like a home, just a house she had been dumped in.

10

'The farm is doing well then?' He looked at the farmhouse.

'The shops are.'

'Ah, yes, your shops and café. They're always busy.' He gave a nod, as though he had used them himself.

Eight years ago she had made the decision to invest heavily in a quadrant of shops where the old stables and field had stood. She didn't ride horses, and her brother didn't want people freely crossing his land on horseback. It hadn't made sense to keep the stables or rent them out to people. Instead, Evie had created a series of farm shops. The cobbled courtyard was idyllically nostalgic of rose-tinted days gone by, a calculated move on her part, helped enormously by cheerful erigeron daisies in milk churns, a subtle reminder to everyone that their produce was as local as any middle-class country homemaker could ever wish for.

'Why not use the builder who built the shops?' He pushed his free hand into the front pouch of his hoody. Evie was hit with an urge to stand closer to him. She backed away, putting some distance between them.

'He retired. It was his last job. I have to go.' Evie took her hands out of her pockets to open the gate. She started to walk away then hesitated. She turned, stopped, turned around and bounced her hand on the gate a couple of times as she said, 'I'll ask Garrett for a recommendation.' She walked away.

Chapter 2

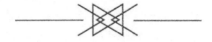

Her brother carried a bottle of his favourite red wine and two glasses into the room. He ducked under the dark wood doorframe that Evie walked through easily. At six foot seven he towered over most people and filled the width of the old doorway easily. He could have been a professional rugby player, but he'd refused that chance, not even playing on the Sunday team with his best friend, Garrett. Those type of things had required a parental presence and they had never had that. It had been their secret to carry silently.

Evie pulled a heavy wooden door to, from an adjoining room and left it ajar. The wood was worn and skewed from age and she never closed it properly. Atlas peeked in the door across from her to another smaller adjoining room, glancing at her daughter's sleeping form, as restless in sleep as she was in life. He gave her a nod to indicate that Rey was finally asleep. She threw a glance behind her at her almost sleeping son and put a finger on her lips, an indication that he was still awake.

Evie had taken over the large suite after arriving back home with a toddler and a baby. The main middle room had become a playroom and sitting room, and the two smaller rooms off it turned into bedrooms. Her own room was just across the landing. Atlas began setting up the chess board near the large antique fireplace. He threw another log on the fire. Flames rose up angrily inside the ancient fireplace to eat the wood inside it hungrily. The house seemed to have been positioned with the sole intention of being as cold and as dark as possible inside. It was angled so that the front faced north west, and the back faced south east. There was no central heating. Evie was already wearing white fleece loungewear and lounge socks. She was colder inside the house than out of it, every day.

Two worn velvet accent chairs, once an ugly deep mustard shade were now draped with teal fleece blankets. Atlas dragged the table with the game board on, and then the chairs, nearer to the fire. Toys lay scattered around. Evie picked them up on her walk across the room, depositing them in a series of plastic tubs that sat in a white frame. That piece of furniture contrasted vibrantly against the dark polished woods and antique furniture pieces they had inherited with the house. Once the floor was cleared, she picked up the rugs and threw them over the white frame. They both sat but neither spoke until the wine was poured.

'How did it go today?' Her brother asked. Straight to the point.

'The waterways are blocked but it's not going to be expensive to fix. Even cheaper if you let me do it my way, mid-winter, after a lot of rain.' She picked up the wine glass but didn't drink from it, waiting for a response.

'Did anyone see you?' The question had serious undertones that only she would understand. Even in the privacy of their home her brother wouldn't directly refer to their gifts.

'I didn't do anything today. I only surveyed. Funny you

13

should say that though because I might have found a builder.' She passed her phone over to Atlas, an internet browser page open on Anderson Builders, exactly where she had left it an hour ago after looking up the company whilst her children cleaned their teeth.

'Where did you hear about these?' He perused the page with interest. His body relaxed with the potential of one of their issues being resolved. Evie took that as a sign and took a sip of the red wine her brother had chosen.

Summer warmed fruits hit her first, sending memories of nights outside, late sunsets, and easy living. She breathed in the scent deeply and let the sensation of her favourite season pass. Her brother's hobby was wine. Although they produced a good farm cider from their orchards, he preferred a wine, each one chosen carefully. This one was relaxed and mellow. She took another sip and let it warm her. Evie answered his question, 'I met one of them in the woods. That one.' She moved the screen with her fingers to enlarge it and pointed Robbie out from the family picture.

'I'd need to meet him.'

'You mean you need to judge him.'

'Yes.'

'They're local.'

'How do you know?'

'Check out the business address. It's the old Oak Hall.'

'They bought the old school house?'

'It was a house before it became a school so we probably shouldn't say that. There's renovation pictures. It looks like a lovely home now.'

Evie showed her brother the pictures. The old-fashioned house they remembered as being their school was now a light-filled spacious home with a pool table, a modern kitchen and large seating area in a fun open-plan style. The page told them that the family had created a seven-bedroomed house. The home was everything she had craved since she was little.

'I'll call them.' He sent the page to his own phone, and moved his pawn to start the game, his fingers grasping the tiny figure over its face and moving it.

Atlas always went first in any games they played. It had always been she who wanted to play. He would have been fine doing homework extensions or extra farm paperwork. She had been the one to push at the kitchen table for a game. At five, six, and seven years of age, she had been too young for the wordy volumes in the inherited library and so she granted him the first move as a bribe. He was four years older than her and she already saw that his shoulders were burdened with the responsibility of the farm due to their negligent, absent parents. Even back then she knew that he had other preferences. Homework extensions were a big thing for him, something that he had forced her to undertake too. His justification had been, 'They'll think we have parents if we turn in extra work.' She moved her pawn up against her brother's, her fingers gently grasping the pointed hat and ears. They played with the set he had bought her for her sixteenth birthday.

Evie had bought her brother a Greek gods figure chess set for his eighteenth birthday in honour of his name. Her friend Genevieve had patiently painted each figure for her, either gold and black, or green and white for the money vs nature theme she had designed. The colours were still present and bold years later. He had gifted her a pale blue and nickel set for her sixteenth birthday with a card that

15

said she was too old for the fairy tales she still indulged in. The nickel pawns were goblins, the other pieces mishappen villains and monsters. Her knights were wolves with ravens sat on their backs, her rooks were worthy of being a Princess's prison. The blue pieces stood proud as beautiful fairy figures, human heroes and mythical animals.

'He used to play rugby with Garrett. You could ask him if they're safe people to be around.' Evie recalled their conversation for her brother. Atlas's eyes focused on her whilst she explained then gave a nod as an answer as he moved another piece. He pulled out his phone and typed out what she assumed would be a message to Garrett. She moved another goblin.

They drank the wine slowly and played the game in companiable silence, the crackle of the fire the only sound in the room. Neither of them were big talkers. Years of growing up together through hunger and neglect, hiding their truth and pretending they were fine resulted in a knowledge that words didn't cover the gulf between how they were used and the deeper meaning behind. She studied her brother's face as the game progressed. It was when he poured himself another large glass of wine half-way through the slow thoughtful game she finally spoke, 'What is it that's bothering you?' she had to pick her moments with Atlas. He shut off and shut down quicker than she did, and she was quick. He preferred to soldier on alone rather than share or talk. She wasn't sure if *preferred* was the term. Taught. Raised. Isolated. Conditioned. They would all be better descriptions of her brother's inability to talk or trust.

'I found a drawing in the back of a cupboard, a seven-pointed star. You know the stuff Genevieve liked to draw, it had names on each point. You, Liberty, Gia, Genevieve, Nina, Tess and Kat.'

'V.V always drew seven-pointed stars. In was in all our birthday cards and Christmas cards, she'd doodle them everywhere.'

'It's not just that though.' He passed her the picture. The paper was the same thick, expensive sketching paper that brought all her memories of V.V drawing flooding back. This was far from the doodles that she was used to seeing. It was partly smudged where it had been folded and pressed up against something but she could make out the leaves on her point, the fire on V.V's point, the gold coin on Liberty's, but the rest was blurred and faded. There was half an edge of something that looked like a demon face on Gia's point.

'Did you ever think that maybe she was like us? She was into all that mystical stuff even back then. I might have been too harsh in shutting it all down. I could have listened more.'

'She used to talk about growing things when doing my tarot card readings. She'd talk about how seeds start in the darkness of the earth, and more stuff about darkness. But to be honest we were teenage girls, Atlas, all we wanted to hear was bright futures and music-filled hot weather summers. Why is it bothering you now?'

'Probably because we've grown up and I see the situation differently.'

'We can't change what is done. I'm more angry at our parents now than I was as a child. I look at my children and wonder how they could ignore that we existed. We were babies. We deserved food and love.'

'I'm angry about that too. I see you trying so hard to

17

be everything that they weren't. You're the kindest, sweetest mum to those kids. It doesn't make me feel any better about their father who never shows up.' A glance up to his angry face showed that he still detested her ex-husband.

Evie didn't speak up to defend her ex. Her hurt still ran deep. It might have been a teenage relationship, it might have been a young marriage, but he had let her down and hurt her. His partying she could take, he'd been a party person when they had met, and so had she. She had needed him, and he had ignored her calls and pleas to come home that night she was rushed to hospital. In the years since she had left him their contact had diminished to letters from lawyers. He never asked about his children. She took another drink of her wine.

'Going back to the builder...?' Evie changed the topic. Her ex-husband managed to find out about every conversation she had that concerned him. In those early messy days when he tried to get her back, he had thrown his knowledge of her private conversations in her face.

'The kids need somewhere to call home, and this was never a home. Not for us, not for them. I don't want them teased about living in the haunted witch house like we were.'

'We're definitely in agreement to go ahead with the architect's plans? I can't wait.' She relaxed into the chair as she sipped her wine, the warmth of the flames finally hitting her, hope dancing her heart as she dreamed of a more modern home.

'Don't go staying up too late looking at pictures of other people's homes. Remember you chose the architect because you love her work and she's done everything for you to create the home you want.'

'And yours.' Evie let her brother top up her wine. His phone pinged. Evie took her turn with her Ice Queen.

'Garrett's in the pub with him now. He says he'd trust any of the three brothers to date his little sister. Funny, because I didn't ask that. And he doesn't have a little sister.' The last two sentences weren't directed at her but typed quickly into his phone as a response to his friend.

Their new houses, two detached properties sharing a large Mediterranean style courtyard, offset with two small one-bedroomed self-contained cabins had been customised to their needs and desires. Her brother had wanted something more traditionally English than she had. Their architect had been extremely clever in how she'd prised colours from her brother and provided deep rich heritage style rooms that flowed seamlessly. By contrast, hers was more Parisienne apartment glamour, light and elegant; even her bedroom had a balcony so she could enjoy summer evenings on school nights. Three years ago when the architect had started to draft the house for her, Max and Rey had been clingy at bedtime. She hadn't been allowed to leave their suite. The habit of her brother coming in for a game of chess and a drink of wine stemmed from those clingy years.

Hidden in a corner hole a tiny mouse stared up at the scene, its sensitive ears picking up every part of the conversation.

Chapter 3

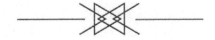

Evie had her quilt and an extra throw over her even though a fire blazed in her bedroom. The quilt, a new mattress, and pillows were among the few basic home essentials she had allowed herself whilst building up the farm enterprises and saving to build the new houses. It was a deliberate choice, the more she was surrounded by the antique possessions her parents had sparsely furnished the farmhouse with, or more likely inherited the farmhouse with, the more it motivated her to dream of clean lines in a new house. An ugly antique bedside lamp cast a glow over the room. A threadbare rug, once beautiful and expensive in an earlier century, surrounded the antique four poster bed she was in. Her tablet was lit up in front of her with access to hundreds of pictures of people's interiors that they had chosen to share. On her other bedside table a white scented candle in frosted glass sent notes of bergamot towards her.

She glanced outside, she always slept with her curtains open. She needed to see the trees and open fields to be able to breathe. Brown cardboard boxes were stacked and hastily piled near the window, labelled in thick black letters as to their destination. Most were for the skips that were coming. An auction house was booked to pick apart their furniture and pieces that could be sustainably repackaged for someone's home. Apart from their clothes, chess sets, and her children's toys, almost every item was going, she didn't care where so long as she never had to see it again. Even the thought of losing the antique furniture made her lighter. She wanted nothing from the house. Evie hated the farmhouse, her parents and the way the locals gossiped. Her past weighed down on her. She didn't want its heritage. She was Evie, not Evelyn Hepburn that lived in The Witch House. It would be the real beginning of her life when the farmhouse had gone and she was in her new home.

A knock on her bedroom door made her look up. Atlas opened the door tentatively, his eyes closed, 'Are you decent?'

'Kind of. What's happened?' Her brother at her bedroom door usually meant a farm emergency. Her shoulder muscles tensed as her thoughts jumped to skipping sleep yet again.

'I was clearing the library out. The grey lady is back. I think she's real.' He was whispering. Evie jumped out of bed and picked up her winter robe, a floor length black fleece with a hood. She pulled the hood up and opened the door.

'Let's get the bitch.'

They walked silently along the corridors of the farmhouse. Halfway down the wide carved wooden staircase they saw the figure. As children they had been terrified of the spectre that floated around their house in the dark. After their parents had left, they had begun to suspect that the spectre was a person, but after chasing her a few times she had returned less and less. They stalled on the stairs as one creaked beneath Atlas's bulk. The spectre turned her face slowly to them, black eyes met theirs. There was no white, only blackness filled her eyes.

Her heart beat fiercely inside her and her instincts told her to go to her children. Despite the fear that wanted to freeze her, Evie pushed through and raced down the stairs, followed by her brother. The spectre froze as though the siblings' onslaught was unexpected, then turned and fled into the kitchen and through the unlocked kitchen door. Evie chased outside after her, her thoughts only focused on the small gap between her and the figure, a gap that she could close. Atlas caught her arm and pulled her back. His strength made her stop. She turned to face him, yanking her arm free from his grasp, anger coursing through her at his interference. She knew she could have reached her and outrun her this time.

'Don't leave the children alone.' They were his only words. She understood his protectiveness, but the wildness inside her still raged and longed to be free to run fast over the fields in chase of the spectre.

'I'd be protecting them better by getting her.'

Inside the kitchen Atlas locked the door carefully and wedged a wooden kitchen chair up against the handle. Evie raced upstairs to her children. Without waking them she checked carefully, they were in a normal sleep, unmarked by the incident. She went back to her brother. He was waiting for her at the bottom of the stairs; without a word he indicated for her to follow him. They walked down the hall with its blood-red carpet and nineteen eighties burnt orange flower pattern to the old library room. Inside her cotton-lined pockets Evie found navy fingerless gloves, a reminder that only two nights ago she had been up late sorting out another room. Fully focused on finding a builder and preparing to move out they had divided the house rooms between them to sort out, she'd gotten the most used ones. She imagined that her brother could breeze through his allocated rooms, that they would be almost empty aside from bits of furniture.

In the library the fire had burnt itself out and the cold was creeping its tendrils back into the room. Small lamps were lit on the walls, casting a glow into the room. Even in here, the rugs were old and threadbare. Their library was virtually bereft of the volumes they remembered from their childhood. Once their parents had moved out and left them alone, at sixteen and twelve years of age, they had burnt most of the books; old, outdated, non-fiction volumes, as kindling over the years. They used this room so rarely that black mould had crept up the walls from lack of heat.

'What were you doing in here? Don't you get up stupidly early?' Evie asked her brother. He pulled a face, then gave a shrug.

'I couldn't sleep. I thought I'd check the library since it's on my list of rooms to clear. I found this already open. I think she was after something in here. Mum and Dad—' He stretched out his arm to a bookcase, a dusty, empty bookcase.

Evie interrupted, irritated, 'I couldn't care less about them. I hope they rot in hell.' She wanted to ask why he couldn't sleep but Atlas was reaching out for something on the bare wall and distracted her with the movement.

'I found this.' Atlas moved a large bookshelf. It swung outwards. Evie saw the dirt and dust trail from years of build-up. It only reminded her that they had to step up their cleaning routines. Atlas used a torch to shine light into the space. Behind the bookshelf was a small room with a corridor leading off. It would have been a secret passage, a servants' passage, except her thoughts weren't on the historical use but at the strange peculiarity in front of her.

She stared at the human sized skull with two stag horns, some kind of once vibrant vine draped around it which was now reduced to a single thread, the numerous burnt candles on top of the layer of wax suggesting previously burnt candles and the gold plate with dried flowers. On the adjacent walls another two skulls were mounted on the wall, a stag skull with full antlers, and a skull carving of a green man which had to be fake. All along the walls hung garlands of faded dried flowers. Evie recognised through the shapes of faded petals roses, canterbury bells, small buttercup and daisy garlands, and pine garlands; there were thorns she recognised as hawthorn, corncockle garlands, cow parsley wreaths. She breathed in deeply, 'Our parents left in August, didn't they? They must have done this.'

'We're looking at some sort of cultish devil worship and you're identifying flowers?' His look of disbelief and frustration was one that she had seen a fair few times before, normally over her love of fairy tales.

'Look at the green man, it's a nature symbol. Is that oak?' She realised it wasn't a skull when Atlas's torch was on it, but bleached wood. It cast an eerie similarity in tone to the bone skulls.

'Yeah.'

'Then it's the green man.'

'And this?' Atlas swung his torch to the stag skull.

'The garlands and vines make me think of Cernunnos.'

'And this?' He shone the final light on the human skull with horns.

Evie shook her head. She reached up to feel the vines. 'Another representation of Cernunnos maybe. Although I'm thinking if it's nature worship this should be a female. I'm certain these are bindweed. The flowers, garlands; it all says it's some sort of nature worship. Given that they were crap farmers... is that a bowl of dried blood!' she exclaimed. Underneath the mounted skulls ran a ledge that held fallen flowers, candlesticks, candle stubs, and a gold bowl that had a suspicious dried brown substance Evie instantly recognised.

'Looks like it.' Atlas had seen as much blood as she had in farming. It didn't faze him.

Their parents had forsaken the farm, and watched as it fell to ruin. They had barely ever left the house. Once Evie had started school they slowly retreated to their bedroom, neglecting their children more and more. Atlas and Evie were used to looking after themselves.

'At least your obsession with fairy tales has finally come in useful identifying myths. They weren't worshipping nature for a bountiful harvest though.' Her brother surveyed the mess with displeasure written across his face. Evie's thoughts joined his in an attempt to try and form an argument for nature worship on the evidence in front of them, illuminated by his torch and her phone.

'If our parents did this it wasn't for the farm's benefit. They only cared about themselves,' she finally spoke, unable to reach any conclusion that didn't involve provoking a rise out of her brother by mentioning witches.

'We have to dismantle this and get rid of it before the builders come in. We can't give them evidence to fuel the rumour that we live in the witch house.'

Atlas started to take the skulls off the walls and toss

them out into the library in a mix of anger and frustration. From behind one of the skulls a photo fell to the ground. He picked it up, looked at it carefully then passed it to Evie. Even as she took it her fingers felt the bindweed before she saw it under the torchlight. It wasn't bound well, she pulled the bindweed from the photo.

The photo was one of her and her friends in Genevieve's perfect garden. Evie thought she had lost her copy of it. Her parents had taken it from her room. Atlas moved another skull and more photographs tumbled out, again each one wrapped in bindweed. They took the bindweed off every photo; photos of her and Atlas over the years, always taken at a distance, always unaware of the photographer. Not once had their parents even asked them to pose for a picture. Evie had whole boxes of framed pictures of her children throughout their lives, waiting to go into the new house.

Evie's hands warmed up with every piece of bindweed they removed. She kept quiet about the soft burning fire in her palms. When Atlas disappeared to get bin bags from the kitchen to dump the altar into, she took some time to really have a good look around. She brushed aside some faded petals to find another bound photograph. Underneath the photograph was a familiar black envelope with a red seal. Her hand visibly trembling at the sight, Evie forced deep practised breaths to calm herself. She picked it up and tucked it into her pocket, checking behind her that her brother wasn't back in the room. She tore the bindweed from a photograph to distract herself and found herself looking at a chubby three-year-old Atlas, a dog next to him and ducks all around, wild birds sat on the ground as though he was feeding them and he had a robin in his open palm as well as a broad smile on his face. She had never seen him smile like that.

'What have you found?' her brother's voice behind her.

Evie passed him the photograph. He took his time studying it. She watched the expressions cross his face, confusion, uncertainty, regret, then a smile.

'You OK?'

'Yeah, it's nice to see I always felt at home on the farm. I understand why they'd bind a picture of you, if this voo-doo witchcraft thing they had going on could somehow suppress your gift. But why me?'

'Don't you get it?' she asked softly. Atlas looked at her, the uncertainty in his eyes revealed that he didn't understand.

'You have a gift too. Look at how the animals behave around you. When did you ever have to put all your weight against a cow to get it to move? Animals instinctively know what you want from them. I think our parents knew. If they knew how to do all this there might be some truth in this being the witch house.' Atlas looked around the little secret room, shaking his head slowly.

'Unlike you I always felt sort of safe here. I knew it wasn't much, except a solid roof over our heads. What if they left because we scared them?'

'We didn't scare them. They didn't love us. They were seventeen when they had you, Atlas. Some grandparent gifted them the farm to live on. They had trust funds and boarding schools and an upbringing only the very privileged get. They just left us. They decided they wanted sunshine and left. They took my dream and made it theirs.'

That was the driving force behind her anger towards

27

her parents. Their desertion of their children and the farm had not happened because they had an idea or a passion, but because they had taken their daughter's dream and decided to live it. Without her.

'Not quite your dream. You wanted a crop farm and vineyard in the South of France.'

'I wanted sunshine and warm weather. Farming was all I knew how to make a living from back then,' she answered softly.

'Do you ever look them up on the internet?'

'No.' She hadn't even thought to. They'd been absent even when they were living in the same house. She'd rarely seen them. Her days were full enough without hankering after distant parents.

'I do. They have three more children. A girl, she's seventeen, and two boys, fourteen and eleven. They all go to a boarding school in Switzerland.'

'At least they learnt a little from their mistakes with us. Send your kids to private day school and you have to feed them at home.'

There had been too many nights when they'd fed themselves, and far too many mornings of making their way to school on empty stomachs. Atlas had taught her basic cookery skills after he'd caught her forcing the wild blackberry bush to grow fruit in midwinter so that she could eat, she hadn't even been four years old. She knew because he'd explained that when she started school she could eat at school.

'They have staff too. Another mistake they learnt from. They still don't lift a finger.'

'Let's clear this and get to bed.' She was anxious to read the card inside the black envelope, but she hadn't let her brother know about the death threats she had been receiving for a few years. He didn't need something else to worry about.

They cleared the altar in amicable silence, making sure that the entire secret room was so empty it echoed. Atlas left the black bags in the middle of the library, 'We'll burn it all tomorrow night.'

'I can make hot dogs or burgers. Max and Rey would love that. A fire night outside.'

'Why do you think they had that picture of you and your friends?'

'Maybe the same reason V.V drew seven-pointed stars and said we were unbreakable.'

'Do you ever hear from them?' He stopped and looked at her, as though realising for the first time that her friends hadn't been around.

Evie gave a sad nod, 'V.V got married the same time I did and disappeared. I see her in magazines occasionally. Thin, blonde and clearly miserable. Gia's in America but she's coming back soon. I talk to her and Liberty. Tess and Kat pop up occasionally to text in group chats. Nina, never.'

'Except in magazines,' her brother remarked.

'She is a model.'

'You weren't unbreakable then.'

'No.' The bound photographs still troubled her. Even if they had bound Atlas and herself, she didn't understand the purpose of binding the one with her friends or stealing the photograph from her.

'I'll finish off. Go to bed.'

'You sure?'

'Yeah, I'll move this lot. Evie?'

'Yes?'

'Garrett says the builder guy likes you.'

'I know what you're doing, Atlas.' She smiled as she turned her back on him and walked to the door.

'I'm not doing anything.'

'You're trying to get me to leave the room with a smile on my face and happy thoughts so I don't think about the fact we're stuck in this nightmare farmhouse.'

Alone in her room she put a small log gently on the dying embers of the fire to warm herself up and pulled out the photograph of smiling twelve-year-old girls taken in Genevieve's garden. Evie had loved Genevieve's house and garden, but her mother would only let them all go round when her father was away on business trips. The photograph had been taken just before the summer holidays. Her parents had been downright neglectful, but Genevieve's father had been violent and controlling. She turned the photograph over.

To her surprise on the back was an array of symbols inside a series of circles, in both pencil and ink, as though it had been done and redone several times. She had to use her phone to look up the meaning of most of the symbols. The only signs she recognised were the earth, air and fire signs. Even with a brief foray onto the internet to look up the messy, hastily drawn stuff on the back, the quick information dump told her it was not good. The symbols and circle had been made to separate them, it seemed to be some sort of a loneliness spell.

As much as she would have liked to keep the photograph, the symbols on the back of it posed too much of a risk. Atlas was right, no one wanted their house to be called the witch house. Whilst she'd had friends at school, she'd also suffered teasing from some of the other children. She wouldn't do that to her children. Evie threw the photograph onto the fire and watched it burn.

She sat next to the fire and reached into her pocket to pull out the black envelope with the red seal. Thoughts raced through her mind about her safety in the house, her children's safety, whether the person threatening to kill her knew about the secret altar, or even how. The card inside the envelope was familiar. Thick and expensive. It had the same cursive writing she was used to seeing. This was about her, but not directed to her, it read as if her parents had received it.

Her Blood is mine.

It will be returned in due time.

Yrsa.

Evie held it over the flames and let it get hot before it caught fire. Then she dropped it into the fire.

In a stone basement devoid of any light except that which came from the lit candles a woman hunched over, grasping her stomach in pain. When she righted herself with a set jaw she breathed out a long controlled breath of silent anger. She picked up a circular gingerbread biscuit from a plate on the table and strode out of the basement to stare across the woods and fields towards the old farmhouse.

31

Chapter 4

A week later Evie was in the birthing barn surrounded by fresh hay, individual pens, and twenty-eight animals; a mix of cows and goats. Electric lights hung high over her head, the metal grid over them only added to her sense of isolation from the natural world outside. She didn't understand the point of farming only to be inside, but it was her brother's farm too, and jobs needed doing. She knew why Atlas had scheduled her into the barn today, it was sheltered from the weather, near the house, and the heat bulbs in the pens generated some warmth if they were needed for the babies. Atlas talked about experienced staff in the birthing barn but neither of them had any experience when they bought their hatchery, or their first dairy goats. They had learnt through hands-on experience.

Her reminder alarm went off midway through a goat's delivery, the vibration in her pocket startling her. She was in a pen with Cleopatra. Cleo was the granddaughter of one of their first goats. With her bloodied hands she had to reluctantly ignore her alarm, she couldn't leave the barn now. The kid she was delivering was breach and larger than average. It was the third such kid for this goat mum and she had to make a mental reminder to tell her brother that perhaps this should be the last time they bred her.

Regret sank in at the realisation she would have to turn up to the meeting, scheduled in ten minutes, in storm blue farm overalls and a matching farm logo-branded cap on her head rather than the clean jeans and jumper that were readily laid out on her bed. Resolutely Evie turned her attention back to the struggling goat, shrugging off thoughts of looking nice for the builder that she hadn't been able to get out of her head.

From an open space in the wall a crow sat unblinking, unmoving, eyes taking in the scene. Unnaturally it fell backwards onto the grass and mud outside the barn. It blinked, righted itself, hopped about, then flew off.

Afterwards she raced up to the house drying her hands on a faded old towel that felt as rough and stiff as the green paper towels school had used. The gate between her and the farmyard was old and ramshackle. It had more nails in it than wood, courtesy of her children who kept *mending* it. Wildflowers hung onto life around the posts bringing out a small smile from her when she saw them. She loved wild plants.

When she shifted her gaze up from the colourful wildflowers to look ahead onto the farmyard drive she could already see a shiny black truck parked, it had Anderson Builders emblazoned across the side in gold yellow. Atlas's muddy quad bike was parked up in the farmyard rather than the barn where he normally kept it, which meant he had made it to the meeting on time. She crossed the farmyard in a hurry, hoping beyond all reasonable hope that Atlas had not taken the builders into the ancient house. She didn't want the rugby playing builder to see that she lived in a museum.

The sun still held some warmth even in its fading strength as they hurtled quickly towards winter. The farmhouse, however, was a constant grey presence in her life.

It frowned upon her as though it was an uptight, bitter, solemn ancestor who disapproved of every life decision she had ever made. Inside wasn't much better. The locals had tried to list the place, the old Stuart era house still had its *updated* Georgian range. The last updates had been to the existing electricity system from the original wiring in the nineteen eighties. The update of modern plug sockets hadn't extended to the whole house, only the main parts.

Outdated, neglected, almost forgotten, such a suitable place to gift to teenage parents not yet out of boarding school. A desolate wasted house to isolate two relatively young people in order to ensure that the world around them did not interrupt their obsession with each other and that they disappeared quietly from the society circles they moved in. No one had ever thought to check up on whether two pampered boarding-school-educated teenagers had enough life skills to survive alone or if they could look after babies. If her daughter got pregnant whilst still at school Evie vowed that she would wrap her up in the comforts of home rather than throw her away to a forsaken house. Not that she actually had a few spare houses laying around to throw a child into.

Her thoughts were interrupted when Atlas stepped out from the kitchen with two very similar looking men. One was her builder from the other day, she recognised his dark blond surfer hair and stature immediately. He had seemed tall the other day, over six foot, but not as tall as her six foot seven brother, now that she saw them together. The other man had lighter hair but the same blue eyes and features, he was just slightly taller. They had to be brothers. Just as she shared grey eyes and brown hair with her brother, they shared blond hair and blue eyes.

Atlas was pointing towards the outbuildings, 'Where the weeds are, those buildings are going, they'll need taking down. That's where my sister's house is going. The back of it will face south. She's designed some joined courtyard thing and the field there will be her garden.'

'The plans are in the kitchen, have you got them?' She joined in the conversation, looking at her brother.

He shook his head as he said, 'Couldn't find them. I was saying about taking down the outhouses.' Evie narrowed her eyes at him in playful annoyance at his description.

'I heard. They're not weeds. Its cow parsley, enchanter's nightshade, and common dog violet. They all have uses for wildlife.' She kept her eyes fixed on her brother. Atlas let out a smirk that silently told her know he had won that round, she had fallen for his taunt.

The brothers looked at her. The one she had met broke out into a slow smile, 'So you do know your plants.'

'More so than my brother anyway.' She shrugged.

'What happened?' Atlas looked at the blood stains on her overalls. His body changed, he was serious now, slightly tensed, as though readying himself for bad news. Evie looked down. She hadn't realised just how much of a mess the birth had left on her overalls.

'Cleo's kid was breach. And large. She needed help. She just timed it well.' The sarcasm in her voice was evident as was her excuse for being late.

'Is she...?'

'Mum and baby are fine.'

'Did you—'

'I left food and water so she can top her energy up.'

'Cup of tea?' Atlas offered.

'Yes please,' she sighed. A cup of hot, sweet tea went down well with her whatever time it was. The brothers had already seen their ancient kitchen. She couldn't hide now. She prepared herself to see their expressions when they looked at the historical weariness of how she lived.

'Let's go back inside and Evie will get the plans out. Evie, you've met Robbie? This is Liam.' The other brother now had a name. Evie followed them all back to the kitchen.

Inside, their kitchen was pleasantly large. Old ceiling beams held numerous large menacing-looking hooks, four of which currently held freshly killed grouse, their feet tied together with rope and strung upside down. Evie shot a look from the new décor of dead birds to her brother who just shrugged, not ashamed of their living conditions.

The kitchen fire in the ancient cooking range welcomed them in. Their wooden table had smooth worn grooves in the wood where people had sat and used it over the numerous years it had been there. As always, a cheery oversized yellow vase held a big bunch of flowers. This week's offering from the florist was deep red sunflowers and orange gerbera that echoed the colours of the fire. Evie stopped at the entrance door after everyone had walked in. She unzipped her overalls and proceeded to take off her outer clothes. At Robbie's look she explained, 'It's a kitchen. I'm not trekking blood and dirt through it.'

She left her wellingtons and overalls outside, entering the house in thick ski socks, leggings and a hoody. Atlas had already lined up four fresh cups on the table. Evie intervened and lifted her vintage teapot from a shelf, placing it intentionally in front of her brother who was about to drop tea bags straight into the cups. Leaving him to make the tea Evie opened a wooden kitchen cupboard that was as old as the table and pulled out two sets of plans. 'Everything is in these folders, the architect's drawings, the storage facility I'm using for furniture, planning permission, the renewable energies we're using. There's no gas up here, only electricity. One copy for you, a copy for me.' She passed them out to each brother so that they could look through and see that they held exactly the same information.

'Atlas says you're wanting a turnkey property?' Robbie spoke.

'Yes. Our architect has everything picked out. Farming is twenty-four hours a day, seven days a week, in addition to running the café and the shops, and my career.'

'Three careers: farmer, TV presenter, and eco consultant, as well as trying to be two parents.' Her brother glared at her.

Evie knew he thought that she had too much on her plate. She had. But she was part-time at everything. Those days when they were younger, hungry and tired with no money would not leave her daytime worries. She never wanted to struggle like that again. She looked at the visiting brothers instead of her own. 'I'm always worrying that one of the jobs can just suddenly disappear and I don't want to be left with nothing. I don't have time to paint walls or build furniture at the moment without staying up all night to fit it in, but my children deserve a home, not a rundown Halloween fun house.' Atlas shot her a warning look at her description of the house. Evie quietened but defiance danced inside her.

'We can do this.' Robbie nodded. His brother was about to say something but closed his mouth as Robbie glared at him before glancing back at the plans. Liam's eyes followed the plans.

'The houses have different layouts?' Liam sounded surprised that they weren't identikit like the cabins.

'Evie needs to breathe. This house stifles her. It always has. She has less rooms—'

'—But more light. The kitchen is huge. Are you sure about these measurements?' Robbie looked at her then Atlas. Her brother exchanged a knowing look with the builder at the plans for her kitchen space.

'She has no concept of how big that kitchen will be once it's built. Measurements are not her strong point.'

'It doesn't matter. It's a room for us to be able to watch movies whilst we bake or cook dinner, to do home-work, play board games and have friends in. Until you've seen children trying to do flips and cartwheels inside you've no idea how much space I need.'

'Can we document this as we build it and put it on our website?' Liam asked. Atlas visibly hesitated. Evie met his eyes. She saw the worry; he didn't have to speak.

'Yes but no pictures of my brother or myself. Or my children.'

'Maximillian and Reina?' Robbie questioned. The long names rolled unnaturally around the room.

Evie realised that he'd done his research on her. The only publicity her children had ever received had been a big joint christening at the insistence of her ex-husband, with their full names published. It had been less about the religious aspect and more of an excuse to get drunk with his friends. He'd arranged the magazine coverage for a fee which barely covered the bar tab at the end of the night.

'It's Max and Rey. Same as no one ever calls me

Evelyn, it's Evie.' She shrugged, self-consciousness getting the better of her. Her parents had been the only people who called her Evelyn. Reina had been her choice of name, but Maximillian had been her ex-husband's idea. It seemed a big name for a baby and a bigger name for a little child to learn to spell. No one had ever used the big name and he was nine years old now. Max suited him.

Atlas asked the brothers for a ballpark figure and then told them to get the work booked in without blinking at the cost. If they were surprised by the immediacy, the brothers didn't show it. A conversation about rugby arose naturally as they walked out of the kitchen. Evie hung back to put her work overalls back on before she went back to the barn. Robbie stayed near her, his hand passed a small black envelope over to her, its red wax seal open. Immediately she wished she still had her comforting cup of tea in her hands.

'You dropped this the other day on the way back from the woods.'

'Oh.' Her hand trembled a little when she took it from him. Habitually she slipped it into the nearest pocket in her clothes. She turned her attention to putting her other leg inside the overalls and pulling them on, pretending that it was just an envelope and it didn't make her heart pound faster or her legs shake.

'Are you alright? If you're in trouble...'

'I'm on TV. I'm bound to get threats occasionally.' She purposefully kept her tone light, but her body was already shutting itself off from any emotion, her brain distancing her from the situation. She zipped the overalls up like they were her armour, trying to shut out anything that could hurt her.

'Death threats?' It wasn't a question as such. His low tone was private and serious, it told her he'd read the note. Her head spun with possible ways to cover up her secret.

She had received it the morning they had met, it had been waiting for her on the kitchen doorstep, weighted down by a stone with a red clover painted on it. Evie had been rushing that day, and now her carelessness meant someone else had found out about the threats. She shrugged and tried to play it down. 'I told the police when it started. They're so overwhelmed with budget cuts and workloads they don't really have the time to deal with stalkers. I'm not the only woman dealing with safety concerns.' She put one foot into a tightly fitted wellington and pulled it on in the hope that he would get the message from her closed off body and lack of willingness to talk.

'It doesn't make it right. I have two sisters. If this happened to them—' he trailed off.

Familiar with how protective brothers worked, Evie offered, 'I have a brother with a farmer's gun licence.'

'You win.' A grudge of a smile crossed his face.

Evie shook her head lightly to disagree, unable to raise a smile, 'It's not a win. A win would mean an end. Please don't tell anyone. I don't want it in the papers. I don't like my life splashed across some gossip magazine. I do publicity when I have to but otherwise, I'm happy living quietly on the farm.' She pushed her foot into the other wellington and pulled as her foot wiggled into place.

'You mean that, don't you?' He looked surprised at her honesty.

'I do. And the house.' She glanced behind her, taking in the ancient range, the lack of central heating and electrical outlets, 'I know cottage-core is a thing but don't tell people we're living without heating or stuff.'

'Real fires are in right now.' He offered a broad smile and a positive aspect.

'To people who don't have to put on sixteen layers to walk from the sitting room to the kitchen in winter,' she tried to keep the sarcasm from her tone.

He seemed to want to stay, there was a pause in which he hung about, then he asked her, 'Have you thought about where you're going to live whilst we build the houses? We'd have to demolish this house and clear the farmyard.'

Evie walked him out of the farmhouse kitchen and closed the door behind her, she pointed to a large patch of overgrown grass behind the outbuildings. There had been a fence once, when she was little, separating it from the actual hard surface of the farmyard.

'That half-field space behind the farmyard will become a garden eventually. We're going to put caravans there. We won't be in your way,' she reassured him. Evie knew she'd go out of her way to avoid him. She might have developed a small crush on him, and his accent might melt her stomach, but she wasn't the type of carefree, open person who would tell him or try to flirt with him.

'I wasn't worried about that.' The slow smile he gave her made her almost wish that she was good at flirting. She had bumped into Damian one night in a club and he had taken a liking to her, they partied together after that and hooked up, she fell pregnant and they got married. Then afterwards, she was far too insecure in herself and vowed to take time out to heal, then as her babies grew into active children her attention was taken. They walked across the farmyard to Liam and Atlas in silence, their brothers

41

animatedly engaged in a discussion about rugby teams.

A hen unfroze in a fallen stone trough and ran off into the grass running between Evie and Robbie's feet.

Chapter 5

Evie had fallen asleep with one name on her mind. In her restless dreams she ran through the woods pursued by the mythical witch of the farm. The woods that she claimed to know so well turned against her with their paths no longer leading to where she knew. Running along a strange path in the dark she stumbled upon a cute little cottage with the lights on. Opening the wooden door, there was only a path leading to a stone staircase descending with lamps on the walls. The roar of a wolf echoed up the stone walls to her, the witch closed in from behind.

On a tree branch outside the bedroom window sat a woman in black, looking in through the open curtains, her mouth moving in a whispered incantation that the wind took away.

A sharp ping pierced through her sleep. She was awake instantly, her arm stretched outward into the dark cold room for her phone. Her shoulders rose with tension, then she relaxed and threw herself back down and sank into the mattress. Atlas was simply telling her to be in the house because the builder needed to come to the farm to complete some checks for the demolition. She felt a smile on her face and hoped that the builder was Robbie. She would like to see him again.

Without the fire, cold air hit her lungs sharply and found its way into her once warm bed. Rising she pulled on her dressing gown. She belted it tightly to stave off the chill and pulled up the hood before she went downstairs to light the fire in the kitchen and make a cup of hot sweet tea. She already had a vision of what next winter would look like when she should be in her new house with instant heating. Her phone pinged again, muffled this time, from her pocket. Evie finished making her cup of tea before she looked at it. It was her brother again, saying that he had passed her number onto the builder and could she please just be normal. Stay normal. Do not do anything weird.

She was used to her brother telling her to be normal, not that she liked it anymore now than she had when she was starting school. He had emphasised it so much over the years. The fact that they lived in the fabled witch house had bothered him more than her when at school. He wanted them to be normal and fit in, and he had fitted in well, he was tall, sporty, popular, gifted academically enough to sit science and maths exams a year early. She, on the other hand, being the wild little sister, used to challenge kids who teased her about the witch house by either fighting them or saying she would cast a spell on them. She had no interest in trying to fit in with the girls her brother dated; shiny haired, perfect, wealthy and sporty. There had been no world for her outside the farm, her dreams of escape, and her six best friends. Atlas had always been more than the farmhouse, but she had never managed to achieve that.

Evie had promised her children breakfast in the café earlier that week, a one-off treat a few months ago that seemed to be a regular weekly event now. She sent a text back to her brother to tell him they'd be a few paces away. She made another cup of tea and carried it upstairs to light the fires in their bedrooms and playroom. She turned on the old brass tap on her bathtub and left it to fill up. She was certain that normal houses didn't require fires in September.

Max and Rey were much quicker at choosing clothes than she was, she left them to get ready and clean their teeth. Evie sank into the hot water and felt her whole body relax in the warmth. She wished for a shower, something simple and easy to use instead of waiting for a claw foot bathtub to fill with water that she loved initially, but couldn't wait to get out of the grey soup it ended as. She'd choose a shower every time over a bath.

Evie thought she was quick to get ready, but she was always too long for Max and Rey. She hastily threw a chunky cardigan over a fine knit jumper and pleather leggings, ever conscious of her contract and how she looked. The TV studio were intent on pushing the city aspect of her life. She would never be forgiven if she looked like one of the middle-class mums in the village with their swishy hair pulled back in the bobble and silk scarf combo, tight jeans and boots, fitted T-shirts and lightweight body-warmers. She looked like she was set for perusing Sunday morning markets in London. She added shades and a nude lipstick.

'Can we go now?' Max asked, as she reached for her bracelets. Evie nodded. She put a couple of bracelets on and picked up her oversized ivory leather shopper from the bed. It was heavier than she had expected, 'What have you got in here?' she looked at the two almost identical faces in her room.

'Our tablets,' her son started the list off.

'A book for me,' Rey added.

'A game.'

'Trump cards.'

'Rey put colouring things in too.' Max added.

'We really need to get you two to carry your own things and see how much you take then.' Evie sighed.

The three of them cut around the farmhouse to the rarely used front of the house. A short ramble through overgrown grass tangled through vibrant patches of sage, thyme, and rosemary; a garden planted by a very young Evie who wanted to try and emulate a walled kitchen garden brought them to face a wet but solid fence half covered with patches of yellow and green lichen. The three of them climbed easily over the fence then walked across the extensive play area to reach the café. Through the glass doors Evie could see straight across the café and through it, into the shopping quadrant. Already people were milling about with drinks in hand, waiting for the shops to open.

Max ordered his usual platter of cold meats, fresh bread, cheese and fruit. Rey went for a full cooked breakfast. Evie settled for a nice coffee and a croissant. Coffee wasn't something that she made at home. It was a treat to have when out, she only ever flitted between ordering cappuccinos and flat whites.

Mid-morning they found their way back to the café. Max and Rey had begged for a slice of cake and a few minutes in the play area. After another rushed week she didn't feel like saying no yet again. Max sat next to her, his chocolate fudge cake two-thirds eaten. Rey was outside with a friend, Evie kept glancing up to look outside and check on her daughter.

'Can I go out too, mum?' Max asked. Evie smiled and gave a nod as he put the last forkful of cake into his mouth.

One of their regular staff brought her another coffee and placed it on the table. Evie picked up a book from her bag, one that she had been determined to sink into all week, one hand went to check her phone sat in her cardigan pocket. She didn't have any messages from her brother or the builder.

Evie had gotten twenty or so pages into her book when someone drifted too near to their table for it to be accidental. She saw old jeans first, muddy but new trainers and then she looked up to a hoody holding a tray with a coffee on. Robbie's hand curved over the back of the spare chair at their table of four.

'Atlas said you'd be here. Can I join you?'

'Of course. He told me you'd call when you got to the house.' She closed her book.

'I came down for a break anyway. I've just come from another client's house to price up a quote.' He took his full coffee cup from the tray and placed it on the table. A passing waitress grabbed his tray, apologising.

Evie looked around the café, she hadn't noticed how busy it had gotten in the last half hour. There wasn't a spare seat in the place, or on the outside tables, and a queue was forming outside. Out of habit she glanced outside at the play area to check on her children. She could see Rey's olive jacket on the haybale, and Max's blue hoody on the rope climbing frame. Robbie looked outside too, clocking her children's whereabouts at the same time she did.

'They're OK.' He said it to reassure her.

She smiled, 'It doesn't stop me checking. Max can be a hothead and go where he wants, and Rey is loyal enough to follow him. That scenario ends in Rey doing something

47

impulsive because she's too much like me and Max doing his best to be responsible and mitigate any damage by himself.'

Robbie pulled out the chair and sat down as he said, 'My brothers and I weren't much different. Katie was mum's shadow. She wouldn't even go to school. Paige on the other hand, acted like she had her brothers standing behind her all the time. There's a twelve-year age gap between her and me, ten years between her and Liam, and five between her and Bodhi. She'd shoot her mouth off and create fights that we had to step in and resolve. She's matured and learnt tact since then.' He smiled at her.

Evie melted into her sea at that smile, 'That sounds lovely. When I was pregnant with Max I dared to imagine a big family. I loved being pregnant. I guess it wasn't meant to be.'

'You wanted more children?'

'Yes. Weirdly. We're not supposed to say that being a mum is fulfilling. I mean, it's also a bloody never ending ride of constant meals and snacks, but, there's fun bits. A few years ago their absolute favourite thing to do was use my bed as a boat and my belts as fishing rods. They'd catch imaginary fish and I'd have to use the imaginary barbeque on the imaginary boat to grill the fish. None of us like fish by the way. I did get to take a real cup of tea onto the boat,' she rambled. Evie mistook his amused smile for merely a polite one, she hastened to add, 'Atlas said you needed some information about the house?' Her tone was already smoothly professional.

'Yes. I managed to move a few jobs around, I can start in three weeks if you're ready.'

'Really? That's sooner than I expected. I mean, yes. I

can sort the caravans and empty the house. We're pretty much ready to pack and move into a caravan.' She couldn't keep the surprise out of her voice.

'That's the fun of a family run business, being able to sit down and delegate. Bodhi's taking over my next job because his client has pulled out at the last minute. Liam, Dad and Bodhi will manage timescales on the other jobs.'

'Your dad still helps?'

'It was his business initially. He never dreamed all but one of his children would follow his footsteps. He wanted us to go to university and be in some office.'

'But you didn't?'

She took a sip of her lukewarm coffee, leaning back into her seat, interested. Robbie shuffled in his seat without breaking eye contact with her. He picked up his own cup and took a sip. His face showed her that he thought carefully before he responded to her question.

'Initially I had plans to study architecture. We moved house and school areas when I was sixteen and I didn't fancy the commute of two buses to get to school and two buses home, and I certainly wasn't changing schools yet again. So I went to college and signed up for construction. My parents didn't know until they had forms to sign.' It was well known that the college in the town was more vocational than academic.

'How old were you when your parents moved to England?'

'Fourteen.'

'That's a tough age. I don't think I could have started fresh in a new school at fourteen.'

'It wasn't the easiest. I did make some good friends at Eastwood though.'

'Eastwood?' Her eyebrows shot up in shock. Robbie didn't appear to be the Eastwood type, he looked nice, he was relaxed and he spoke gently.

Eastwood Academy was on the worst side of town, where her friend Liberty had lived. The school had a reputation for its tough as nails pupils who resided in one of the most deprived parts of the town. She tried to backtrack on her initial shock. Normally she wouldn't have bothered to make the effort. This man was going to build a house that would be her children's home, she didn't want it messed up by her rudeness.

'I thought you lived in the village?'

'We do now. My parents live in the old school house, so they're told. I have a house on Sevenoaks Close that I'm refurbishing on weekends. But starting off in a new country is hard. Dad says we were lucky to come over with money and be able to buy a house for cash after emigrating costs. That side of town meant we had no mortgage.'

'I looked at a house close to Sevenoaks Close when Damian and I first split, Leatoft Street. I didn't want to be a burden to my brother. It's a nice street.' It was an expensive street, she knew that. Leatoft Street, with its faded grandeur of Georgian detached houses and larger gardens, was marginally more upmarket than its mid nineteen hundreds built neighbouring street. Originally part of the old village, it had been swallowed up by the farm before being built on again in the early twentieth century.

'But you chose to stay on the farm?' He looked interested in their conversation.

'I sank my divorce money and a bank loan into this instead—' she indicated the café and shopping area they were in. It teemed with life. Robbie looked around, his face showed appreciation of her achievement.

'I bet it was hard work getting it off the ground.'

'There were a few sleepless nights and a lot of tears. There were times when I thought it wouldn't happen. It was definitely a learning process.'

'Would you do it again?'

'Yes. Would you go into construction again? Knowing what you know now?' She smiled. He laughed and shook his head. Evie watched his eyes crinkle and deep lines form along his face when he smiled, a warmth radiated from his eyes that indicated he was genuine.

'No way. I wake up in a morning and feel ten years older than I am. Every joint is starting to ache. Can I ask you a question?' His tone changed from playful to soft with that last sentence. It changed their bantering conversation and made her pull back. She didn't answer personal questions. Evie looked at him, her response was a question in itself and indicated that she would choose whether to answer his question.

'Yes?'

'Why do the locals call your house the witch house?'

'It's something to do with a local myth. Like fairy tales have a witch in the woods. When the house was first built, the oldest version of the house, a witch lived in it, apparently. Ever since it's been the witch house. Either it has a witch living in it or it's haunted by a witch depending on the version you hear. I've only ever caught snippets; I don't know what the actual stories are.'

'It has a witch living in it,' he confirmed, looking at her.

Evie felt that comment, it cut her inside and froze her blood. Without realising it she stiffened slightly. She hid her unease by taking a sip of coffee and carefully put it back down. Usually, she shut down any conversation about witches and the farm immediately, with an uninterested tone and a dismissive shrug.

'Really? What else do they say?'

'That the witch made your parents leave in the middle of the night and raised the two of you herself. In fact, an old lady told me the pair of you were cursed and not to take the job. Of course I told her straightaway that you're perfectly normal people and I was happy to take the job.' The smile he gave her was supposed to be conspiratorial. Instead, she was frozen. It took a few moments to pull herself together. She took a sip of her coffee as he started to apologise. She didn't let him finish.

'No, it's fine. I know they talk about me. My parents did leave us. It's gossip to them. We were already running the farm, like, really, truthfully, nothing in our lives changed because they left. I don't know why it got to me hearing someone say it.'

'How old were you?'

'Twelve. My brother was sixteen.'

'That's young. I thought you'd have been at university when they left.'

'I suppose that's why people thought there was an adult of some kind around. We ran the farm and turned it around. We did the farmers' markets, and the country shows. Those shows are vital.'

'How did you go from farming to TV?' His gaze was steady now.

'Damian. I married a footballer. It's the only reason the press was interested in me. I was this wild party girl he fell in love with.'

'Sorry, I'd forgotten about that. I remember now. You two were all over the front pages constantly. Mostly falling out of a club.'

She remembered that. She had forgotten about the tabloids too. The blinding flashes as they stepped drunkenly out of clubs and parties around the world. In the beginning Damian would hold her close. She used to hide her face with her hair. Then she became accustomed to it and stopped hiding, stepping up her attire as she received free clothes from labels for the sole purpose of being photographed coming out of a club in the revealing outfits. Which in turn had only resulted in more attention on her, the wild partying university student in the latest clothes dating a footballer.

'I had a guest spot on a couple of shows. I performed well enough to be invited back a few times then one of the shows offered me a contract. By that time I was already pregnant with Rey, I was doing my masters degree and Damian was pissed at me because I had changed, and he... I had a chance of a job that paid well and I took the contract irrespective of whether it matched my career dreams.' She played with the way the gold band of the bracelet folded around her wrist, restraining herself from saying anything about her ex-husband, especially in public.

'You had changed?' He looked genuinely interested in their conversation, in her. Evie took a second to answer, then realised that she couldn't hurt any of the several reputations she had by telling the truth.

Her voice lost any of its remaining playful edge as she admitted softly, 'I wasn't a wild party girl anymore. I put being a mum first. I lost all my university crowd, they were still partying and drinking. I couldn't inflict that lifestyle or

53

a constant stream of babysitters on Max. Stuff happened, and…' She shrugged. The rest was history. The media made it known what happened. She walked out. She left the nation's darling footballer and took his children.

No one knew the truth of that night. Alone, bent over in pain because it was the only way she could breathe, a screaming, colicky baby on her hip and a tired toddler that couldn't sleep through his sister's crying, Evie had to call for an ambulance. Damian had refused to even answer her texts and calls pleading for him to return home to look after his children. Atlas had turned up at the hospital after one text with borrowed car seats and beds made up on the farm. No one knew about the hospital, that was too personal. It highlighted that she hadn't been capable of looking after herself, much less two children.

'Did he ever try to step up? To be a husband and a dad? To understand why you'd put a baby first over a party?' Robbie asked.

Evie shook her head, 'No. He wanted things to stay the same. He wanted me to remain the same.'

'Then he's a piece of shit.' He finished his coffee and stood up. Evie stood up too. In the time it took her to pack her children's things away in her handbag he had already picked up her shopping bags.

Hidden in the corner a slight figure, face obscured by a baseball cap, in baggy clothing, lifted a phone.

The black envelope was waiting on the kitchen doorstep for her. Worn grey stone presented the card to her much like a butler would. It was weighted down by a small but heavy stone. Painted on the stone was a daisy.

'Your favourite flower, mum.' Rey smiled, handing her the makeshift paperweight with the glazed, professionally painted daisy on. Evie smiled tightly and took it from her daughter. Robbie took it from her and examined it whilst Evie picked up the envelope.

'What's in the envelope, mum?' Rey looked interested.

Evie smiled, 'It's a party invitation, baby girl.' Evie lied quickly and easily. She avoided Robbie. His eyes on her back were like lasers at her lie.

'Are you going?' Rey believed her.

'No. I don't do grown up only parties unless I have to, you know that.' Happy with that explanation her children rushed inside, tablets in hand, chatting about an online game they were about to play together.

Out of habit she stepped into the kitchen and threw another log on the kitchen fire. They tried to keep it going from breakfast until after dinner, so that Max and Rey never had to walk into to a cold house like they had. Behind her she heard the soft swoosh of the door as Robbie closed it, the only door in the house that worked properly. She turned around and ignored the questioning expression on Robbie's face. He knew what the black envelope was. He knew that she had lied. Evie slipped her work mask on and asked him, 'What did you need to look at?'

'The walls. I need to know if they're solid and what they're made of. The roof trusses, we have to take them out one by one and not just demolish. We have to strip out the house before we can knock it down, so all electric cables, windows and doors need to be removed by hand.'

Evie hesitated over his words, just because he'd seen the kitchen didn't mean she was ready to let him see the rest of the house. Her mind flashed through the rooms, rooms like the library with its mould ridden walls. Or the children's playroom with rugs thrown over the toy organiser to try and keep it all clean, the general lack of cleanliness in most of the rooms because she never managed to get on top of the cleaning, not for lack of trying.

'You can't just come in with machinery?'

The alarm must have showed in her face because he chuckled and shook his head, 'No.'

Evie swallowed. Even on its way to demolition the house still held power over her emotions, humiliating and belittling her. She thought about the new houses and how much she wanted them built. To have the chance to finally start their legacy fresh without any ties to their past. She breathed out slowly, 'The quicker it's done the quicker it's over,' she said, more to herself than to Robbie, and led the way out of the kitchen.

If she expected criticism or laughter, or both, Evie didn't receive it. Robbie treated the house like a professional. Evie took him into the dining room, one of the more presentable rooms, with an ornate fireplace, a huge space designed for entertaining. The curtains were moth eaten but the space was clean. Robbie made his checks and wrote some notes in a pad that appeared from a pocket. Off the dining room they had a fairly well used sitting room, full of throws, cushions and blankets, antique furniture, books and games. It was bright, it was lively, and it said that she lived there.

'This is a nice room.' Robbie smiled at her.

Evie shrugged, 'It's one of the nicer rooms in the house. We don't use the rooms on the other side; the library, the old billiard room and the drawing room.' She watched Robbie check the internal walls and windows for whatever he needed to know.

'When we got to England we moved a lot. Dad's goal was to get to this side of town, into the village because living in a cute English village was their dream. We started off in a terraced property, a two-up two-down with a tiny square patch of land at the front and the back. We had to do an attic extension just to have a bedroom. We went from there to a three-bed semi which was a mess. It had been burnt in a house fire so everywhere was damp and charred. We renovated that place from top to bottom and added two attic bedrooms. With the money Dad made on our free labour he bought a big early twentieth century four-bed detached near Elm Fields Academy. Mum wouldn't live in it until we'd stripped it out. It took months to get it to a liveable state. It belonged to an old man who had had birds and cats and other rescue animals like hedgehogs. It was infested with rats. The bathrooms were unusable. We took out carpets, dealt with the rats, pulled off tobacco-stained wallpaper. We all puked outside on several occasions, it was that nasty.'

'That's a very extreme case of buying the worst house on the street and turning it into the best.' Her eyes widened with alarm. She understood his kindness though. He was trying to tell her that he had been in houses much worse than hers.

'The old school house was a breeze compared to the ones before it. At least it was clean.'

'When did your parents buy it? Surely I couldn't have missed you living in the village?' She leaned against the doorframe as he looked in the fireplace, a rare flirtatious side emerging from her like a butterfly coming out of a cocoon. She was rewarded with a quick turn of his head to look at her and a smile, a beaming, genuine smile.

'I was almost twenty-one. I had already bought a couple of investment properties by then, just two-up two-down places back in Eastwood. I was living in one and doing it up in my free time. If my parents had moved to the village when we first emigrated, I'd have noticed you.'

'I wasn't the best person as a teenager. I was young and wild.'

'So Garrett has told me.'

The twinkle in his eye and smirk on his lips told her Garrett hadn't held back with the stories about her either. Robbie stood up and walked towards her. Evie turned quickly and led him to the unused billiard room. The heavy closed door was stuck. She tried to push it open but it wouldn't move. Robbie tried using force. The frame split, bending the wood around the door inwards but the door stayed shut.

'Does this happen a lot?'

'Yeah, it's an old house. It should have been brought up to date or replaced. When our— when we were old enough to notice the endless repair list in the house, we figured it had stood up long enough that a bit longer would be fine. By the time we were adults and the farm was turning a profit we realised it would just be easier to knock it down and start again.'

'What's it like living in a house this old?'

'The worst is the gossip, the witches, the ghosts. I mean, I walk around in a black hooded dressing gown with the hood up. I'm pretty sure someone has seen me from the road and gone home to say they saw a hooded figure cross a window.' Evie tried to dismiss the rumours and deflect Robbie from thinking that the house was haunted.

She needed a builder, and she needed to not live in The Witch House. She looked at the door in front of them, 'We probably haven't been in there for a good seven months. It's got skateboards and rollerblades in from last winter. We had a bouncy castle in the room last Christmas. There's an axe in the outbuildings. I'll sort it out.'

'If you're going to destroy it, I can get a chainsaw and save you the hassle of using an axe,' Robbie offered.

'OK.' Evie accepted the help. She didn't care what happened to the house.

'There's three external walls in that room, right? Is there a fireplace in there?'

'Yes. Almost the same as the living room.'

'Do the skateboards need rescuing?'

'Please. Rey loved hers. They both got off-roaders in August, so they've been on those a lot lately.'

'Why August?'

'We all have birthdays in August. Atlas, me, Max and Rey.' It was strange to say it out loud.

Robbie raised an eyebrow, a quizzical look on his face, 'Was that planned?' There was humour in his voice that suggested otherwise. Evie laughed and led him to the old library.

'Not at all. Max was due the last week of July but came late. Rey wasn't actually due until the beginning of October but D—' she cut herself off and rephrased that sentence in her head. Robbie waited patiently for her to carry on. Evie found the words she needed, 'Rey came early. As for Atlas and me, I think it was accidental too.' She turned to look at the empty library and gasped.

Black mouldy walls in the empty library were adorned with red paint that echoed the threats she received in the envelopes:

I am watching you.

I am waiting.

I am owed your blood.

The secret door was ajar. Evie stared between the writing on the wall and the secret door. Inside her own head a muddled stream of thought gradually became clearer. The spectre had long since taken free rein of the house, roaming it after dark for as long as Evie could remember. Evie remembered being terrified when her parents had said they couldn't see the grey lady. That the strange woman was likely to be responsible for the altar, and responsible for binding her, for the spell that separated her from all of her friends made more sense. Having thought it over, she suspected her parents had been working with the spectre woman. She must have a key to the house.

Robbie closed the door. Evie knew that he was trying to shield her from looking at the threat any longer, but she pushed it open again. She turned to look at the kitchen entrance, judging the distance from the door to the library and wondering if someone had gotten in through the kitchen. Robbie's eyes followed hers, knowing exactly what she was thinking, his eyes flickered to the wide, sweeping staircase. Evie reached the same conclusion, 'My children aren't safe.'

'None of you are safe here.'

'There has to be another way in. She can't have come in through the kitchen door.' The words were whispered to herself as she walked into the room. Robbie walked in too. They searched the room in silence.

Robbie shouted her over to a window. He showed her an extra piece of wood painted to look exactly like the frames. Demonstrating his point, he lifted the window to show how the piece of wood had a makeshift handle on the outside and could be used to prop open the window.

'I'm certain that's how they got in.'

'I'll close the shutters.' She started to unfold the heavy wooden shutters that had an iron bar to prevent anyone coming in through a window pushing them open. Robbie saw what she was doing and began to help her by opening the shutter on the other side of the window.

'Please don't tell anyone.'

'You should tell the police, Evie.'

'Atlas and I confronted an intruder the other night. She must have come back to do this.'

'A deranged fan isn't a good sign.'

'You don't understand.' Evie sighed.

'Enlighten me? You said *she*.' He raised his eyebrow as though challenging her to share her secrets. Evie looked at the red paint on the wall again and started.

She told him about the other night when they had chased the Grey Spectre out of the house and her brother had pulled her back when she had been merely inches away from being able to reach out and rugby tackle her to the ground.

'Maybe you're hiding it well, forgive me for saying, but you don't seem especially shocked or upset about having an intruder. From the way you speak I'm guessing it's not the first time?'

'No. It's not. It's not just her either. Every Halloween there's people trespassing because of the myth. Some-times, especially when we were younger and less careful, they'd get inside the house too.'

'I can see why you're so determined to get rid of the old farmhouse and have new homes. You're changing the landscaping too?'

'Definitely. I grew up with furniture and rugs older than I am. I'm over the antique museum look. The court-yard is going to make it easy to walk outside with a cup of tea and sit down next to herbs and—' She cut herself off from rambling.

Robbie smiled, but took the hint and checked the room. 'This woman who was in your house, who you've seen before, has it been often?' His question caught her by surprise as they walked into her bedroom.

'A few times.'

'What's a few times?'

Conscious that he had already asked about the witch myth Evie skimmed over the bare facts, not actually telling him much more, only that it was more than a handful of times. Not enough so she would encourage the myth to have space in his head, but enough that she covered the base truth.

'This isn't healthy.' The expression on his face clearly contrasted his childhood to hers. Evie acknowledged that he had a point. They were in the children's room now, the open playroom was scattered with cosy rugs, blankets and cushions; the old fireplace contrasted against modern, flat pack furniture that provided toy storage.

Robbie checked the well-used fire whilst she answered, 'I know, and once we're in the caravans, then the houses, we'll be so much safer because we'll be the only ones with keys. This house has been in the family for over a century or more, who knows how many people have a key to some part of it?'

'How soon can you get those caravans in? My house isn't furnished but you're welcome to move there.'

'We've survived this long. I'll get the caravans this week. I have a feeling this is just part of a game for her.'

'You don't know who it is?'

'She runs too fast for an old lady. But if she's been doing this since I was a child, she can't be that young either.'

'Unless it's the actual witch.' Robbie's smile and his playful tone was meant to be a joke but Evie had dark shivers running down her spine when he said those words, she didn't like the way he watched her response and grew serious himself.

Chapter 6

At work the following day Evie yawned her way into hair and make-up to a smile from Maria, who waved to a spare seat, indicating that she would be one minute. Walking uncomfortably to the chair in wardrobe's choice of a dress for the day; a smart, tight fitting office dress belted like a corset and paired with an extra high heel, Evie was glad to take a comfortable seat. She placed her mug on the counter and pulled out her phone, going directly onto the farm's emails and started to reply to the several hundred that had been sent in. Maria interrupted her with apologies and a remark about how tired she looked. Evie tilted her head and closed her eyes. She really liked that Maria didn't try to make small talk while she did her make-up.

When the brush swept over her lips applying a final coat of red Maria said in her low voice by Evie's ear, 'Be careful out there today. I don't know how you've pissed Yvonne and Jess off but they're out for you.'

Evie wouldn't have thought anything of Yvonne and Jess huddled together at the edge of the set without Maria's warning. Ice Queen Yvonne ran the team, and she ran a tight ship. Not only was she the self-appointed anchor, she had also managed an executive producer position and had the current producer wrapped around her little finger.

Jess was in her normal skirt and blazer business

workwear. Yvonne, as always, had tried to stand out. Standing behind a camera Evie assessed the scene in front of her with a more critical eye. Her normal seat in the centre of the five presenters had changed. Young favourite Elsy now had that place. She was on the edge opposite Yvonne on the horseshoe-shaped table. Inwardly she suppressed a smile as she realised her whole side profile would be on camera. Her eyes glanced over to Yvonne who was designed to capture attention in a red jumpsuit.

'Evie, a minute please.' Her producer caught her arm.

'Can we schedule this? I don't have a minute.' Evie checked the gold watch and bracelet on her wrist, a delicate gesture in an attempt to remind her colleagues of the time and that she needed to be at her seat. The watch had a face of unfurling leaves, different shades of greens that changed constantly in the light. Damian had found it in a shop and bought it for her, very early on when they were still unofficial. It was one of a handful of items from their time together that didn't remind her of him. It was hers, Damian hated nature, to the point where she hadn't been allowed houseplants, only hothouse grown, modern sculptural pieces, delivered already arranged in a vase from a florist, and the garden of their expensive house was immaculately landscaped to a soulless modern, paved party area, sprayed frequently with weedkiller and insect poison. She had died inside herself a little bit more every time the contracted gardeners had turned up to cover the patio with chemicals and sterilise it from any plant life. Even the cooking herbs had been dried, supermarket packaged items instead of her preference for fresh plants.

'You know the terms and conditions of your contract?'

'I believe so.' She was deliberately vague, still in the

dark about whatever action she had undertaken to cause such a fuss. Jess's face was blank, but Yvonne's red lips were twisted in a smirk.

'The part that says you agree to the image we present to the public. The carefully crafted image of you that we've built up as a sophisticated, intelligent, and educated woman.'

'Yes.' Evie hoped they had a point to make. She took a slight offence to the *carefully crafted* description, she was all that they made her out to be, only less sociable.

'So this is flying around social media. I like the outfit. That's not so bad. The location however, and the choice of boyfriend...' She twisted her phone screen round so that Evie could see a picture of herself with Robbie, the two of them chatting over coffee in the farm café, and another picture by its side, of them walking back up to the farm with him carrying her shopping, Max and Rey in front of them. Although only the backs of the four of them were shown, it was clear that they were all walking back to the farmhouse. It took her a minute to respond as a lump of anger lodged in her throat and threatened to unleash a torrent of abuse. It was pushed down into the pit of her belly. Once the danger of being unprofessional had passed, Evie spoke, 'What about them? Clearly I didn't take the photo or post it.'

'I'm more concerned about the boyfriend and the location.'

'You know where I live. That's not a secret.'

'The boyfriend?'

Evie stayed silent. She refused to answer the question. Robbie wasn't her boyfriend, but she wouldn't give her producer the satisfaction of knowing that he was her builder. That comment would somehow have found a way onto the social media page of the show and it would be phrased in a way to belittle Robbie and elevate herself. She'd watched them do this too many times, especially to the other presenters, which was one of the reasons she kept her head down and her social life non-existent.

Her producer sighed at the silence, then said, 'You need to be seen with more suitable people. I'd like to set a date up for you on Saturday, in the city, an invite-only party. The press will be outside.'

'No.'

'You're not in a position to say no. We have to do some damage control. Fuck the working class boys if you must but maintain your image.' Those harsh words came from Yvonne.

'No.' She stood by her refusal even if it was uttered softly. Evie knew what would happen, they'd give her less shows, cut her hours, until eventually, she would have to find another job because she wasn't earning, and she was paid per show, not an annual salary. She had seen it happen to more than one ex-colleague who had been perceived as offending Yvonne. She had stood by silently, retreating further into herself when she should have spoken out.

Jess spoke next, her voice full of her authority, 'I'll send you the details. Also, I have another job for you. Our Halloween special fell through. Yvonne had an amazing last minute idea. I'd like to get paranormal investigators into parts of the village you live in. The pub have agreed, the B&B, a coffee shop on the high street, we have permission to film in the church graveyard. I'd like you to go along with the team and present, since it's your village. I'll have someone pass you all the details.' Evie gritted her teeth at being asked to pull a night job. She had so far refused to leave Max and Rey.

'Elsy is the one that believes in that stuff.'

'You presented a nicely balanced view when we spoke about it on the show. You said you were open, but you'd never had any experiences to convince you. If I remember rightly you said ghosts were like vampires, faeries and werewolves. Elsy will be going on some other ghost hunts. She's doing one in the woods.'

'The woods are private property. You'll need permission to film in them.'

'There's public rights of way. As long as we don't stray from them onto private property we can film. Anyone would think you don't want us on your land.' Yvonne stared at her. Evie could just tell that she had done research into her life thoroughly from the warning in her tone and the narrowing of her eyes when she threw out that statement.

'I'd prefer not to do this.' Evie directed her remark to Jess. Yvonne was as cold as the frost that covered the ground in winter. Except she didn't thaw like the frost did.

'It's just a little ghost hunt. Oh, Yvonne wanted to change seats and shake things up a little today.'

Evie should have expected the surprise conversation on air, the segment on *class* dating and whether dating outside of one's *class* ever worked out. She threw every socialist argument about the class construct she could fit into the discussion, using academic jargon and a strong, insistent voice. She was rattling Yvonne each time she debated back. Evie could see behind the mask. The smile might be in place, but it never reached Yvonne's eyes, unlike Robbie's smiles yesterday that she still remembered. Evie understood Yvonne enough to know that Yvonne thought the new seat and the conversation was a punishment.

Instead of allowing the punishment to rattle her, Evie played it to her advantage, showing off legs that were normally hidden under the table. The jumpsuit that looked great when Yvonne was stood up, rumpled and creased throughout the show, meanwhile Evie kept one heel on the set floor and another perched on her stool, her stomach sucked in and back straight. Heated, intellectual debates happened few and far between on the show presently, in fact ever since Yvonne had talked her way into an executive production position and had a say in the running of the show it had turned into fluffy conversations of short duration, not a notable meeting of opinions on present day issues.

Then it was over. The next day's planning was talked through over coffee and a plate of gingerbread biscuits and she was free to leave. Evie raced to her car in the outfit she had turned up in; a long wool coat, new jeans, cream jumper and ballet flats. Her car reflected parts of city gleam back but equal parts mud. The conversation with Yvonne and her producer sent a fire coursing through her as she stared at her car, not seeing the vehicle through her messy thoughts. The Halloween presenting job was supposed to be an opportunity but they both knew that it was a punishment disguised as opportunity. She stared at the car as she tried to think her way out of it all and put her colleagues' schemes into a strategy that made sense.

'Sad thing, winter. The rain really does ruin the work of the carwash,' a male voice said at her left ear. Evie jumped and spun around to look. A tall red-haired man stood next to her, his worn tweed jacket and woollen jumper a giveaway, even if she hadn't recognised the veteran country presenter.

'Andy!'

'Yes. I've seen you. I don't watch your show though, sorry.'

'Don't be. It's a trifling magazine show where we get ten minutes to discuss huge issues without any depth. For some reason people like it.'

'Your face just then seemed to indicate you could use a friend. Production issues?'

'A producer issue.'

'It washes off, the mud,' he nodded towards the car.

'I live on a farm. The mud isn't an issue. I'd rather be in wellingtons than dressed up on set.'

'Why didn't I know you lived on a farm?' He picked up on that casual statement instantly, just as she had hoped.

'I'm not allowed to say. My producers want people to think otherwise.'

'Look, it might blow over and you'll be happy, but we're opening up to new presenters. Ideally we wanted an unknown who knew what they were talking about when it comes to the country. How long have you lived on the farm?'

'All my life. I grew up with crops, later animals. If it helps my application, I have a degree and a research-based masters in Plant Biological Sciences with emphasis on native plant conservation and adapting to climate change.'

'Can we swap numbers? I'm meeting my producers now. I'll throw your name into the ring and judge their reaction. What farm do you live on?'

'It's called High Lēah. An hour-ish from here,' she

replied. The farm's official name was High Lēah, even if the villagers just called it the witch farm, or occasionally the Hepburn farm. He looked at her sharply, his eyes narrowed and frown lines appeared. Evie steeled herself for another rejection, their reputation clearly extended further than she anticipated.

'You're joking! I knew the McGregors. I grew up with their sons.' His accusatory tone immediately had her on defensive.

'I did not force them out. I made an offer for their farm.' Evie stood her ground.

'A low offer.'

His words were a relief. If making the McGregors a low offer for their land was his only issue with her, he clearly hadn't heard about her or her farm. She took the opportunity to tell him the truth, 'Not really. They'd used pesticides for years so we can't extend the organic label that we worked hard for. Their orchard trees are rotten inside and all need replacing. They were proud, like all farmers are, and didn't ask for help but no one really understood just how much needed repairing or replacing. We had several long conversations about what my brother and I would do with the farm before they agreed to sell to us.'

'I didn't realise.'

'No one did. Out of respect don't say anything. Let them have their dignity, please.' Evie knew that they didn't have much left, but they were old now. She could have said more, and made it worse, but she preferred that she never had to hear their name again.

He gave a nod and then a smile, 'I'll see what I can do. It might be to our advantage having a known face around.'

'Just, were you friends with their sons?' The answer that he would give was dependent on whether she wanted to work with him or not. She had to know if she was swapping Yvonne for another version of Yvonne.

'Not really. Our parents ran in the same farmers social circle but they're a pair of bullies. Anyone could see they were going to turn out bad.'

Relief ran through her body.

It was dark when Atlas filled the doorway to the play-room, a bottle of wine open, two glasses in his hand and gave a quick nod to the chess table. Evie looked up from kneeling on the floor, tidying away Lego into white plastic baskets according to size. She glanced over at the chess set, high up on the shelf and gave a responding nod. He put another three logs on the dying fire and stoked it. He made certain that it was blazing. Without saying a word, he set the chess board up and poured two large wines, the entire bottle going between the two glasses. Evie stood up and put the baskets away.

She took a seat opposite her brother, 'Sorry I snapped at you.'

'It wouldn't be the first time.' He moved his piece.

Evie played her rook pawn instead of meeting him in the centre of the board. He raised his eyebrow at the change of tactics and looked at her. Silently he moved another pawn. Evie moved her rook. She knew by the questioning look he gave her it was probably the wrong move. She wanted to try something different.

'My producer has set up a date for me. Apparently, I can't be photographed on my own farm or in the presence of a man without people making assumptions. I have a fake date on Saturday night. I thought she was joking.' She explained the reason behind the bad mood she had been in since arriving home.

'She saw the photographs on the internet?' Atlas assumed.

'You've seen them?'

'Most of England have,' he told her.

She shrugged in reply and picked up her glass. She took a long, slow mouthful of wine, then another. 'She thinks Robbie is my boyfriend. I didn't correct her because I've seen how they put people down and belittle them. She said Robbie wasn't the type of man I should be seen with and I had an image to maintain.'

'I'll babysit, of course, but are you going?'

'No. But if I don't go, I could lose my job.'

'Lose it. There's enough work on the farm. On the other hand, if they're playing games with you why don't you play back?'

'I tried to. I feel like a sacrificial pawn right now. I swear the producer has spies everywhere. Whoever took those photographs was quick to get a perfect shot that made nothing into something.'

Atlas quickly killed every piece she had as she tried to move her outer pieces around the board the protect the inner pieces. They set up for another game.

Nestled into a corner in the wall a little mouse sat perfectly still and listened.

Chapter 7

Their caravans — big, pale grey, static, unattractive containers — were moved into place at the same time she was filming the Halloween special. Sunset occurred quickly, one minute it was daytime, then an orange glow, and then dusk happened in what seemed like seconds to Evie. Between the extra work and the other jobs she had that week, including an eco-plan presentation she had worked a year on, she was ready to fall asleep standing up.

Evie chose to walk from the farm into the village for filming rather than drive her car. Her eyes were fighting to stay open. She didn't trust herself to drive back safely later. She had already driven into the farm's driveway posts once, at eighteen, the solid stone causing her small, cheap car more damage than the car had painted onto the stone. Atlas still brought it up occasionally when reminding her to be careful and normal.

Despite the chill in the air, she warmed up on her brisk walk down into the village. The night wrapped itself around her, enveloping her in its darkness. Evie kept her eyes on the closing distance between her and the first of the street-lamps that lit the way into the old village. It cast a halo down to the ground and the yellow light filtered into the blackness rapidly, as though it wasn't strong enough to survive far from its source. Evie understood not being strong enough to survive far from a source; back in the initially beautiful house with Damian, the lack of greenery inside and out had held her in a straightjacket. She had started to leave earlier and return later, always walking the scenic route through parks and tree-lined streets from the house to university, and back, Max in his buggy or toddling next to her looking at insects, grass, flowers; he had needed the outdoors too. Underneath that first streetlight, a smoky grey cat passed through the patch of light moving slowly and gracefully, glancing in her direction with slit eyes that disdainfully glanced at her for a fraction of a second.

When she reached the coffee shop Evie was surprised to see Yvonne there. Head to toe in black, her blonde hair sleek and shiny, set to fall just so perfectly down her back by heated appliances and products, she was basking in the attention of the locals. Evie held her head up and approached from the back, her eyes seeking out Maria like a comfort zone. Maria waved at her from a monstrosity parked a few yards down the street. Evie went straight to her. Maria talked about trying a new pin curl and different style in her hair. Mutely Evie nodded, too tired to think or care about how she looked. Her eyes closed as Maria gently combed through her hair.

She woke up to Maria's fingers removing clips from her hair and her assistant placing a coffee in front of her. Maria told her it was a flat white, she'd ordered it for her. Evie was grateful but doubted that caffeine alone was enough to keep her awake. Caffeine usually had the opposite effect on her than it did to everyone else.

'My sources tell me they're planning to surprise you with a tarot card reading and a personal palm reading as a warm-up tonight. Yvonne received a lot of backlash over her having a dig at you about dating that man and calling him lower class so she's here to make out you two are best friends and do some damage control.' Maria's words seemed friendly; a passing innocent remark, until Evie met her eyes through the mirror. It was a warning not to fall into a trap that Yvonne was setting of laying a honey cage for a later date. Maria had worked on the programme longer than she had. If Evie knew that Yvonne liked to reel people into a safe spot before dropping them in shit over and over again, Maria must have seen it many more times. Evie nodded her understanding. Maria continued, 'Yvonne had an idea that since she's in black she wanted you to be in white. Wardrobe left you some clothes and a coat. They'll be back in ten to check you.' Evie glanced over to where Maria had nodded, a white winter dress waited for her, a beautiful coat, a scarf and brown boots that matched her hair colour.

'Is it as bad on your side of the camera?'

'Yes. Everyone wants to get on in the industry and no one wants to stay on the bottom rung.'

'Have you ever thought about moving on? There must be places that aren't as bad as this.'

'I might not be there for my girls in a morning but at least I'm home to make dinner, listen to their day and do bedtimes. Maybe when they're older. I'll put your lipstick on when you're dressed.' Maria waved a pinky-brown neutral tub at her.

'No red?'

'Yvonne said no red today. She wanted natural glam since it's your home village, something about people seeing you how you normally look but better.' Evie looked at her face in the mirror, the suggestion of smoky eyes and hint of blush on her pale skin had all been done in natural, soft colours. It was how she looked every day, just thicker and heavier for the cameras. Her stomach churned in anticipation of Yvonne's unspoken schemes. If Yvonne was this involved in the planning, she was pulling unseen strings and manipulating an attack.

For all of them, their normal look onscreen was nineteen forties/nineteen fifties full make-up and red lips. She wanted to know what Yvonne's plan was but she couldn't ask. Dressed and with her new lip colour on, Evie wandered out of the large truck to the front of the café. Yvonne was posing for photographs with members of the public. Evie slipped into the shop quietly unnoticed whilst all eyes were on the attention-seeking presenter. The décor was different from what she had expected; the soft, pastel pink kitchen area caught her eye with its pretty cake stands in the glass displays, surrounded by a mix of vintage gothic seating and decor, all very carefully put together. The ghost hunters were loud about arguing over where to go first. Two wanted to start in the basement whilst another wanted to go upstairs. A senior member of staff stood with them and several cameramen were trying to resolve the dispute. A woman with pink hair, lots of silver rings, head to toe in flowing black apparel and thick eyeliner sat shuffling tarot cards.

Evie stopped by her first, sliding into the seat opposite, 'Hello.'

'Hi.'

'I'm Evie.'

'Harriet.' The woman was cool, even indifferent to her.

'Do you regularly do readings for people?'

'Are you trying to say I shouldn't?'

'Not at all.'

'Or perhaps I'm not as good as you because I don't come from such an established witch family.'

'I don't come from a witch family,' she protested, her stomach lurching and the two bites of pizza that she'd forced down rising to the back of her throat.

'You do. We all know it. All the locals know. Stop pretending to yourself. That's the witch farm up there and no matter what you do it will always be The Witch House.'

'Nice to meet you, Harriet.' Evie got up and walked away.

She was grabbed by Yvonne. A hand around her arm stopped her from moving. The other woman slipped her arm through hers and directed her outside, whispering that the fans wanted them both outside. Reluctantly a silent Evie accompanied her, disliking that she had *fans* in the very village that gossiped about her. She pushed a professional smile onto her face and posed with Yvonne, as she was expected to do. Maria's warning stayed in her head.

When she turned to pose for a picture with a fan, Evie took the opportunity to have a quick one-second glance down the romantic picturesque stone-built high street and saw the pub garden was packed with people watching. She smiled for the camera then looked back over to the pub. Her eyes found Robbie and Liam sat on the low boundary wall around the beer garden, coats on and pints in hand, looking her way whilst having a conversation. They were illuminated by the mournful ground level lighting the pub had installed around its boundary, and the dark attire of winter coats looked sombre and moody. She waved at them even as her stomach sank to the ground after what had been said onscreen.

'Let's go over and say hello.' Yvonne was dragging her over before she could say anything.

'An apology would be more appropriate than hello.' She broke angrily out of Yvonne's iron grip and stood still, facing the other woman with a defiance she had never shown her before off screen. Evie did not want to face Robbie. His name hadn't been mentioned, nothing about him had been mentioned. But the conversation on air had clear undertones. Their exchanges since had been nothing but professional.

'Is it serious enough for those feelings already?' Yvonne managed to mix the disdain in her voice with a neutral expression.

Evie bit her tongue against the outburst that she wanted to give Yvonne and said simply, 'You were absolutely awful about the whole class thing. It's outdated. Maybe we should do a feature on tradespeople outearning university graduates.'

Yvonne took her arm again and pulled her forwards. They walked on, nearer to the pub. Evie's stomach heaved and threatened to retch with each step. 'That, actually, could be a good idea. At one point tradespeople and farmers were highly regarded by less literate and able people in society. It was as though they held secret knowledge. Then society progressed and the industrial revolution happened. We should do that. It's almost like a full circle.' They had reached Robbie and Liam now.

Evie's body shook, whether from cold or nerves, she couldn't tell. Robbie and Liam looked the pair of them up and down as they approached. Evie replayed the entire conversation that had happened on air through her head in seconds, recalling everything that had been said, finding faults in her own behaviour and gaps in her arguments. She wished she could explain that her producers had all made assumptions, she didn't want to have to explain how she had let those assumptions pass without correcting them.

'Bit rich, coming over after what you said on your show about us,' Liam remarked.

'She stuck up for you.' Yvonne still managed to project scorn through her body language and voice, keeping more of a distance from the pair than Evie did.

'I'm sorry that happened. If it had been run past me in the pre-show meeting, I would have said no. Sometimes they throw topics at us and catch us off guard for authentic reactions,' Evie apologised, with a glare at Yvonne.

'I'm still not sorry. Any publicity is good publicity. Which reminds me...' Yvonne turned deliberately to Evie. It was clear she was about to drop the manipulated, planned bombshell announcement on her. Evie stared her down, her heart beating fast and fingers shaking. Yvonne believed that Evie and Robbie were a thing, this would be big enough to drive a wedge between them. Evie had watched Yvonne do this to others. Yvonne let the pause extend for exaggeration. Finally she announced, 'We need you to film the promotion after this. It's going to be a "Get ready to go ghost hunting with me" type thing in a hotel room, you'll be in lingerie and you'll have to be sexy.' She turned and walked away.

'I hope you fucking fall off that power trip platform you're standing on.' Evie said softly at her back. Robbie chuckled at her side.

'She's your friend?'

'No. She thinks she's in charge of the show. I really am sorry, you were just being kind and then those photos—' She looked at Robbie. Liam choked loudly on his drink.

'Sorry. I'll go and get another round. Wine, Evie?'

'No thanks, I can't afford to relax around Yvonne.' She shook her head.

'You look tired. It's the fourth night this week you've been filming, right?' Robbie said to her as Liam walked back into the pub.

'It's the last night. All I have to do is my job, hope Andy messages me soon and apologise to your partner for the photographs.'

In her head she could hear her brother's voice talking to her teenage self when she was in trouble at school yet again, Depersonalise the situation Evie, do not let them think they've gotten to you. Apologise and be a normal person, it'll blow over.

Robbie's next words surprised her, 'There's no girl-friend, just me. Andy? Is he someone you fell out with over the photos?'

'Andy Bassingham. The presenter on the weekend country show?'

'Isn't he married?'

'Yes.' Suddenly realising how the conversation sounded, her hand flew up to her mouth at her mistake. Then she smiled and shook her head. 'It's not like that. There's nothing going off between us. The show is looking for another presenter. We had a chat about it. I'm waiting for a yes or no answer.'

'Do you want the job?'

'Yes. You've met one of my colleagues, there's a whole crowd of them in the studio,' she said wryly, and shrugged.

He let out another chuckle.

Out of the corner of her eye she saw Liam emerge from the pub with two pints. With a goodbye she walked back to the coffee shop, lighter in step than before she had spoken to Robbie. That was one awkward meeting over. She hadn't realised how much she had dreaded seeing Robbie until she saw him sat on the wall with his brother. Some of the weight in her stomach lifted.

The film crew had moved the café tables around and set Harriet up at a cosy looking but large table with a black tablecloth over it. She was on her phone, reading a text message then replying to it. Yvonne was looking at the set up through the camera and was snapping at someone. All the smaller tables had been set up in crescent arrangements around the table with lit candles. Yvonne pointed to a seat and told Evie to sit. Yvonne took it upon herself to film the introduction instead of Evie.

Harriet started with a palm reading for Evie. She ummed for a minute, holding both of Evie's palms open with her hands. Evie could feel her own hands shaking in Harriet's steady ones. Evie tried to focus on her breathing to calm down, she reminded herself that most individuals who claimed to be able to do this generally made vague statements that could be applied to anyone. Harriet must have been able to feel the unsteadiness in Evie's hands too because her eyes lifted up to Evie's, a slight shocked surprise showing. Evie held her gaze even knowing that the fear was visible in her own eyes.

'You didn't want to do this, did you?' she whispered.

Evie shook her head, 'No offence or reflection on your abilities,' she whispered back. Yvonne joined them, sitting next to Harriet. Harriet looked back down at Evie's palm but didn't show any emotion or speak out.

Instead, she picked up and used a thin black sharpie to draw the lines and shapes that she was looking at on Evie's hand for the television audience to follow along. Her soothing, calm voice surprised Evie after the way Harriet had talked to her earlier. Her finger was light as she traced the lines rhythmically on Evie's palm when she talked. Evie realised that it was on purpose, she was trying to get Evie to relax with her warm fingers. The sharpie, by contrast, was cool and the synthetic fibres pulled on her skin. Her palm became full of black shapes as Harriet talked for the next thirty minutes.

'You're kind, giving, very accepting of people for who they are. You don't hold preconceptions about people, you find it easy to take people as they are and not judge. You should be careful because you have many enemies, one in particular is determined to see you fail at something big. This shape here means you have gifts that you have been blessed with by your ancestors, blood gifts that not every descendant will be given. Seven will become a very important number for you, as it once used to be. You struggle with decisions because you see a lot of sides to every choice and that can lead to self-doubt and questioning, you are able to look at the same situation from multiple points of view.

'You need to be wary of burning yourself out in being all things to all people. Your heart line is broken in multiple places but from this point here, it looks like around the age of twenty-eight to thirty-two it runs deep and unbroken which means one long lasting relationship and true friendships will start to form or be reformed. You have ambition but not in the traditional sense of carving out a notable career, it's more do to with the background that people don't see, there's ambition to achieve something in your private life that pushes you in your professional life. I see something to do with greenery and nature. You're not a city girl in your heart, I see flowers blooming rather than farm crops and cosy nights inside. This is interesting, this collection of lines that align with the greenery suggests you're tactile, you'll seek out reassuring hugs and touches from a lover, you're not emotionally distant or logic based, rather you let your emotions control a relationship and if it's not right you pull away quickly.

On all your lines it suggests that something is going to happen in the next couple of months, something significant that will change your private life even if the public don't see any change in you. The dual fate line here, it's very interesting. Usually there are dual aspects like male logical thinking and female emotional thinking but the lines and shapes here, they suggest, just suggest, that there are two paths you will be asked to follow. The longer one requires deep sacrifice and self-work. There's something you're not accepting. The shorter line here, there's a sudden stop as though it's cut, possibly by someone else rather than your-self, as though they're in control of you from that point onwards if you don't accept difficult truths.' Harriet was interrupted by Yvonne at this point asking a barrage of questions.

'Can you tell us more about the next two months for Evie?'

'Not really. It's a slow build up to something big, all areas of her life are linked, professional, private, sibling, self-acceptance, health; the journey is something that is done alone, without friends, although I see some love

84

coming her way, perhaps unknown, that develops.'

'A romantic love?'

'Yes.'

'That's what we like to hear. Is this new relationship threatened by all that's going to happen?'

'Not really, it looks solid and long term once it gets off the ground.'

From the way Yvonne glowered at Harriet and Evie they both understood that this wasn't the answer she wanted, despite that, she answered Harriet with sweet words, 'I'm so glad to hear that. We'll have to keep our viewers updated on Evie's love life.'

They took a break for a drink. Evie was sipping a flat white, listening to another argument between Yvonne, Jess, and the ghost hunters. They were short on cameras and the ghost hunters wanted to start. Yvonne was determined that the planned tarot reading would happen next. Evie hoped they'd argue it out soon and they could get started.

'Weird how we think of people and they turn out to be something we least expect,' Harriet said, suddenly appearing next to her. Evie jumped, she was so tired that everything was startling her.

'Sorry?' She turned to look at Harriet, her pink hair had been pulled back into a messy bun.

'That was my way of trying to apologise. For judging you before.'

'If I'm right you were raised listening to the village talk about me anyway. It must be hard not to form judgements.'

'That's true. But I really did not expect your reading to go like that.

'Where did you learn to read palms?'

'My great grandma had the patience to sit with me, whilst I studied her hands. Her own grandmother taught her about their Indian heritage. I saw how open you are, how accepting of people, that's rare. Although it makes sense, having been judged your whole life for being a witch, born into the witch family.'

'It shouldn't be rare. I don't get why people judge others. It's like having children, you can fight their nature and try to enforce your idea of who they should be, or you can accept that they're born with their own personalities and work with them to guide them as they grow.'

'That's how you raise your kids?'

'Yes, there's enough tension at work. I don't need to bring it home and take it out on my children because they're not being programmed robots.'

'Yvonne is a piece of work.'

'Everyone seems to be the same in this industry.'

'Want to take a break?' Harriet offered her an air pod, she had the other one in her ear. Evie took it. The music felt like home even though she had never heard it before. It resonated deep in her soul.

'What is this?'

'Viking metal.'

'I really like it.'

'I thought you would. Even if you look like butter wouldn't melt there's a steel core in you. Not that I'd say that in front of the bitch from hell.' Harriet nodded towards Yvonne.

'I appreciate that.'

'She keeps helping herself to my gingerbread biscuits.'

'Yeah, she has a thing for gingerbread.'

Chapter 8

Evie left the old hotel, previously a coaching inn in an older life, in her own clothes and her coat wrapped around her. A mist had risen from the ground, it perpetrated everywhere. She was thankful Maria had slipped samples into her pocket when Yvonne announced a wrap. The cream balm had melted off the make-up and there had been enough for two cleanses. The moisturiser was enough for tonight. It wasn't a full skincare routine but it was enough to go home with a bare face and be able to clean her teeth before falling into her bed.

She set off home. There wasn't an inch of the village, the farm or the woods she didn't know. The walk home was a straight line up the lane. A glance along the village high street showed yellow lights glimmering through the mist. She was certain some belonged to Harriet's café. The street was empty of the film crew, they had packed away all the cables, cameras and associated paraphernalia.

'Hey, Evie!'

Her heart jumped into her mouth and her blood froze. The reality of the threats hit her as her heart and thoughts raced faster than she could gather them. Robbie emerged from Harriet's café, pulling on his coat. He shouted out again, 'Evie, pop over here a second.' Harriet came out behind Robbie. Evie walked towards them. Her heart sank into her stomach when she saw Robbie say something to

Harriet. There was an unmistakable familiarity between them, and it ripped through her in a flash of hot lightning. She had never felt that emotion before. It was strange how it made her insides tear and something like disappointment flooded through her. Evie pushed the emotion aside before she had time to analyse it. She walked over to the pair, 'Just, would you mind giving me your hand a minute?' Harriet asked. Evie was confused but too tired to argue. Thinking that Harriet had made a mistake in her original reading she offered her hand.

Harriet held her hand, and Robbie's, peering at something on both. She looked satisfied with herself when she met Evie's eyes again. She gave a nod and looked directly at Robbie when she spoke, 'You have the same love line. Same events, same deepness, same length. Your lifelines indicate a long and happy relationship too.' Robbie pulled his hand away. At the gesture Evie pushed her hand into her coat pocket. Her eyes were closing, she should have been relieved that the night filming had reached its conclusion, instead, all she was looking forward to was falling into her bed and sleeping.

Robbie picked up something, a glass, and handed it to Evie, 'I couldn't get you a glass earlier. There's no Yvonne so you can relax now.' Evie looked at the bubbles rising in the clear drink and took a sip. It was prosecco and it was exactly what she needed after work. She took a sip and closed her eyes briefly in appreciation.

'I needed this,' she sighed, knowing that Yvonne had gone home before she even started to take her make-up off.

'Goodnight. Don't be a stranger, Evie.' Harriet shut the door and started to lock it.

Evie was left with a glass outside a locked café standing next to Robbie. She was confused about a lot of things, she had questions about what had just happened, but all she wanted was her bed. Her eyes started closing. She tried to give Robbie that glass back, 'I need to go home.'

'I'll walk you. It's your drink.' He refused to take the glass back. He gave her a shake of his head.

'Why would you wait up to walk me back?' she asked, her brow furrowing as exhaustion began to confuse her senses.

'Because I like you. If it's inappropriate until the build is over that's fine. I'll ask you out for a drink afterwards. I just wanted you to know before someone else got in there first, because I definitely had a scare when you mentioned Andy earlier tonight.' They started walking back towards the hotel, heading for the lane that would take them through the village and up to the farm.

Evie heard the words but they took a while to translate their meaning from her ears to her brain in her overtired state. She took a sip of her drink then suddenly stopped walking in the middle of the high street as the words hit her, 'You like me? Me?'

'Yes, Evie. You're beautiful and sweet. I like that you know your plants and you put your kids first, that you read books and that you work somewhere you don't even like to give your kids a decent life.'

'You're not with Harriet?' she asked.

He swore. Then shook his head, 'Did we give you that impression? We tried to date. It didn't end that well. We're trying to go back to being friends. Since we're asking, you stopped yourself from saying something about Damian the other day in the café. What was it?' Evie glanced around, cautiously, checking to see if they were alone. Robbie followed her gaze. He looked at her, puzzled.

'I'm still wading through some stuff with him. Every time I think it's finally over, he comes back with something. I'm scared if I say anything negative someone will hear. He can be nasty. When he's partying and drinking, he's the nicest guy, the most generous person you'll ever meet. But when he's sober, the anxiety and self-hate kicks in. He took it out on me quite a lot after Max was born.' She started walking again. Robbie kept pace with her.

'Physically?'

'No, he's more verbal. He never hurt me. He might have taken my confidence and ground it to a powder with comments about how often I was texting and calling my friends instead of paying him attention when we were at home. He had this snarky way of making remarks about my appearance post birth, but he never hit me.' It was the reason she had been hiding behind the farm, and the reason she had let the studio do what they wanted with her image, because at the time her self-confidence had been non-existent.

'Is that what you were going to say about him?'

'No but, I can't, there's things I don't want finding their way back to my children. If I never say them, no one knows.' She dropped her head and looked at the ground. She couldn't dump that knowledge on someone else, never mind a stranger. It hurt to keep it inside, but it would hurt her children more if they found out. She had to remain silent. She couldn't let it be revealed that her ex-husband had thought it an achievement to get her pregnant and married, but when he had a baby to hold, he didn't want to be a father. It would hurt Max and Rey to know.

'Back at the house, when you said Rey was born early, you gave the impression that he did something?'

'He had an outburst. It was a horrible prolonged one, and what he said was a shock. By that point he was already sleeping in a separate room, living a separate life and I was pretty much a single mum. He didn't help out at all. One of my university professors actually had Max whilst I gave birth. Damian was off somewhere. We were never more than two people who got drunk together, once we lost that we had nothing.' Evie still felt guilty that she hadn't been able to absorb his vitriol without it affecting an unborn Rey.

Robbie didn't push her further. His hand reached for hers and they walked slowly back up to the farm. Evie sipped on her drink, her feet growing heavier. She enjoyed the heat from his hand that made the bones inside her own relax. She wondered how someone who had seen inside her house could like her. But he'd also seen the new house plans too, plans that were much like his parent's house. Suddenly it occurred to her that he might not like either house at all, 'What is your house like on Sevenoaks Close?'

'A mess. I've just put a couple of steel beams in downstairs and I'm waiting on my plasterer to have a free weekend so we can crack on together and do the whole space. I've been helping him put a new kitchen in his house at the weekends. His wife is due to have their baby at Christmas so their needs trump mine. There's hardly any furniture because of the renovation. It's not going to be my house anyway, that was never the plan. I bought it to do it up and rent or sell. I never saw it as a home for me.'

'So what's next?'

'I don't know. Looking for a home is different to

91

looking for a house. Home is something that speaks to your soul. Doing a house up for the mass market, that's easy. The Sevenoaks house was always going to appeal to a family, all I've really done is take out the dated décor, and opened up the smaller rooms into a more modern layout.'

'How?'

'The kitchen was tiny, the dining room was separate but large, I've knocked the wall separating the kitchen from the dining room and added new central doors straight to the garden so it's a decent kitchen diner now. I've created space for a utility by making one of the lounges smaller and turned it into an office or a playroom, depending on the family buying it.'

'Do you think my kitchen is too big?' Doubt ran through her, wondering if she was creating a large, cold, soulless space.

'No.'

'No?' she teased, remembering his face when he saw the plans. He grinned and relaxed visibly. He gave her hand a playful squeeze.

'I admit I was shocked when I saw the measurements. What are your plans for the space once it's built?'

'The kitchen sits in the middle third and I know that's a big kitchen by itself. The large island is so we can make breads and pizzas and biscuits. We're not overly amazing but I love doing that with them whilst they're little, creating memories for them, and skills to look after themselves when they're adults. On the north side of the kitchen, I'll have a big dining table with huge velvet chairs for cold evenings and board game nights. On the south side I was thinking big comfy snuggle chairs. Maybe some shelves or high console tables behind the chairs for vases of flowers, recipe books and house plants.'

'That sounds cosy. I can picture that now. Do you do a lot of board game nights?'

'We try to play after dinner on school nights in winter. Weekends are movie nights, and when the lighter nights start and the weather gets warmer there's usually extra to do on the farm or I try and fit in some gardening, then I lose track of time and I'm not ashamed to say they go to bed much later than most English parents would approve. I'm not a strict bedtime mum. My brother and I play chess in the children's playroom whilst they fall asleep.'

'I noticed the chess set in there.'

'It was my sixteenth birthday present from him. He thinks I'm a little bit too obsessed with fairy tales.' Her fairy tales weren't light and sweet, they were dark and grim, much like the mist filled night that they were currently walking in.

'Are you?'

The question made her pause to think. Perhaps she was, she sought solace in fairy tales because of her gift. They took her to a world where her gift was possible. She liked Robbie and he had already seen the darker side of her life. He was walking her home in a gloomy, cold mist. She tried to keep her answer light, 'I like the idea of magic and monsters and wearing pretty dresses without being cold. It's England, we have about three days of dress-wearing weather then it's raining or cold or both.'

'I work outdoors too, those hot days feel like a year in themselves on site. Monsters?' Evie heard the amusement in his tone.

'In fairy tales, books, films... you know who the monsters are. Here, they're other humans and harder to

93

distinguish until you're too close, or tied into a contract, or whatever.'

'Are we talking about fairy tales, or Damian and Yvonne?'

'Who would be your monster?' She avoided the question by asking one of her own.

He shrugged, sighed, and there was a long pause. Evie thought maybe her question was silly, maybe her brother was right, she was about to say something else when he answered, 'Maybe two things, my family has this thing of decontaminating, purging, sanitising and refining certain buildings. You know the type of house that people walk into and get instant bad feelings about and nobody ever buys, we see those as a challenge. The other, that eternal task of finding someone special to come home to at night, someone who makes you want to go home.'

'That wasn't Harriet?'

'Harriet is... a great person. We ended up talking late into the night a lot more than we did dating. She was my sister's friend first, and became mine over time, initially because we share the same music tastes. We got confused that we liked each other because we talked a lot, but we're friends.'

They passed the last streetlight and walked up the dark lane in silence, the mist always just beyond an arm's reach around them. The further they walked the more the light pollution faded. The woods hovered as a blurred blue-black mass behind the almost transparent white veil in front of them, until the narrow road curved slightly to the left and the entrance to the farm slowly became visible with each step nearer. The closer they got to her door, the slower they both walked. Evie knew the short respite from real life had to be over.

'I never asked how the last bit of filming went?' He got in there first just as she had steeled herself to say goodbye at the gate. He walked her down the path to her door whilst the remains of gravel crunched under their feet.

'Mortifying. I managed to convince them to let me put a hotel robe on over the thing Yvonne wanted me to wear. I argued it was more suitable for daytime TV. It's done though. How was your Friday?'

'Tough on my knees. We laid the floors in the client's house. Can I take you out for a drink? A meal?'

'I don't go out. I have Max and Rey. My brother has been amazing this week, but he deserves a break. They need a parent that's there for them.'

'OK.' He took a step back from her. Evie suddenly wished she had said yes. Her whole body felt cold, a block of ice settled between her and Robbie. The distance between them seemed more than a step.

'But we eat at the farm café Saturday evenings and we're spending Sunday morning there again this week, in case you wanted to somehow, just drop by. Max and Rey will probably spend most of their time outside in the play area and I'll be alone with a book.'

'Yes.'

'Yes?' Her mouth curved into a smile of its own accord. The ice block melted, she had imagined it.

He cupped her face in his hands, 'I'll send you my number. Text me the time and I'll be there.' He placed a gentle kiss on her lips.

Everything about that moment was soft. His look, his lips, the kiss. She understood it was a gesture to show that he liked her without coming on too strong. When he pulled back a second later it was clear that he hadn't meant the gesture to be anything more than a sign of affection. She gave in to her instinct to stand on tiptoes and kiss him properly. Her lips crashed onto his a little harder than she had anticipated and demanded more than she knew she could promise. He tasted of beer and pub curry. Their kiss deepened, his hands moved to her waist and pulled her body closer to his until even air couldn't fit between them. She cupped the back of his neck with her free hand, not wanting it to end. The last few years melted away and she was Evie again. Just Evie. She pulled back slowly, a smile on her face, and said goodnight.

When her foot hit the kitchen floor something felt off under one of her boots as though the floor was lightly raised. Evie closed the door before she looked. She used the light from her phone and shone the screen downwards. A small black envelope lay there with a red wax seal. Evie's fingers slipped as she tried to pick it up. She placed her phone on the table and opened the envelope, her hands were as unsteady as her irregular heartbeat and her fingers stumbled when she broke the wax seal. She lifted a piece of rectangular card from its place in the envelope and read it:

The time is coming near

Exasperated and tired she threw the card onto the cold fire without thinking and made her way to her children's bedrooms to check their sleeping forms before collapsing naked into her own bed.

4500 BCE

He had separated from the group and gone into the vast forest alone. He wouldn't find her with a group. His hand gripped the hilt of his sword as his horse walked softly through the dry forest paths. It had been three years since their last meeting, he had searched often for her. She was elusive. He had begun to think of her as less than human, as a spirit of these islands.

She waited by a tree as he walked past. He stopped his horse and made it do a quarter turn towards her, four trees further into the forest from the path he was on. She took a bite of the fruit she was eating, 'Anders, son of Eric.'

'Release the curse.'

'It is already done. The words were spoken, the price is paid.'

'What is the price to undo it?'

She looked at the ground, regret passed over her face. 'A price I won't be part of. Find another.'

'What is the price. I can pay!' he shouted.

She shrank backwards, into the trees, seemingly merging with them.

'To change the course of destiny is to change your bloodline,' she shouted, before disappearing.

He turned his horse around, then charged towards where she had been, slashing at the air around him as if it

97

would project her body forward onto his sword. She had vanished.

Chapter 9

Atlas had unexpectedly joined her for dinner the next evening in the café and stayed for a drink afterwards, even after she had explained that she had arranged to meet Robbie. Evie chatted to her brother about the farm as she prepared herself to mention her unvoiced plans to open a plant nursery and garden centre when Robbie walked over. Atlas glowered at Robbie.

'Sit down, we need a chat. According to my sister you walking her home last night was a surprise. So explain the set up. Was it a bet?' Atlas pulled out his phone and showed a picture. Evie leaned forward over the table and grabbed his phone to look. It was a picture of her and Robbie kissing outside the farm door, and another of them stood by the open farm door, hand in hand, Evie walking inside. The image insinuating that they entered the house together. Evie looked at the top bar, it was a social media gossip page.

Immediately she opened her own phone and found the photograph plastered across the gossip pages, the preferred headline seemed to be *Builder takes footballer's girl*, nothing about her and Damian having been divorced for six years and separated before that, nothing about her having her own career, nothing to say that she was a real person and not an object to be owned, a trophy to be taken. Robbie didn't seem as surprised by the photograph.

He calmly placed his pint on the table and the tray on a neighbouring table, taking a chair. He moved Max's things a little to the side and pushed the chair in his hand closer to Evie before he sat down, close enough so his leg rested against hers under the table.

'I appreciate you looking out for her. If it was my sister, I'd be mad as hell too. All I can say is I genuinely like Evie. I intend to stick around. I didn't see anyone when I kissed her last night. If I had it wouldn't have happened. Not the kiss, but the photographs. I swear I didn't see or hear anyone spying on our privacy.'

'If I find out you had something to do with this—' Atlas muttered in a low voice.

'I didn't. I like the woman I met in the woods who was exploring a ditch. I like the woman that came to our meeting late in bloodied overalls because helping a goat give birth was more important than the houses she's spent two years fighting planning permission for. I like that she drew boundaries last night and didn't invite me in because she puts her children first, because that's what I'd want for my own children. I'm not here because she's on TV.'

Unlike others, Robbie didn't shrink from her brother's large frame and deep voice. He held his ground calmly, his leg against hers, elbows on the table, leaning forward to speak to Atlas privately. He didn't announce the conversation to the whole café in a loud voice. Atlas sat opposite him, absorbing these words, different expressions appearing behind his thoughtful eyes.

'You hurt her and I'll hunt you down and watch whilst my dogs rip you to pieces.'

'I don't doubt it.' They stared at each other across the table for a few seconds.

Atlas turned to Evie, 'Don't put the houses at risk. Wait until they're done. You, Max, and Rey deserve a home.'

'I agree. We all need those houses built. I'll take it slowly,' she nodded.

'I'll get another round. What are you drinking Robbie?' Atlas stood up despite the fact that not one drink on the table was finished. He fixed a hard stare at Evie who knew what the look meant. Be normal. Robbie shifted in his seat and put an arm over the back of her chair. He looked amused.

When Atlas left, he said, 'My brothers and I have those conversations. The ones where eyes and expressions speak all the things we can't say in front of a client.' Evie had noticed, she remembered Liam had been about to object to providing a turnkey house when Robbie jumped in and said they would do it.

'He's picked up more of my messes than he can count. He got lumbered with a wild child when our parents left,' she commented.

'I don't think you're much wrong on the wild part.'

'Have you been talking to Garrett again?' she teased.

Their conversation flowed easily. Atlas came back with a trayful of drinks, including more for the children. When Max and Rey came inside for a quick drink Atlas introduced Robbie as a friend of his and their mother's. The fact that the introduction to Robbie came from their matter-of-fact uncle rather than their mother made the children question it less, they darted back outside to play. Inevitably, the conversation turned to rugby and Evie took a second to look at her phone whose pinging messages she had ignored throughout the conversation at the table. As she bowed out of the conversation for a minute to reply to a friend,

Robbie shifted again, so that his arm no longer rested along the back of her chair but on her thigh under the table whilst he laughed and chatted with her brother about different players. Between texts Evie put her hand over his. She alternated between the conversation and Gia's messages.

'Gia's coming home!' she announced suddenly, she blurted it out in the middle of their conversation. She hadn't meant to say it out loud. She looked up, alarmed, 'Sorry. That wasn't meant for either of you. I'm just happy.'

'Gia?' Robbie questioned.

'Gia Roselli, the writer,' Atlas answered, before Evie could, as she paused mid-way through typing a reply to look up. He downed his pint and stood up, 'Want me to take the kids back?' Evie shook her head.

'I'll be an hour or two. They asked for dessert and we haven't had that yet.'

'We close in half an hour,' he told her. Evie looked up from her phone. She hadn't realised how long they had been talking.

'Oh, I'll get them to box it up then. Do you want anything bringing back?

'If you stay till closing and there's still strudels left, I'll have those.' Atlas left, carrying his glass back to the counter and handing it over to the staff.

From the other side of a café a figure in an oversized black tracksuit lifted a phone.

Evie put her phone down on the table and placed her hand over Robbie's on her thigh. He shifted in his seat again so that he faced her. Both his hands cupped hers. Silently they interlocked fingers. Their eyes met. Evie dipped her eyes down to her jeans before looking back up. She was about to speak when he smiled, 'Cute phone cover.'

'What?' she glanced at her phone, the clear case held sellotaped daisies, pressed real ones and childish drawn ones between the transparent case and gold back of her phone. She smiled at it, 'It makes me happy. Max and Rey pick daisies for me. They love that they can give me my favourite thing instantly. I love how happy it makes them, that there's no pressure on them to go to the shops to buy me something. Jess and Yvonne hate it, if we have an evening work thing, like an awards ceremony, they'll message me and tell me to change my phone case. They're petty like that.'

'They control you that much that they think they can decide your phone case?'

'It's for the show, my career. Apparently PR think I'm more sellable if we leave the children thing at the door. But I don't mind in a way, it leaves something that's private at home.'

His hand tightened around hers, 'If my phone case was full of my kids' gifts, I'd tell them to fuck off. I was raised to be proud of who I am and my roots. Have you heard about the other job?' Evie glanced up before she answered Robbie's question as a group walked past their table. The café was emptying, people knew it was closing time and they were leaving.

'Not yet. I wish we could have a bit longer. I really didn't know Atlas was coming tonight or that Gia needed to talk urgently. She was worried about coming back.'

'We have tomorrow morning, don't we? Leisurely coffee here?'

'You still want to? Even though I've been talking to Gia?' She had been rude, it was supposed to be a date, but

103

as always, she struggled. She thought to apologise but Robbie placed a hand on her thigh.

He leaned forward and smiled, 'Everyone needs friends, and friendship isn't one-sided, Evie. I'll always tell you to make time for them. Your brother isn't going to scare me off by looking out for you. Does he know about the threats?'

Evie shook her head at his question, 'He's dealt with enough. The farm is in a good place right now, but he's been working on it since he could walk. I want to let him have some time when things run smoothly and he's not fighting something.' She hadn't worked out what to do in the library yet except close the door and hope that he didn't go in. From the slightly raised eyebrow Robbie had the same thought.

'How did you build the farm up? People say that the fields were overgrown with brambles and gorse and you had to dig it out by hand.'

'We did dig it out. I remember doing that. It took years to get those fields ready. We started off with food for ourselves, then we took the excess to the farmers' markets. One day I had a wild idea that we could sell eggs, but we didn't have any animals to get eggs from. About a week later I negotiated our farmer's markets takings for some ducklings from another farm. Atlas was furious but I knew I could make it work, and he fell in love with them so much that those ducklings lived in the house with us until we fixed up the duck barn, which is now part of the turkey enclosure but that's another story. It's all new now and built to farming regulations. We eventually bought hens. We slowly put money away from the hen and duck eggs to buy dairy goats which ate those overgrown fields faster than we could clear them by hand. From the goats' dairy products we saved to invest in cows. Atlas always wanted animals. I'm happy with crops, we both have our own thing with the farm. Crops made it all happen though.' Her wicked grin and light tone showed her love of farming and crops. She wouldn't reveal her secret to those abundant crops, but her brother knew that without her gift the farm would never have happened.

'Suddenly I'm getting a new appreciation for being able to go to college and work with my dad. How old were you? Twelve?'

'No, we started growing crops a long time before my parents left. We— I might have been around seven or eight when we started the local farmers' markets. Old enough to be able to do maths and work out change. I remember getting better and faster every week. I'm going to get the desserts boxed. Do you want anything?' She stopped talking suddenly, and shook her head, her shoulders tensed with unspoken, shameful secrets. Her parents had only been interested in each other.

'No, I'm good.' The way he looked directly at her with a smile, silently telling her that she was all he needed right at that moment was enough for her to take a breath and relax. All she had to do was pretend to be normal.

Chapter 10

The skies broke to a warm grey the following morning and soft delicate light started to fill the milking shed. Evie pushed a slow cow into a stall, Atlas was ready with the equipment in an instant. Evie patted Flora's rump and moved onto the next cow. They had already milked one herd and her goats. Max and Rey had her phone to call Atlas if there were any issues at the house, but both were still asleep when she had nervously left. The staff who helped Atlas deserved at least one day off, but it didn't make her feel any better about leaving her children alone. She used to bring them along when they were very little. Lately they had begun to moan about getting up so early. Evie had been mindful that they too, were juggling their own heavy schedules of school, hockey team training and match games. Max's ambition was to eventually make the national junior team, whilst Rey was just happy to be on the school team with her friends. They had the additional schedule of figure skating lessons for Rey who was more than good enough to start competitions but was not inter-ested. Evie had no desire to make their lives any more rushed or stressed than they already were by pushing Rey. They ignored most of the school set homework, everything she did was to create a calm, soothing home for them, space to be a family, not endless work after already working in school all day. Evie carried around with her an internal worry that no matter what she did as a parent, it would never be enough, never good enough. She did try to keep up with the reading.

Atlas nodded to the muted sky she was looking at as those thoughts tumbled around inside her own head, unspoken.

'That sky is going to build until it throws itself down mid-afternoon. Reckon the rain'll settle in for the rest of the day. You should take an umbrella to the café. You don't want to catch pneumonia again.'

'Atlas, I don't catch pneumonia, it develops.' Despite her protest, she'd had pneumonia enough times for the count to be in double figures. Nevertheless, it was always at the forefront of her brother's worries, even though they didn't have to be concerned anymore.

Initially, when their parents had left, her pneumonia was a problem. They could explain solo visits to the doctor with her brother, but they agreed that their excuses of busy parents would not work in a hospital. She didn't pull her full weight on the farm in winter because he didn't allow it. Not since that second winter after their parents' departure when the doctor tried to hospitalise her with severe pneumonia. That was the winter mould really started in the house. She stayed in her bedroom for three weeks and every morning Atlas would try to bring enough firewood up to her to keep her warm throughout the day, he brought and subsequently took, her schoolwork in, and carried the extra textbooks, papers and messages as though they were nothing. He sourced some DVDs that winter, halfway through her second week of sickness, for a popular teenage vampire vanquishing show from the past, and a DVD player for her, way before they had money for subscriptions. Nowadays Atlas tried his hardest to make sure she was near the house, that she rested, and that she was done before it got dark so that Max and Rey weren't out on the farm like they had been as children.

He changed the subject, 'You're meeting Robbie again?'

'I am.'

'I like him.'

'Because you two can talk rugby?'

'Yes.'

'You never gave Damian a chance.' Her words were soft, not accusatory, just in wonder that he'd give a man a chance after his hatred of her ex-husband.

'I never liked him. He was full of himself, he took you on a destructive path you didn't need to go on and then he walked away from being a father and left you alone when you needed to be in hospital. With pneumonia. You were on a fucking ventilator to breathe, Evie. He never showed up. I told you when the McGregor boys were growing up next door that footballers are assholes. You're far too full of second chances with people.'

'I dealt with the McGregor boys,' she hissed through gritted teeth. Every time he brought up the incident anger flooded through her.

'At great expense. You told the ivy to wrap itself around them and pin them down before you broke the eldest one's nose and his rib. They saw you use your—' he cut himself off. The McGregor boys were men now, but they didn't have names. To use their names was to acknowledge the years of bullying the pair of siblings had inflicted upon them. Even her brother had struggled when it was two slightly older boys against one, they had usually planned their attacks and relied on catching Atlas and Evie unaware and alone.

'He's in prison for assault and rape now. I wasn't the first or the last. But I made damn sure he never came over on our land to try anything with me again. Do you ever think about what would have happened if I hadn't used my—' She stopped as she caught her brother's look. His face was thunderous.

'I do. And that haunts me too. We got our revenge. I still remember how you told me that night you'd make certain you owned their farm one day. What worries me is with phones these days all it's going to take is for someone to get it on camera and one person to take it too seriously and you're in a lab being tested on for the rest of your life. I don't want that for any of us. We belong under open skies in the fields, Evie.'

'I know,' she whispered.

Atlas's phone pinged. He looked at it and froze, 'House.' He started running. Evie ran after him.

They ran into the kitchen to hear screams from Max and Rey. Evie shot up to their room. Her children ran into her, colliding with her as she sank to her knees and wrapped her arms around them.

'What's going on?' Evie panted, out of breath after the speed they had raced at. She had known immediately from her brother's tone that something had happened to her children.

'The grey lady came back, she was in your bedroom. I thought it was you.' Rey sobbed into Evie's clothes, holding her so hard Evie's top crinkled and pulled into Rey's fist. 'I sent you a text instead of calling so she didn't find out we had a phone and take it.'

109

'You did good, Max. It was all I needed. You kept your head. It takes a lot of effort. Which way did she go?' Atlas praised his nephew.

'She came in here after Rey, she saw me with the phone but I'd already sent the text, then she left the room and turned towards the stairs.'

'I'm going to find her.' Evie stood up, detangling herself from Rey, determined to remove the threat from their lives. The house was quiet around them, holding its creaks and whispers in, as though to protect whatever hiding spot the Grey Spectre had.

'Stay. I can manage a woman by myself,' Atlas told her.

'What if she's like me?' Evie threw at him. He stopped and looked at her, his gaze going to Max and Rey then back to her, his expression clear that he had never considered that.

'I want to find her too,' Rey spoke, her crying easing, 'No one scares me like that.' She slipped her hand into Evie's. Max took Evie's other hand with his.

Happy to keep her children close by, Evie looked at her brother, 'Let's go.'

Before they could move a step they heard the echo of the internal kitchen door slamming in the way it did when a gust of wind caught it. Evie looked at Atlas. He ran to the kitchen. She followed more slowly with her children. Their grip on her hands hurt, but she didn't say anything. Atlas was already at the open kitchen door.

'We're too late. She must have hidden in one of the rooms and slipped out. You stay here. I'll manage the cows alone.' Atlas was visibly angry.

'I'm going to check the house anyway.' Evie knew she

had heard the internal kitchen door. She didn't trust that the Grey Spectre had run out the house as much as her brother did.

In a dilapidated outbuilding a grey hooded figure stooped to avoid part of the rusted metal roof that was falling inwards, anger crossing her face at the interference from the children. She hadn't finished her weakening spell in Evie's room. Evie was due another bout of pneumonia, it would lessen her physical strength and her powers, for the time was approaching when she would call them her own. Shrugging off the grey cape and soft shoes to reveal a basic plain black sweatshirt and leggings, she hid her hair and face beneath a plain black cap. She folded the grey cape into a black gym bag and lifted out a smart watch to complete her outfit, designed to blend unnoticeably into a crowd. She pulled out a small case from the bag, opened it, and put the circular shapes into her eyes. She did a final check to ensure she left no trace, then began to make her way to the café and shops, a phone in her hand encased in a plain dark cover.

In the busy café Evie and her children made their way to the only reserved table. Evie had changed from farm overalls to jeans and a pale blue/grey T-shirt. It was still a mild day, despite the threat of rain. A young waitress, she could barely be fourteen, stopped them and told her the table was reserved with all the haughtiness that only a teenager could manage. Before Evie could even respond, regular waitress Josie came up behind with apologies, and told them to take their seats even as she pulled the new waitress away to whisper that she never stopped Evie again. Evie suppressed a laugh; once she had been a teenager who thought she knew everything too.

Max and Rey unloaded their unwanted jackets and bags onto chairs and the table whilst Evie placed the light-weight showerproof jacket she had carried with her over the back of her chair. Both children were still subdued but they'd helped to finish off milking. Rey had opted to bring her drawing things and three books, Max had brought a gaming console and a magnetic thing that amused him to take apart and rebuild. A glance outside showed that the palest warm grey skies from that morning were now steadily growing to a mid-grey. Her brother was right, there wouldn't be daylight today, only a soft wintry yellow/grey glow and it would be dark with rain by mid-afternoon.

Forlornly her thoughts turned to spending the evening in the house. She could set up a movie night in her bedroom. Or a boardgame night.

A sudden voice made her look away from her own thoughts and re-enter the café, 'You look a million miles away.'

'Just planning dinner tonight.' She smiled as she looked up to see Robbie.

'Any conclusions?'

'Not really. I'm leaning towards steak, chips, and a salad.'

'It's Sunday. Aren't you supposed to have a traditional roast dinner as a farmer?' He put two hands on the back of a chair and leaned forward slightly. His eyes never left hers. Evie liked that. He wasn't looking around the café, just at her.

'I don't really like roast dinners.'

'What do you prefer?'

'Raw and natural food. Salads, rocket especially. There's three exceptions,' she flirted, her mouth curving into a smile.

'And those are?' He leaned forward slightly more.

'Cheese, pasta, and pizza.'

'Not desserts?' He faked looking shocked.

Evie shook her head, 'Not really. Maybe a lemon cheesecake. But not a baked one. What about you?'

'I like all foods. Chocolate brownies are my downfall. Liam and I have had physical fights over the last chocolate brownie. Not recently though.' He laughed at the memory.

'Are you going to sit down?'

'Shall I get us coffees first?'

'Please. Cappuccino.' There was a pause as he waited for her to continue. She lifted her arm in an expressive gesture to question his hesitation.

'That's it? No special milks, syrup pumps, extra foam, shot of something?'

'No. Just a cappuccino.' An expression went over his face, something that she couldn't decipher, before asking what drinks Max and Rey wanted. It left her wondering if her order was too simple for a supposed twenty-first century city girl. She liked simplicity, she liked understated and uncomplicated.

In that way, she understood why her brother and son loved the farm so much. The routines were familiar, they had time to watch the seasons pass in a manner that had been a lifeline for so many generations before, not that many people noticed the seasons changing now. They noticed the big weather, the rain, the heat of the sun increasing, the leaves dropping, the snow, but she doubted that they saw the tiniest green buds on the trees in February, the emerging greenery before the earliest crocuses and daffodils came out, the increase in insects, the migration of birds, or even the way the wildlife snuggled down in sheltered spot`s before the rain.

She talked with Robbie through another coffee and then breakfast. Robbie's warm leg rested against hers the whole time he laughed with Max and Rey over childish jokes, their tales of school, and chatting about their general lives whilst they ate. When Max and Rey ran off to play before the rain, Robbie and Evie sat with the last of their coffees. His phone pinged, he glanced at it from the corner of his eye towards where it lay on the table. He moved away from her and opened it up.

Robbie turned back towards her and silently passed her the phone. Evie wrapped her hand around his and angled it so she could see better, having already taken in his masked expression. She looked at the screen. The text from his brother had a screenshot attached from a social media site. Side by side pictures of them yesterday sat together after her brother had left, and right now, sitting, drinking, chatting together. The accompanying text was simple, 'Saturday evening and Sunday morning. They hid it by arriving separately but IFYKYK.' Evie shot a glance around the café. At least half the customers were on their phones instead of talking to the people they were out with. Her stomach sank to the ground and her happiness dissipated. She reasoned that it cut more deeply because it wasn't an instantaneous, random shot posted, it had been carefully planned.

She took a moment before she responded, 'I'm sorry.' She released her hand from his, already worried about her producer's reaction. She moved her leg away from his. He reached for her hand with his free one and held it.

'I'm not worried for me. I guess I never really thought

about what it's like to be recognised everywhere. I moan about village people knowing everything but to experience strangers knowing who you are and posting photographs, that's a whole other level.'

'At least they left Max and Rey out of the pictures this time.'

'Do you think it's the same person?'

'Yeah. Probably some kid hoping to use the photos as a platform to turn into an online influencer. I can't exactly ban phones in the café. I'm not Luke Danes.'

'I actually know who he is.' Robbie grinned.

'I should go. I've got our clothes to pack up today.' She didn't move, she found that she liked a relaxed Sunday morning coffee with Robbie, and she didn't want it to end.

'How about another drink first?' he offered.

Evie smiled back, 'I'd love that.'

They stayed in the farm café through lunch, sharing touches and conversation as though they had been together for ten years and were a couple completely comfortable with each other. The rain started at lunch. Max and Rey stayed out until they were drenched, at which point Evie had to reluctantly accept that they needed to go home. Rey surprised her by asking outright if it was a board game afternoon and a movie night. Evie nodded that they could do that, but they definitely needed to get changed.

'Can we have a pyjama day?' Max asked, hope filled his quiet voice.

'I think a rainy afternoon merits a pyjama afternoon.' Evie smiled and dropped a kiss on the top of his head. They both cheered and shouted, and told Robbie that their friends talked about having pyjama days. The problem was that there was always a list of jobs to be done on the farm, and in the rare instance of all jobs being completed, they had a back list of repairs and non-urgent jobs.

'Can we wear our new Halloween pyjamas?'

'Yes.'

'Are we safe at home? Can't we get the caravan and move in, Mum?' Rey asked.

Robbie looked at Evie, 'What happened?'

It was Max that told him, standing in the café in wet clothes. Robbie listened carefully, crouched to Max's level. Rey chewed on her lip. Evie packed their things away into her bag. She wanted her children to talk, as opposed to her own childhood when secrets had been hidden and shameful. But she did not want Robbie to know about the latest incident at the witch house. The way those blue eyes kept glancing up at her with pity, concern and then worry, she didn't need that. Evie hurried her children out of the café door and into the onslaught of rain.

Robbie's hand caught her arm, 'Are you going to be alright by yourself?'

'We'll be fine. I've got chocolate, crisps, marsh-mallows, we might even make chocolate crispies in the kitchen with cereals and I'll put a movie on my laptop. They like watching movies and baking at the same time. I'll make it a comfort afternoon. Board games with blankets and snacks. Dinner. Another movie in bed in my room. I'll keep them in my bed for tonight.' They were all getting wet now. Raindrops ran down their faces, her showerproof jacket did nothing against the hard downpour, rain soaked straight through it.

'Can I walk you back?'

'You'll get wet.'

'It's just rain.'

'He can help us bake, mum, and if he comes with us we can play that game we never get to play because it's two or four players and you always say we argue too much over who plays first because we both want to play it with you, and you have spare men's Halloween pyjamas that you bought, in your room.' Rey slipped her hand into Evie's.

Evie cursed her children for telling truths, 'I'm hoping they were for your brother rather than anyone else,' Robbie whispered in her ear, his breath on her neck.

'A joke present, but yes, matching Halloween pyjamas for us all.'

'They're just black with white skulls though.' Rey frowned at Robbie, 'She never buys us cartoon ones.'

Evie rolled her eyes. The pyjamas Rey complained about were tasteful brushed cotton ones from an expensive store. The pyjamas Rey wanted were cheap fast fashion. Evie didn't argue though, she let Rey make her point. They ran to the farmhouse beneath dark skies and pushed through reeds of rain.

Chapter 11

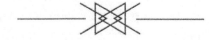

Evie looked at the parcel sat innocently on the old wooden table where they had all baked and played games on Sunday, distrust running through her entire body. Behind it was a large vase of fresh flowers, this time a subdued apricot bouquet. She never received parcels, not from people she knew. The occasional unwelcome fan parcel came in the post, whilst she loved the friendship bracelets that arrived, she didn't like the expensive jewellery or worse, the underwear men seemed to think was appropriate to send.

Despite her children urging her to open it she shook her head each time, uncertain that the contents would be suitable for them. Occasional fan parcels turned up in the mail, but this box, it whispered *money*. The people she knew who had money like that were her parents. Evie wasn't accepting anything from her parents. She doubted that they even knew they had grandchildren.

The parcel had stayed on the dining table for two days, until her children were at school and she had a free day. It was their last part week before construction began. A part week because Robbie and his team would arrive Thursday to start stripping out the house. Atlas had already loaded his caravan up with his clothes, the slow cooker and the toastie maker. He'd left her the pans and ovenware. Evie had bulk ordered store cupboard essentials for the both of them, things like stock pots and stock cubes, passata, pasta, rice, and other bits. Their biggest fear was a lack of food, a deeply rooted fear whose tendrils ran back to their childhood days of foraging for food, because their parents had forgotten to feed them yet again. She could still remember the retching of an empty stomach, waking in the darkest hours of the night with stomach pains and a feeling of wanting to be sick from the hunger gnawing inside and gouging its way into both her physical body and her mind.

With a freshly made hot cup of tea in her hands she sat in an old wooden chair by the fire, staring at the parcel. She stood and walked slowly over, and proceeded to examine the parcel again for half an hour without touching it. Woven black gracefully textured paper encased the contents without a hint. With hesitation Evie pulled the delicate ivory satin ribbon. It fell apart elegantly. Underneath the ribbon, the black paper was folded in a series of intricate folds to create a seven-pointed star. The star opened to show a set of leather-bound notebooks. Sat on the top was the type of small black envelope she knew. Her heart skipped a beat when she saw it.

On the enclosed card was a familiar loopy, exquisitely artistic handwriting she knew instantly as her friend Genevieve's. In blue ink Genevieve had written:

> *Thank you for breaking the spell Yrsa*
> *made to separate us. I could never find the*
> *source. You need these, so study carefully.*
> *Do not let anyone see them, do not talk*
> *about them, do not let Yrsa into your life.*

See you as soon as I can, V.V

Evie stared at the note that somehow made a lot of sense and very little sense at the same time. Her thoughts drifted back to the reference Genevieve had made at the beginning of her note. The spell to separate them. She remembered the photograph of them all with the strange symbols on the back that she had thrown into the dying fire.

Evie picked up a book. The leather was soft and worn, as though lots of hands had used the book over the years. There was no title, no label, nothing to indicate the contents. She opened it. In ink, in English, someone had written that the books had been translated from original sources in the 1940s during the chaotic times of World War Two to ensure that the original knowledge and material was not lost to future generations. The next page talked of the Circle of Leif, named after Yrsa's second son and fifth child, the first to be sacrificed, and his magical abilities gifted to Yrsa for eternity. It failed to tell her who Yrsa was, although it did say that the family lines had been traced for hundreds of years and Yrsa took whatever gifts from her descendants that she required.

Intrigued, Evie flipped further through the book. Mixed in with spells and instructions were descriptions of sacrificed powers and bloodlines. She came to a page with a beautifully illustrated picture of British woodland, a raven in one tree, an owl in another, various animals peeping through hedgerows, a tiny mouse eating a blackberry, a family of hedgehogs in the undergrowth of a hawthorn hedge. She read the page. It talked about projecting consciousness into the animals to view situations unfolding without having to be physically present.

She was so lost in the books her cup of tea went cold and she jumped when her phone alarm went off. Hastily she gathered the books up and slipped on her shoes. Picking up a key from the hook by the door she ran across to the field behind the farmyard and opened up a beige door.

Inside the caravan was filled with unpacked boxes. Evie ignored all of them and went straight to the bright white double room that was going to be her bedroom. She closed the curtains then opened a part of the overhead storage that hung over the bed and placed the books into the clutch of the darkest corner of the cupboard. She locked the caravan securely and placed the key in her pocket.

On the routine drive to the school to collect her children her thoughts turned to the black envelope, the same black envelope that her threats turned up in. Her parents had received that envelope too. Genevieve possibly held all the answers to her questions but was still uncontactable. Evie pictured the last time she had seen a photograph of her in a magazine. Genevieve had stood in the background of some event, aloof, regal, with no light in her eyes. She had stopped being their vibrant V.V years ago. And yet, she was reaching out as though she knew Evie needed someone.

She pulled up into a parking space near Oak Hall. The well-kept private school buildings gleamed in the autumn sunshine. Her phone rang and filled the car. Evie was tempted to ignore it, but lifted it from her bag to see who the caller was. Andy's name flashed at the top of the screen. She chose to stay in her car and answer it.

'Hi, Andy.'

'Evie. Good news. All we have to do is the contracts and HR stuff. We're ready for you to start as soon as you can, possibly next week if you can juggle two schedules. It turns out that if you go up the chain far enough the same company that owns the network which produces the country show also owns the different network that produces your lunchtime show so they're communicating an early contractual release for you. Lyssa and Col are really impressed that there's a known face out there with experience of actual farming. They've dropped the search for other presenters for now.'

'That's great, what do I need to do?'

'You'll get an email asking you to confirm that you still want the job so look out for it. It should be plain sailing from now onwards.'

'I can't thank you enough for putting me up for this opportunity. I'm looking forward to working with you.'

'Likewise. I'm driving home now. Hope to see you at work soon.' Andy hung up. Evie got out of her car with a huge smile.

Her smile extended as her phone pinged with an unexpected message from Robbie, telling her that he had hit his hand with a hammer because he had been thinking about her instead of concentrating on his job. She typed a flirtatious reply back as she negotiated the school path to her children's classroom doors with her eyes down as she pretended to be busy on her phone. Her smile disappeared when she saw the Headteacher making a direct line for her, her eyes fixed on Evie as she walked with purpose, a grave air of seriousness pushing everyone else away. Evie's memories of constantly being called into the Head's office over some misdemeanour or infringement of the numerous rules she thought to be ridiculous flooded back. She reminded herself that she liked this dark-haired lady and forced a smile onto her face. She watched her approach in her light blue blazer and trousers.

'Hello, Ms Hepburn. Could we please have a word in my office.'

Evie knew from the way her name was spoken that this was a formal meeting. She followed the Headteacher silently.

The office was minimal and neat aside from the number of box files with pieces of paper poking out at the corners. The only indulgence seemed to be a glitter mug with the remains of a cup of tea. The carpet was functional cold dark grey thin carpet tiles, against which the warmth of the Cornish cream shade on the walls clashed. Framed certificates from universities and pictures of various school events were hung on the walls.

'Can I get you a drink? This is going to be an uncomfortable conversation I'm afraid.'

'No. Let's just dive straight in. Who did what to whom?'

'It's about you.'

'Me?' Evie tried to think of ways she had recently behaved that could have necessitated school involvement in her life. All she could think of was the photographs of her and Robbie. She waited for the Head to get to the point, ready to fire bottled up anger towards her if it was about her personal life. Far too many people thought they had a right to an opinion about her personal life lately.

'We've received this today in the post. Our staff opened it because it had the school's address on, so we weren't certain whether it was intended for the school or yourself.' The Headteacher passed her a black envelope.

It was the second time that day she was seeing the thick card envelope. This one, with its unique red wax seal, was instantly different to the earlier one. Genevieve's hadn't been sealed. The envelope had already been opened and read. Evie opened it carefully, the message inside was simple:

I know everything.
If you fail to give me what I want,
I'll take it from the children.
Their lives for yours.

Evie spun the card around and around in her hands, wondering how to explain it away.

After too long a pause to be able to fake a nonchalant response she looked up, she couldn't even speak before the Head did, 'I already have the police here. They've seen it and recorded it. We're going to be bringing them in to talk about safety to all the children. We'll be especially vigilant around Max and Rey. I'll bring the police in now. They would like to talk to you.' The woman stood up.

'I told them when it started happening.' The words tumbled from her mouth, unbidden. Evie shook her head as the woman stopped mid step to look at her, but that didn't change the fact that she had spoken, she was unable to take the words back.

'They didn't seem aware.' Her tone was less authoritative now, more hesitant, she looked human as the professional mask dropped.

'It was after I left my husband. The threats have been increasing in severity every year. They weren't bothered then. They told me to be careful but that they didn't have staff to deal with every female who reported an ex or a stalker or someone acting suspiciously. I understand they've taken a brutal share of budget cuts since. If they didn't have the staff then, they certainly won't have the staff now.'

'It looks like this person is stepping up, if they're sending threats via the school.'

'They are.'

'And you've no idea who it could be? Your ex? It's no business of ours but we've had to do some research, all the school fees, the trips, the extra curriculars come out of your bank. Your children never see their father or talk about him. He's never been to one concert, assembly or parents evening. We don't have a great view of him here at the school. It's a safe place if you wanted to talk about anything that might have happened.'

'I might brush off the odd threat towards me as part of my job but anybody that puts my children at risk would be shut down immediately. I understand your need to bring the police in, but they don't need to waste their time seeing me. Keep Max and Rey safe whilst they're here. I'll work the rest out.' Evie stood up as the bell went signalling the end of the school day. She passed the card back.

'They'd still like to talk to you. Feel free to stop by my office any time. We can make alternative collection arrangements for Max and Rey if collecting them from the gate is a safety concern.'

'I know from experience that feeling different as a kid is a huge stress by itself. They're already very aware that their dad isn't around like their friends' fathers are. I'd prefer to try and keep things as normal as possible for them, for as long as I can, Mrs West.'

'Call me Rachel. Don't brush your own welfare under the carpet either. There's far too many horror stories around at the moment. I've left an abusive relationship with a young child myself. I understand the fear, not just of leaving but of having Social Services involvement. There's no judgements here.' The look of concern on the other woman's face was genuine.

'Evie.'

'You know, a few of the teachers here still remember you, in the senior part of the school.'

'In which case I'm sure they've delighted you with stories about my behaviour. I've calmed down.' Evie let out a small smile to reassure the other woman.

'I have no concerns about your parenting. Max is a delight to have in class, and whilst Rey is a bit more of a handful, she speaks her mind. I can easily understand why and how those stories came about if you were similar as a child. Stay and talk to the police. I'll have Max and Rey taken to the after-school club for a bit. I do mean it, my door is always open for you.' Her voice was softer, encouraging rather than stern. She left the room.

Evie was given no choice unless she wanted to make a scene. In the moment that passed between Rachel leaving and the police entering, Evie's hands started to burn. She should be cowed, she should be scared. That had been the purpose of the note, her stalker had attempted to show off, to say that they knew everything about her life, all Evie felt was a dissipating fear and a growing recklessness.

Chapter 12

Evie walked up to the caravan feeling remnants of warmth from the lunchtime winter sun, marvelling at how quickly October had disappeared. Her hands carried full shopping bags from the farmers' market shops in her farm branded totes and her head was elsewhere as it sorted through the current crop rotation. Although she saw Robbie as he jogged over to her in his workwear, she didn't snap out of her thoughts until he fell into place next to her holding something metal in his hands. He wrestled the heavy bags from her and passed her the item. Shards of light hit her eyes as the winter sun glinted on it. It was cold in her hands and she registered that it was an old toffee tin, the bonnets and clothing frills on the women in the pictures giving away the age of it.

'I thought you were working.' His statement reminded her that she still had perfect studio styled waves in her hair. The crisp shirt, jeans, and country boots with an equally country jacket made her look the part. Her lunchtime show hadn't officially let her go, she had already started pre-filming slots for the country show which was where she had been earlier.

'We finished early. We got lucky and I was only filming on the farm anyway, the producers are wanting to start a focus on my farm and Andy's as well as usual countryside issues. I was going to get the plough out and try to get at least one field done but I needed to get the food first.' She reached into the pocket of her country jacket for the key to her caravan. She had tried to do it the other way around, contemplated just heading straight for the plough whilst driving home, but she couldn't, a voice inside her head wouldn't rest until the caravan was safely restocked with the items from her shopping list that sat heavily in her bag.

'Do you have time for me? There's some things you really should see. Not just the tin.'

Evie looked at his sky-blue eyes, the way his eyes crinkled into deep weatherworn lines when he smiled at her and knew she'd always have time for him. Inside her stomach butterflies and moths began to dance. Previously unveiled secrets from the house had taught her caution. A runaway hen stopped by her feet and looked up at her. Evie looked down.

'If I try and pick you up, you're going to move aren't you, Winnie?' Winnie answered by pecking at the ground and running away when Evie bent down.

'We've noticed the hens.' Robbie smiled.

'Those three are really good at escaping; Winnie, Joy and Vivienne. We try and round them up. They're nosy and like to see what's going off. Have you looked inside?' she asked. The tin looked old, like turn of the last century old.

'I glanced at the contents. It was under the floor-boards in the old pantry area off the kitchen. But there's more.' The hesitation in his tone told her enough.

'I don't want to know, do I?'

'People are going to talk. You should at least see why.'

'OK. Let me put the shopping away.'

'I'll wait here.' Robbie looked down at his workwear. Evie shook her head at his gesture. Dirt didn't bother her.

'Come on in. I'll put the kettle on.' Despite her words Robbie removed his boots and outer neon clothes.

His jaw dropped a little at her caravan when they walked inside. Evie didn't notice until she turned and indicated to put the shopping bags on the dining table. He was staring at her caravan. It was the complete opposite of the farmhouse and probably more in tune with her celebrity persona than her farmer one. The caravan was small but luxe, she'd opted for white and gold, having taken the children with her to choose it. She liked white but Rey adored all things winter, snow, ice, wolves; and therefore lots of white. They had both agreed on the white scheme whilst Max had gone off with Atlas. Her brother, along with her son, had chosen a masculine wood and leather caravan. She opened the white-fronted dishwasher and took out two black mugs with their farm logo printed in white. Robbie was still looking around. The tiny kitchen was all white and uncluttered except for an emerald vase holding white flowers.

Evie tried to see her living space through his eyes. Her settee had blankets and cushions in a variety of blues strewn over it where they had watched TV and films. Her king-sized midnight blue blanket was ruffled in the middle, Max's double cobalt blue blanket was trailing from the settee onto the white rug. Rey's blanket, icy blue with white snowflakes, had been thrown to the other side of the small corner settee. A row of baby snake plants in textured ivory pots adorned the sitting room window. Underneath the raised settee woven baskets hid various toys and personal bits, board games, and books. A cheap silver tinsel Christmas tree was draped with a string of skull fairy lights and decorated with tiny hanging jet demons and gargoyles collected from trips to Whitby; her daughter liked the dark and macabre in winter. Pottery ghosts from York sat between plants. Dried honesty stems shimmered in translucent pearl shades inside crystal vases, they created a frame for the TV with their tall, elegant beauty. The dining booth was scattered with cushions in soft dawn pinks. A matching pink glass vase held more white flowers on the table.

'I'll change the Christmas tree for a proper Christmas one. I let them have their choice when it's Halloween.'

'How do you keep it white with children?'

'Shoes off and slippers on the minute we get in. I have a cleaner twice a week from the village. She'll do the entire caravan Tuesdays and Fridays. It's why we use the door nearest the bathroom and bedrooms as the entrance, we go straight into the bedrooms to change.'

Her cleaner was new, and a revelation after trying so hard to keep on top of the farmhouse. She explained to Robbie that they had put the old washing machine in an unused storeroom that had water already linked up so any item of clothing that managed to get filthy, like her farm overalls, didn't come near the caravan.

'Hence your boot room with utility, shower, and its own entrance.' He gave a thoughtful nod, remembering the plans for her home.

Evie gave a wry smile at the memory of rushing to their meeting after helping Cleo the goat give birth. 'You've already seen the sort of mess I can create for myself on the farm. Tea or coffee?'

'Coffee if you have it. Is this how you'd choose your home?'

'All white? Probably. I chose our architect because I

love how she visualises family homes. I've followed her work for a few years since she revolutionised a family home on a TV show when I was at university. She took this Victorian terraced house in London with small rooms and made it a beautiful glamorous light-filled twenty-first century home with all the gadgets like hidden speakers to play music in every room. She did my favourite cocktail bar in London. She uses colour but she's used it so differently in both houses. Mine is light and airy, my brother's house looks moody and reflective.'

'She's managed to capture both your personalities in the houses. I like how she's given yours a bit of nineteen twenties luxe. The green bathroom is beautiful and slightly ironic for someone who's demolishing an old Stuart era building,' he said. Evie laughed.

'She asked me what my favourite books were, now and growing up. One of them was *The Great Gatsby*. The escapism of his parties was probably the catalyst for my own partying lifestyle. She took a little of that era and brought it into the house. I'm not a period house person. I think sometimes, for some people, growing up with furniture older than you that you have no choice over and never an option to change, forces an intense dislike of antiques. Max and Rey will probably hate mass produced white flat-pack furniture.' She filled her white textured kettle with more water and turned it on.

It seemed natural for Robbie to take over making the drinks whilst Evie put away the fresh bread, meats, and vegetables she had brought home. She had turned the heating off when she had taken the children to school and she felt the lack of it inside the caravan. The old farmhouse kitchen had provided some relief from the cold with its almost eternal fire. They stood in the kitchen area with their hot drinks as Evie perused through the old toffee tin Robbie had found between sips. There were two letters, one addressed to her and one to her brother. She put those aside for later. A jar held a string that had some sort of metal with amber beads on. A pair of blue baby boots and Atlas's hospital plastic tag from his birth were inside. There were three rolls of bank notes. She opened them and laughed about how big money used to be, passing them to Robbie to view. The five- and ten-shilling notes were cute, she had no idea what their modern equivalent was. The one pound and ten-pound notes from various years were much bigger than she had seen before. As the value of the notes went up she felt surprise, and hid it by pushing them back into the box. There was an old Christmas tree ornament, some thin candles and a very old box of matches. The last item she pulled out was a tiny book, its small pages filled with pencil writing. Dangling from a ribbon attached to the book was a tiny pencil. Evie put it away for later.

She finished her drink at the same time as Robbie. They looked at each other from opposite sides of the clean white kitchen, a mere pace away from each other. She moved next to him and put her cup down in the sink next to his. He smiled at her and wrapped his hand around her wrist, his grip gentle and warm against the cold of the caravan.

He pulled her closer to him, his other arm encircling her waist, 'You're so beautiful when you smile and laugh.' His lips touched hers, warm and inviting.

Evie leaned against him, relaxing into his kiss. Outside a sudden sound make her jump. She looked sharply in the direction of the sound, then she let out a small laugh at herself and rested her forehead on Robbie's shoulder, 'Sorry.'

'You OK?' he breathed the words out in a quiet tone meant for her only. His hand came up to cup the back of her neck.

She liked that, heat from his hand helped uncoil her spine, she found the touch reassuring. He didn't need to say the threats were on his mind, it was evident in his whisper. She took a moment to savour the words as she breathed out, her head on his shoulder, the weight of his hand on her neck was a thousand times better than a massage. It made her head quieten. Then she pulled herself back together with her next breath in, raising her head and stepping away, 'Yes. Shall we go and look at the old pantry and whatever it is that I don't want to see?' she asked.

'Can't we stay here?' Despite his words he had a quick smile and made a move to walk out of the caravan.

'I wish we could,' she whispered back, mostly to herself. The thought of putting the heating on and spending the day in the bedroom was much better than getting colder ploughing a field.

Outside, only the ground floor rubble remained of her old farmhouse home that had been standing the previous week. The site was eerily quiet, a contrast to the sunbeams poking holes through the thick clouds and highlighting spots in the farmyard, one of the last reminders of summer before winter fully descended, and any warmth wouldn't return until March. The sun, if it did come out, would be a yellow orb in the sky, a decoration, much like she had been with her ex-husband.

Robbie picked his way through the rubble, turning once or twice to help her before he realised she was a capable person. In the area that the pantry had once stood the old floor had been cleared away to reveal steps down to a stone floor and a hidden sublevel. A bulldozer sat empty, stone piles next to it. A small brown hen stood on the stairs, 'Which one is that?' Robbie asked as he nodded at the hen.

'That's Joy.'

'We found the tin under the floor. But this is what you needed to see.' Robbie bent down, signalling for her to look closer. Joy stayed where she was.

Evie crouched down and looked. In faded chalk she saw a pentagram and a circle that spanned the width of the unknown basement level. She sighed. They were never going to lose the witch house myth. She took her jacket off and dusted away the faded remains of chalk.

'There.' She needed to wash the jacket now but at least the evidence was gone.

'You OK?' Robbie stood up. He looked directly at her.

'Yeah. No. I'm, confused. Why would you put a floor over it when it was easy to clean up?'

'Maybe to preserve it?'

'Just redraw it?'

'You'd be surprised at the lengths people can go to in order to avoid what they view as unnecessary tasks,' Robbie said.

Evie studied the stone floor, contemplating his words. She let out an impatient sigh, 'I have a field to plough.'

Voices and the sound of heavy work boots crept into the distance behind her and she guessed the tea break was over. That was confirmed with a glance over her shoulder and she saw the takeaway cups and bacon sandwiches in the builders' hands.

'Would you like to get dinner one night this week? With Max and Rey? Just dinner. I know it'll be a school night and they'll have a bedtime. I'd like to see you,' Robbie asked.

Evie thought fast. She wanted to say yes, but the weeknight schedule was almost packed with after school clubs and extracurriculars. Friday was their only free day and she fought to keep it clear. She took the whole day off, changed the beds and made sure she spent time with them both listening to the bits of their week she had missed. She wasn't ready to let him into their Fridays yet. But instead, she heard her voice betray her, 'Friday? You might have to sit through a movie and Guiseppe's though.'

'I've never been to Guiseppe's.'

'You haven't?'

'I've heard good things about it.'

'It's the best Italian food you'll ever eat. Guiseppe is so sweet. He always comes out of the kitchen to say hello to us, and his staff are nice. It's not so upmarket that we have to dress up like its black tie, but it's not the farm café where you can walk in wearing leggings and a hoodie either.'

'So I'd have to change,' Robbie joked. His eyes crinkled, telling her he was teasing.

She smiled back, 'I love your workwear, it's quite sexy, but yeah, you'd have to change.' She gave a nod.

'Max and Rey like movies?'

'They love movies. We all do. I—' she cut herself off and turned around as men entered the space, 'I'm going to go and plough that field.'

Joy the hen sprang to life and ran between the men towards a quieter space.

After a risotto dinner that evening, she showed Atlas the tin and its contents, leaving him alone whilst she supervised her children's teeth brushing. She left them tucked up in their beds with a book each to read. When she went back into the main living area of the caravan with its white and gold gentleness, she almost wished she'd chosen Atlas's wooden cosiness instead. The letters were either side of the chess board he had set up. Two glasses of red stood next to the chequered board. He looked up from his phone, 'These certificate things, they're worth a lot of money Evie. They're issued by the Bank of England.'

'Yeah?' her tone was bored, uninterested, so was she. They'd made enough money by themselves. She wasn't going to take anything more from her parents.

'It's enough to set Max and Rey up for life and that's just a portion of it. Let's compare letters whilst we play.' Atlas's expression meant he understood her tone and wasn't going to push the subject further than he could. He moved his pawn and took a long sip of his wine before opening his letter.

Evie sat down. She matched his pawn with her own move and opened her letter first. The paper crackled and tore unevenly, creating jagged edges which reminded her of trees on the horizon. She raised her wine glass and the fruity dark liquid rose to meet her nose. She took a sip, then another, barely tasting the complex notes, willing her shoulders to relax into a normal position.

'Shall I just get you a bottle of rum to down?'

'Shut up. I appreciate that I've trained you to bring wine. I'm doing your future wife a favour.'

'She'll end up drinking rum and coke with you.'

'If that was going to happen then you'd be with one of my friends.'

'Talking of being with someone, Robbie sent me screenshots of the pentagram.'

'Did they all take a picture?' She let out an exasperated sigh.

'Probably. They're working on the witch house, they found something witchy. Even if they're not locals it's a story to tell their mates.'

'Shit.'

'We're fucked. Even when we try and make things better the witch house fucks us over.'

'I thought you were the optimistic one, Atlas.'

'It's hard these days.'

'The farm is doing fine.' She didn't understand. After all their years of struggle she wanted him to be able to coast along and enjoy the moment. He deserved that much.

'It is. We're making profits. I know that's your doing. Your ability to grow things from nothing got us started at the farmers' markets. Your stubbornness with the local council over the café and shops made the houses happen.'

'And you've got your animals, so why are you so down, Atlas? We're not struggling. We're not fighting anyone or anything. We have food, we'll have our own homes, we made the farm a success, we bought the McGregor farm. What's left except to keep it working and enjoy it?'

'I'm so used to fighting for something. Even for my corner of the farm when it was clear you were the more natural farmer with the crops. I'm not sure what to do now.'

'You enjoy what we've created.'

'I've tried. I can't. Then there's this bit of gossip I heard...'

Atlas had a tell. Evie had learnt it by now. He narrowed the inside of his eyes, right by the tear ducts. It usually meant she had done something wrong. She waited. Atlas took a sip of his wine, moved his piece and looked at her again. She shrugged and met his move. Atlas refrained from raising his voice but his angry whisper was enough when he did speak again, 'Were you going to tell me about the threat that was sent to the school? The cards you've been getting or the writing on the library wall?'

'No. It's my problem and I'm dealing with it.'

'I don't care if you're dealing with it. I care that I didn't hear about it from you.'

'How did you know about the cards?'

'I found one in the kitchen fire. I know you, this isn't new,' he challenged her.

Sitting straighter Evie met his eyes, 'The first threat was years ago, when I came back to the farm after being in hospital. I am scared but also over it. If they want me, they can come and find me, I'm ready for the fight. I've handled bigger and stronger than me before.'

She had pulled one of his ex-girlfriends to the ground at twelve, feral and wild. The sixteen-year-old pretty princess had been spreading rumours about her brother. One bright July day Evie had seen the girl laughing on the high street, the wind had carried her brother's name towards her, without even thinking she had charged at the girl and tackled her to the ground, the pair of them falling without any major injuries. She had sat on the girl and pummelled her with her fists before her friends dragged her off. Not one shop owner or passerby had intervened. V.V had told her that the locals were both scared by Evie and repelled by the older girl's manipulative lies. It was a lesson for the village, the siblings stuck together, neither were to be crossed.

'Evie!' The slight slant of his head, the way his shoulders stiffened, his arms crossed.

'Atlas, it's not a mess you can clean up for me. I don't think they're going to do anything now. If someone wanted to hurt me they'd have done it after a few threats. I think that's why they've brought the school into it. They want to shock me again, get me back into being scared. It's been years. Just like the Grey Spectre.' Her brother stared at her for a while, then gave a single nod to show his understanding behind her reasoning.

'Do you think it's the Grey Spectre sending the threats?'

'It's the only thing that makes sense. We know the Grey Spectre is a woman, she's real, and she used to scare us as children. Now I'm more angry than scared and so the notes start, little threats, like she's trying to get me scared all over again.'

'Why?'

'Because my gift isn't as fluid if I'm scared, it's harder to bring it to the surface. It's all connected to the witch thing. I just don't know how.'

'Let's read the letters.'

'What if they were planted? Why would our parents write us a letter then hide it?'

'Why would you be suspicious of a letter?'

'After years of threats I'm suspicious of practically everything and everyone,' she answered, separating the letter from the jagged, torn envelope and unfolding it.

Evie,

We've been binding your gifts yearly but despite that you're getting stronger. Much stronger. We cannot help or aid you. Or your brother. Your father and I, we cannot understand the concept of having something unique. Somehow, you've chosen to surround yourself with friends that are the same as you, even if you haven't all figured it out yet. Genevieve knows. Genevieve's parents are in the same network as we are. She will explain it all to you. Yrsa has banned us from talking to you about it. She has her eye on you like a cat playing with a mouse.

This farm is the original homestead of Yrsa and her husband. They once owned the whole area that is now the village, the town and several farms. Yrsa is someone to be feared, she has honed her craft over a thousand years upon this earth. She changes appearances and careers. Only one person has ever gotten the better of her, her great granddaughter Genevieve from the line of Leif, the one your friend is named after, who enclosed her in a magical circle on this island and she can never leave these shores. The lore goes that Genevieve escaped to what is now called Belgium.

There are five lines of descent from Yrsa – Tyr's line, Freya's line, Rhiannon's line, Thyra's line, and Leif's line. These are the surviving children she bore to her husband before poisoning him and claiming the land for herself. Her last claim on the farm and the village was as the young and widowed Lady Ursula Leah-Campbell of Hightly Hall in the period between world wars.

Yrsa will kill you for your magic. To view her properly when she is not in character is a sight to bring fear into the bravest of people. Her brown hair is braided into braids of braids, her skin is as flawless as a white cloud on a summer's day, her eyes are black from the darkest of magic that she welds as both armour and sword.

Ophelia and Jasper

Atlas looked up at her. Silently they swapped letters.

Atlas,

Good luck in the future. You've shown yourself hardworking and capable. I've already put the farm in your name, in trust until you turn eighteen. When Yrsa comes for your sister stay out of it, it's not your fight. Nightmares you cannot imagine will happen if you try and intervene.

You need to know that you are of Freya's line. One day you will be asked and you will answer 'of Freya's line'. The money is one of Yrsa's stores. Do not touch it or cash it in, unless the fates change and somehow luck favours your sister in defeating Yrsa.

Jasper and Ophelia

Chapter 13

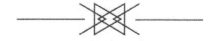

Atlas's eyes glimmered faintly in the dim light when he looked up from reading her letter, a slight glow of the amber in the greyness. Evie thought that it was the caravan lamps reflecting weirdly. She watched as he struggled to control the anger. His eyes definitely changed. Grey, then a flash of amber, slowly fading to grey, then amber again. The inside of his eye narrowed with each amber flash.

'You need to control your anger, your eyes are changing colour.' It hit her then, that her concern for her brother and his control outweighed any surprise that she had about his eyes. It didn't startle her or freak her out, she found it unusual but vaguely familiar, as though she had seen it before.

Suddenly she placed glowing amber eyes in two places, as though her brain exploded with memories. Angry Atlas with a small glow in his eyes after the McGregor brothers had tried to sexually assault her. He'd exploded but calmed down quickly when he saw she had the situation in hand. Before that incident it had happened once, after their parents had left them. No note, no goodbyes, his eyes had lit up the dark bedroom, empty of their parents' belongings, rumpled sheets on the bed and the smell of sex still heavy in the air. Atlas had flown across the room and opened the windows and curtains.

He spoke again, bringing her attention back to her

caravan and out of the darkness of that overwhelming room. 'Not just my eyes. Ever since we found that hidden altar in the library weird things are happening. I don't think we should have destroyed it.'

'You specifically said no one could find it, or any item from it,' Evie pointed out.

'I don't have all the answers!' he snapped.

Evie leaned back and looked at her brother. It was rare for him to have an outburst. She swallowed what she wanted to say down and forced a calmness into her voice that she wasn't feeling. Angry Atlas looked indomitable.

'What can I do to help?'

'It's all my fault. That's on me. I've spent years shutting you down every time you tried to bring up our gifts. I've denied that I've had any luck and it was all just hard work with the animals. I destroyed that altar willingly because I didn't want the witch house label to carry on. The locals used to say we were cursed. It's beginning to feel that way.'

'I disagree. We've made everything a success. I mean, neither of us has much in the way of a personal life but the farm is a success, the shops are a success, I want to open a garden centre and plant nursery.' She picked up both letters and crumpled them into balls. She held the balls between cupped palms.

'Evie,' Atlas objected half-heartedly. She curved one half of her mouth up in a mischievous smile and carried on regardless. Her hands grew warmer, green liquid made a ring around her index finger before disappearing. When she opened her hands a few seconds later, a tiny sapling with four leaves appeared in place of the paper.

'Aspen, that figures,' Evie said.

'Aspen? We covered that in classics. It's something to do with myths and legends.'

'Aspen gave heroes a pass to the underworld to return safely. The tree was revered as a connection to the fae until Christianity pushed that out.'

'Will you ever not love fairy tales?' He moved his black bishop on the chess board. Evie chose to ignore the fact that lumping myths, legends, and fairy tales together was wrong in her view.

'No. I refuse to believe we're alone on the planet in having gifts and I think fairy tales and folklore are clues that things used to be a lot different at some point in history.' She checked him with her queen.

'You know what happens to witches in fairy tales though?' He moved a knight that had been the only piece protecting her queen from his bishop. She could take his bishop, but that would walk her straight into whatever strategic trap he was setting up to take her queen. Atlas was the one that played on long-term strategies. She tended to change her direction whenever she felt like it.

'What if only the bad ones made it into someone else's story? The ones that minded their own business and didn't try to eat children lived happily enough. You know there's far fewer evil stepmothers in the original tales. At least half were natural mothers being cruel, but that didn't fit the stereotype of the wholesome motherhood vibe for the new mass printing era, so it was changed.'

'Give me an example.'

'Hansel and Gretel. It was their parents' decision to leave them in the forest in the earliest versions.'

Atlas shook his head and argued back, 'I don't believe it. No mother would—' he trailed off, 'except ours.'

144

'We got left on a farm with woodland instead of the middle of the forest. We have one of those mothers, yet you still don't want to believe because it contradicts the narrative we're fed about women,' Evie pointed out.

Atlas glanced in the direction of the bedrooms. 'But you're a good mum. You care. I thought you were too young, I mean you were at university.' He shrugged.

'I make mistakes all the time. I'm growing up with them.'

'But you care,' he repeated, looking at her as though she had a magical answer as to why she cared for her children when their mother couldn't care for them.

Evie didn't have an answer. She couldn't describe the reaction of taking that first pregnancy test, already knowing that she was pregnant without the confirmation. The intense protective surge and love she had for the little bean sized Max had hit her like a truck. She hadn't expected that. She hoped Atlas got to experience that for himself.

'It's not like they got a perfect version of me. They didn't get a father that cares. You know Robbie asked me out to dinner, and then said to bring Max and Rey along too without a breath in between.'

'That's good.'

'I think it might be.' She didn't dare raise her eyes to look at her brother. Instead, she stared intently at the chess board.

In the years since splitting with her husband not one man had ever asked for dinner with her children. Every single one had expected her to get a babysitter. It took a few declinations and a lot of talk about her children before men got the message that her children would always come first. Robbie had come along and seemed to fit right into whatever sized slot she had free, whether it was walking home after work, breakfast, or dinner with the children. He made his time fit hers. In a world where she was meant to bend and shape herself to be everything to the public that they demanded, it was refreshing to feel that someone saw her for who she really was and willingly changed their life to match her free time.

In the morning she woke up to several messages, including a gleeful one from Yvonne with the caption. *It's dropped, be ready.* Evie knew that she didn't want to click on the video attached but she did so anyway and found herself staring at a stranger. The Evie in front of her was sultry, sexy, mischievous, and the hotel robe did very little to hide the lace teddy Yvonne had decided she had to wear. On the hotel bed sat a little tray holding breakfast for two and a glass of champagne. The Evie on the screen held the other champagne glass in her hand and invited the public to go ghost hunting with her and get a personal palm reading.

The other messages were mostly from Yvonne, with reminders that the show still controlled her image and that they would be using the photos of her and Robbie to back up the statement of a new man entering her life as per her palm reading. Evie tried to read between the lines, to see if it was a last attempt from someone who was losing control and knew about her moving shows, or if Yvonne was fixated on her because Evie had stood up to her.

Her phone pinged again with a message from Robbie, asking her if she had seen the ad yet and adding that he'd choked on his coffee that morning. Evie checked the date on her phone to see how long she had to endure the ad, the stares, and comments on the show.

Another ping came from Yvonne called her to an early meeting to discuss the Halloween special and arrogantly informed her that she would be required to be available every day for the following week of lunchtime shows. Evie read the message and sighed. That new fact hadn't been mentioned before and she was scheduled to pre-record some more for the country show. With a sigh she kicked off the covers whilst dialling Andy's number to attempt to solve the issue, and threw on a lightweight long jersey dressing gown and slippers to make breakfast.

She had barely flicked the charcoal plastic switch that turned on the heating in the caravan and put the toast into the machine for Rey when a knock at the door startled her. Staring at the door she thought she had imagined it until a sleepy Max popped his bedhead face around his bedroom door. 'Someone's at the door, mum.' He closed the door and disappeared back into his bedroom.

'Get ready for school,' she called after him, knocking on Rey's door to wake her up.

A muffled shout of, 'I'm already up,' came in response. Evie opened the main door to the caravan. Robbie stood there, a cardboard carton in his hand holding two take-aways and bending down to pick up a black envelope. Evie bent down to get the envelope, making sure she was faster. Their eyes met, he smiled, and his eyes crinkled deeply, the lines starting to curve down as they deepened. Evie loved that about him. The genuine warmth from him.

'Morning, I brought you a cappuccino.'

'Um, why?' Aware of her morning breath she drew back slightly, taking the envelope.

'Truth? I was sent the ad by a friend who'd seen it on

147

YouTube and I thought you might have more than a few men outside your door. My excuse was going to be that I had to be on site early and I stopped on the way.'

'Do you want to come in? I've just gotten up. I'm making breakfast for Max and Rey.'

'Of course I want to come in and see you in that whilst you make breakfast.' She watched his eyes roam over the jersey fabric.

Her eyes widened and told him that she saw through his words to the truth, his lopsided grin at her response admitted it, but the sparkle in his eyes challenged her to speak it. She shook her head slightly, but turned away with a smile, 'The heating is on. You might want to lose the coat,' was her only allusion to the fact that she was naked underneath her robe.

Evie left the door open and walked away to finish breakfast and chat with Andy over the difficulties of conflicting schedules. She made toast for Rey, with butter and jam, a sliced apple and their own farm yogurt drizzled over the apple topped off with a bit of honey. Rey wasn't a big breakfast eater. Max liked fresh bread, cold deli meats, cheese, a sliced apple, their strawberry yoghurt with a handful of berries and crushed nuts. All the while sipping the coffee Robbie had brought her, Evie heaped two spoonfuls of Greek yoghurt into a small bowl and lightly topped it with honey and nuts, asking Robbie if he wanted anything.

He shook his head, 'I'll get a bacon sandwich from the café when it opens. I don't want to hold you up, I'm enjoying watching you.' The flirtatious remark was unmissable.

She grinned back, 'Making breakfast and talking on

the phone?' Disregarding his remark, she put a frying pan on and threw some bacon into it.

'Yeah, it's sweet. It's making me think that maybe one day we could have normal mornings like this. You on the phone whilst we make breakfast and me with my jaw on the floor thinking how beautiful you are. Obviously, I'd need to impress you and build the houses.'

'The fact that you can even build a house is impressive. It'd be nice if it stays up though. I'll make my mind up about you after that.' Her tone was light as she flirted.

'After the house stays up?' He held her eyes but took a step towards her.

'Yes. I'm just wondering how long I should give it before being suitably impressed. Maybe five years?' she teased.

'Five minutes?' His hand slid round to cup the back of her neck. She smelled coffee and men's cologne as he leaned in for a kiss. Breathing in, Evie met his lips and kissed him. They managed a minute before Rey shouted that she couldn't find her school tie.

Evie pulled back, instantly reminded of where she was and who she was, and her priorities, 'I'm sorry. I need to get ready.' Her walls were already back up as her mind went to her children, their schedules, her work.

'I'm looking forward to Friday night with you all.'

'Robbie's coming on Friday night?' Rey came out of her bedroom, her shirt untucked, her pleated skirt twisted, her knee length black socks at mid-calf height and wrinkled around her ankles. Max rushed out of his room, still putting his blazer on, neat and preppy as ever.

'Robbie's coming too?' He looked at his mum, his

expression told her that he wished it wasn't true.

'If it's alright with you two. I'd like to get to know you all a lot better. Plus it would really help me when I build your house if I know what you like.'

'Depends.' Max picked up his breakfast and walked over to the dining area.

'Sit down,' Rey spoke to Robbie but followed her brother in picking up her breakfast and sitting down. Evie smiled at their little interrogation tactics, she knew what was coming.

'Good luck,' she laughed, putting his bacon sandwich together then floating off to her room to get dressed quickly.

She picked out washed faded charcoal jeans and a cosy grey knitted jumper and threw them on as quickly as she could, applying her skincare in between items of clothing. She applied a light five-minute fresh-faced make-up over her suncream as she listened to the conversation, the thin caravan walls did nothing to muffle the interrogation from Max and Rey.

'Can you be quiet through a film? You're not one of those people that has to make comments about stuff?' That was Max.

Presumably Robbie just nodded to that because Rey was next, 'What films do you like?'

'Um, lots of genres, action, horror, family.'

'More specifically, do you like space films?' that was Max, he loved science fiction films.

'I love them.'

'Do you know mum's favourite films?' Rey asked.

'No. Do you want to tell me?'

'Alien. Labyrinth. Pan's Labyrinth, and a really bad one

called Krull.'

'Do you have a family business like mum and Uncle Atlas?'

'We do. It started off as my dad's business. My two brothers are in it, my sister runs the office side, and my youngest sister is in her last year of midwifery training.'

'What does your mum do?'

'She's a nurse at the hospital. A Senior Staff Nurse.'

'What food do you like best?'

'Everything. I love food.'

'Do you fancy mum?' Whatever response Robbie had to that set Max and Rey off into giggles.

Evie walked out to laughing children and Robbie with his finger on his lips. Robbie looked up as she announced her entrance by dropping a pair of pointy grey flats on the floor, the same soft shade as the jumper. Her other hand held a soft, cotton scarf in a delicate pink.

'You look nice.'

She met his eyes at his kind words, he looked genuine. The words hit a small hole that had opened up in her armour around her heart. 'I look OK. I would prefer to hide after this morning. But I can't.' She avoided his gaze.

'Ah, I can take Max and Rey if you'd rather hide?'

'No. I have stuff to do. For work.' The way she spoke the last two words let him know that she'd rather be elsewhere.

'Is it one of those duvet days mum? Mum lets us have duvet days. She prefers to read but I like to watch films, she lets us order takeaways too.' Max's wide, shining eyes told everyone how often they had a takeaway.

'Do you have plans for the rest of the weekend?' Robbie changed the subject, looking at Max and Rey.

'No.' Max shrugged.

'Yes. We go to the café on Saturday nights and sometimes Sunday mornings.' Rey glared at her brother like it was crazy that he forgot.

'That's not a plan, that's our routine,' Max shot back with fire in his eyes.

'That's a plan. If it's arranged in advance, it's a plan.'

'It's a routine. Unless going to school is a plan?' Max argued.

'It's both.' Robbie didn't raise his voice but he did lower it, 'something can be both a plan and a routine. When my family gets together mum likes to fuss around us and make sure there's cakes, and baked goods, and a proper dinner. Dad makes a plan once a month to take her to the pub for the afternoon with as many of us as he can get so she sits and enjoys being still around us. It's his way of trying to look after her. Our monthly pub meet up is both a plan and a routine wouldn't you agree?' Two little heads nodded slowly, their faces thoughtful until Rey said to Max.

'You always order the fried chicken sandwich on a Saturday with chips, that's routine not a plan.'

'You order it too. It's nice. I like Saturdays knowing I'll get the fried chicken. You always ask mum for the same chocolate.'

'Hey, we're allowed to like different things, remember? Rey, for some of us home is all we crave, adventure is in little things like the seasons changing, finding the first grasshopper of the summer, seeing the first dormouse, the first tadpoles and watching them change into froglets, surviving lambing season. It's not always flights to snow covered lands that have green skies at night.' Evie settled the argument that was erupting for the sake of falling out.

Chapter 14

Evie slowed down in the corridor as she approached the room designated for Yvonne's important unscheduled meeting. Around her people hurried about, most intent on their destination or task, some shooting looks at her discreetly, others looking openly in awe. Nerves mounted inside her stomach with each slow step nearer to the conference room door. Evie stopped outside, took a deep breath, put her hand on the old-fashioned brass knob, turned it to release the latch and walked into the pre-Halloween meeting, dragging her stomach behind her on the floor.

Propelling her forward was the very real thought that she needed to work, otherwise she would much prefer to be hiding under a duvet. Smells wafted to her that churned her stomach, prompting a wave of nausea. Since Yvonne had gotten herself an executive producer position three years ago the happy vibe across the whole workforce had been eroded away and gradually replaced with fear.

Inwardly Evie was still kicking herself for prioritising this meeting over filming. She didn't know why the sexy Halloween advert affected her, but the dread of the village gossip had made her attend, as though she had a chance to control part of it. People, mostly women but a few men, were gathered in the tired and dated room. Some seated, some talking in small groups, others perusing their phones, a couple had headphones in their ears. A range of tired looking breakfast foodstuffs was laid out, as though they too, lacked the willpower to be fully present and enthusiastic about the meeting. She moved her eyes from the food to the corner quickly enough to see a smug expression cross Yvonne's face at her presence. It suddenly occurred to Evie that the other woman had been worried that Evie would miss it. As their eyes met it was replaced by deep venom. Evie held the glare and didn't avert her eyes.

Yvonne was dressed head to toe in raspberry, her blonde hair tied back in a chic bun. Evie dropped her mushroom leather handbag on the floor, the studs making a satisfying thud. Faces turned to her, faces already wary from dealing with Yvonne's unpredictable and ever-changing moods. Evie felt for them. The relief of not having to tip toe around her co-presenter and producer for longer than necessary was immense. A weight lifted from her shoulders as she realised that she never had to do another meeting like this with this team again. The power shift was addictive, but she wouldn't be Yvonne, she wouldn't sink her claws in and be a bitch to own moments like this one.

'I'm not staying,' she announced, her voice crystal clear and deliberately carrying to every quiet corner of the room, 'I'm done trying to get some agreement with the production team about leaving. I quit.'

'You can't, we only need you another week and a half. Hold it together until after Halloween for us, Evie, and we can release you.' Jess looked scared and desperate at the thought of losing her before Halloween. It dawned on Evie that the intended *punishment* necessitated her actual presence for Halloween. Without her, the show had no significance that week.

155

'I don't like your outfit, I think we should put you in green today, get you on air.' Yvonne shot a pointed glance towards Sallie in Wardrobe. Sallie picked up a pen and made a note of Yvonne's wishes, her eyes not even daring to meet Evie's. Evie didn't like herself in green. Sallie knew that. Green was far too near her gift to be a comfortable colour for her to wear. It would be the same as broad-casting her ability to grow plants on air and announcing herself to the world.

'I'm not scheduled to be on air today. I'm pre-recording for the country show.'

'I want you on air. We've had a great response to the ad. You can take Faith's spot.' Yvonne didn't even give her the courtesy of looking at her when talking, she drifted over to the breakfast table and selected a coffee and a syrup-coloured gingerbread biscuit, throwing the words at the wall where they bounced off and filled the room. The only thing remaining after her words was silence as people waited for Evie to back down. Everyone held their breath.

'I quit, Yvonne. I'm done.' Her voice was calm. She was calm. Outwardly at least. She picked up her bag and turned, prepared to leave when Yvonne's next words stopped her.

'I own you,' Yvonne hissed, turning around and staring at Evie with wild eyes. Looking around at the shocked faces caused Yvonne to shrug, 'I do. I was the one that suggested we gave her a contract following her guest interviews. I was the one that shaped the wild party girl image into a city sophisticate, I'm the one that controls wardrobe choices and what topics we discuss on your days. You're throwing it all away Evie, to be an uncultured country girl on a stupid country show that a random few people will watch?'

'I'm not throwing it away. I'm both city and country. I can eat a miniscule five course meal in a nice dress under city lights just as well as I can grow crops or plough a field. There's balance, Yvonne, one doesn't trump the other, it's not a war, there's no sides. Just because I'm a farmer doesn't stop me appreciating art, or music, or the theatre.' Evie stared Yvonne down.

Silence stood as heavy as stone in the room. Evie shrugged and picked up her bag, 'And afterwards, when I'm done filming for the country show, I'm going home. I'll make dinner, put my children to bed and read a book instead of watching TV or scrolling through social media because you tag me in far too much shit like we're friends when all you're doing is promoting yourself.'

'Once upon a time you were all over the media. It made you into someone.' Yvonne's accusation had sour notes of envy.

Immediately, her sentence clicked in Evie's brain and she understood. Once upon a time, falling out of clubs with Damian in miniscule clothing had been her life and it had been splashed all over newspapers and social media sites. It had made her famous without any effort on Evie's part. The more she tried to shield her face from the photographers, the more they tried to get a shot of her. Yvonne wanted the same, she craved that same level of attention.

Evie tried to summarise Yvonne's career before Evie started to date Damian. She couldn't. Yvonne seemed to have appeared as a new presenter after Evie's unplanned rise to fame. By posting pictures of herself with Evie online, Yvonne was trying to reach the same heights as Evie had achieved simply by dating Damian.

Jess stepped in front of Yvonne, suddenly freed from Yvonne's vicious need for control. She became the calm and collected producer Evie had seen before Yvonne had secured a role as an executive producer. 'What do we need to do to keep you, Evie? I mean keep you, not just for a week. I agree on the balance thing. I really like that we don't have to pitch the country and the city against each other,' she asked.

Evie looked around the room. Several hopeful pairs of eyes met hers. Maria gave a small encouraging nod, almost indiscernible, so as to remain undetectable to Yvonne. Elsy's expression went from despair to brightly hopeful. Evie looked back at Jess. The calm eyes seemed to know who they were losing. Evie decided to see how far she could push. Standing up straight she channelled the person she used to be, before Damian had destroyed her confidence. Confidence that she was slowly regaining.

'My wage needs to be discussed. Hours negotiable depending on other projects. I want freedom over my career to do other projects, and I control my image, not you. Ring me when we can discuss it calmly without Yvonne's input. I'd really like the old work environment back, and less trivial stuff on air, more experts, more politicians, bigger topics like we used to. I don't care that some celebrity has had plastic surgery, we should be discussing the rise of how unaccepting we are of women aging. And I want a book club, we should be encouraging reading for adults and children.' Evie couldn't believe that she was considering staying. She turned and left, ignoring Jess's cry to stay, pulling out her phone to let her cameraman on the country show know she was on her way to the village.

Back in the room, a young cameraman looked over his phone with lovestruck eyes to Yvonne. A subtle, single nod from her was all it took to upload the scene to social media.

4500 BCE

He had crawled along the mud with a pain where the axe had hit. He remembered that. Now he was in a place that had a fire, that smelt of pine and juniper. He lifted his hand, it was clean. Someone had cleaned him, wrapped him in blankets, carried him here to this enclosed place where he could see the stars, feel the fire and still be sheltered from the rain.

'Anders, you are awake.' Her voice was soft. She was drinking from a cup next to him.

'What? What magic is this?'

'It is not magic. It is care. You will be better and strong again,' she responded. A man's voice in a language he didn't understand cut into the conversation. Anders turned his head and witnessed a soft exchange between the woman and the man, secret smiles, soft faces, eyes full of love. The man didn't even look at him. He touched her round stomach. He tilted her chin, gave her a lingering kiss, then left. She sat down.

'You have—'

'No need to state the obvious. Rest and be quiet.'

'You cared for me when I would kill you?'

'Would you? You hesitated once.' Two small girls ran up to her and she smothered them in hugs. She cleaned their faces and gave them cups. Then she instructed him to raise himself and gave him a cup too. Two small faces, identical to hers, looked at him with amusement.

'You have sons.' She caught him watching the girls.

'I do. Four so far. It is time for a daughter.'

'Your gods do not have a daughter for you, Anders. You shall only have sons. Strong boys that will live until adulthood and continue your line.'

Chapter 15

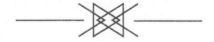

Friday came around quicker than she was ready for. The week lurched from disaster to disaster. Jess called her everyday asking, then begging her to return for the live Halloween show before threatening legal action over breach of contract. With an exasperated sigh that muffled her hidden anger and frustration at life, Evie agreed to do the live Halloween lunchtime show but refused to do any interviews on their sister evening show. The country show team were trying to get her released from her contract, but Yvonne and Jess were digging their heels in. She was reassured by the production company that things were happening higher up behind the scenes and no legal action could be taken but it didn't satisfy the worry that gnawed at her stomach over the battle of wills.

The leaked video of her trying to quit and losing was as popular as her teaser for the Halloween special. She was stressed, anxious and losing sleep over people so keen to control her image that she had jumped at a shy request to help a member of staff from her local spa start an online presence.

On Friday morning she flew out the door into a clear cool day that held a sharp chilly breeze and white cotton clouds, clad in uncustomary tracksuit bottoms and a matching hoody with no make-up. Robbie was walking to her door with a cardboard tray holding two coffees. He had taken to bringing her a cappuccino every morning before he started work on her house, and she made sure she always had bacon in. Max and Rey climbed into her car holding plates full of their breakfast. She picked up her cappuccino from the cardboard holder and gave him a quick kiss on the lips, noting his scruffy work clothes that she loved; how soft, worn and faded the materials looked.

'Why the rush?' Robbie asked, watching Max and Rey get into the car.

'Jae's setting something up, an online business venture, and they've asked me to help at the salon.'

'You're qualified to work in the salon?' His expression of disbelief matched his tone and elicited a laugh from Evie who wondered when she would have found the time to train in that area.

'No. Sorry. That was a rushed explanation. Jae works in the salon. They've booked a room on their day off and they need a model to make a video for their online debut into the ASMR world. I messaged the salon to say I could really use some time there, I didn't care if it was a massage or nails or anything, I just need time out to relax. I've agreed to be their model in return for a full day of treatments. I know it's my privilege showing and I'm not even sorry right now. We're taking the Halloween teaser that I hate and twisting it into a *Relax with Evie* sort of thing for her video. It's not perfect but it means that I get to take back some control of the direction Yvonne chose to take my image in.'

'Jae? Short brown hair, the one we can't figure out?'

'Figure out how?'

'Whether it's a man or a woman.'

'Jae is non-binary.' She caught Robbie's look, she'd

seen it a thousand times before. The unspoken judgement, the perceived challenge when something affected the villagers' norms. She cut in before he could say anything, 'Jae's pronoun and non-binary choices don't impact anyone else's life so just let them be.'

He changed topics with the warning tone in her voice. 'Are we still on for tonight?'

'Yes. I'll see you at six. Shall I pick you up?' she glanced at the van Robbie used every day.

'I was going to offer to drive, and pick you all up.'

'Do you have anything that seats four people?'

'Yes.' She watched him smile as he answered the doubt in her voice. She loved that smile already, the way it matched his eyes, the lines it made around his eyes and how his eyes lit up.

Evie didn't have an argument against him driving, even though she could tell he was ready to protest the issue if she tried, 'OK. I've had shit week, I could use a drink.'

'I've had a good week. I'll drive. You drink.' He relaxed. Evie had thoughts of Damian and his drinking in the back of her head, his promises that failed to materialise into actualities, the time he had promised to take her to a scan with Max when she was first pregnant with Rey and she had tentatively trusted that he would turn up with their shared car and drive her. Instead, she had stood outside Max's nursery holding her paperwork waiting, and then called a taxi when it was clear he had forgotten. She pushed the thoughts back. She was an adult. She had options and resources. Robbie hadn't let her down yet.

'What's been so good about it?' she asked, taking a sip of coffee.

164

'I got to see you every day. I love the simplicity of walking into the coffee shop and asking for a flat white and a cappuccino. I know you're upset about the other video, the meeting one, but I like you standing your ground. It's good for Max and Rey to see you're not a pushover.'

'More like a punchbag. I've got to get Max and Rey to breakfast club.'

'They're eating breakfast on the way to breakfast club?' His face was a picture of confusion. She glanced at the two children in the car who were tall and slim, they seemed to have grown in the last week alone.

'They're on growth spurts and breakfast club food is limited to what is deemed acceptable portions for their age group. So yeah, breakfast on the way to breakfast club and another one at breakfast club. Being full helps to concentrate in lessons. They like breakfast club, they have board games and daily riddles to solve and the library is open with reading corners for them.'

'Sounds fun. I'll pick you up at six.' His rough hand made contact with the sensitive skin of her neck when he cupped the back of her neck just underneath her hair with his free hand and leaned in to give her a kiss just at the same moment her children shouted at her to hurry up. He chuckled and made it a quick, light kiss. Her shoulders dropped when his hand lingered awhile. He looked surprised.

She winked at him, 'Told you. Shit week. I like the way you touch me.'

In response he squeezed his hand against the taunt muscles in the bottom of her neck, 'You are tense.'

'I always am. Not this bad though. I'll see you tonight.' Before he could respond she got into the car and started it up. He lifted his hand to wave them off.

Jae was sat quietly in the gaudiest red and gold reception area in a plain black salon uniform, reading through handwritten notes when Evie walked in. Evie pushed her car keys into her front pouch pocket and finished off the last of her coffee. Jae raised brown eyes from the faux leather tub chair in the reception area and smiled broadly at Evie, the first genuine smile Evie had seen on a person other than Robbie that week; even her children had been unusually moody, something that, after assessing the past few weeks, she put down to a mixture of factors from stress of moving into a caravan, being ready for half term and growth spurts. Evie smiled back, thanking Jae for making room for her.

Jae shook their head, 'It's a pleasure, I'm glad you're letting me use your name to get a head start.' Jae took the empty coffee and threw it away in a hidden bin under the reception desk.

'I've had enough photos and videos released about me recently without my say.' Evie shrugged, it was good to be in a position where she could bring most of the unsolicited interest in her back under her control.

Jae acknowledged the social media posts she was referring to with an understanding nod but didn't pursue the topic, 'Did you get a chance to look at the ASMR videos I sent you that are similar to what I want to do? I've done a few practise sessions with my sister for the technical side.'

'I loved the videos. I found them relaxing. It might be my new favourite thing.' She had fallen asleep to the sounds of someone having their hair brushed. Evie didn't say that sitting in bed with headphones relaxing wasn't something she was used to, and sleep had come to her so much quicker that night. She was usually fighting to stay awake to get her consultation reports finished.

Jae flushed with happiness, 'I'm glad. I'll show you the room. It's all set.'

Evie followed Jae to a room at the back of the salon, away from the noise of the entrance and the hair salon and entered a warm room. A corner was set up with candles, the scent of jasmine filled the air from the delicate yellow flames, a few plants were strategically set next to a display of towels and oils. The white walls made the small room light although little daylight filtered through the heavy curtain that had been thrown over the room divider blocking the window. Evie stood still and took it all in.

Jae saw her looking at the window, 'I thought it would try and stop anyone taking pictures. We'll be working in front of it. It's forecast to start raining in an hour anyway. I want to see if I can capture the sound of rain too.'

The next hour reminded Evie of how she and her friends had used to play with each other's hair and practise hairstyles. Jae brushed and combed her hair with different brushes and combs, plaited it and unplaited it whilst whispering to the camera what she was doing. The brushes started with soft bristles, threatening to frizz her hair up before moving onto plastic, then wire before Jae spritzed water over her and twisted it into curls again. Evie closed her eyes to concentrate on the sensations. It was the only way she knew to stop the commentary running through her head, the worry that Jae would somehow take advantage of the camera and reveal more than agreed.

Closing her eyes allowed her to focus only on the sensations of her hair, the gentleness of the brushes, the smoothness of the combs, the tingles when her hair was lifted and combed and the pulling of the plaiting and the twists, the way the hair pins scratched her scalp when they were put in.

Jae reached over to a hanging robe that Evie thought was there for atmosphere and gave Evie the spa robe to wear before a shampoo and condition to get rid of the oils in her hair from the Indian head massage. Afterwards, Jae made them both a cup of tea whilst they took a short break.

They kept looking at her hair, so when they asked the question, Evie wasn't surprised, 'How do you feel about changing your hair colour?'

'I like it brown, I've never considered another colour.' As a child she'd had light brown hair like her brother, the type of European light brown that lightened from the sun in summer before fading again over the autumn and winter. As a teenager they'd all changed their hair colours multiple times. She had thought she was so amazing doing a custom mix of pink with a hint of red on her brown hair to give a soft warm glow. It was only at university with Damian's money had she ventured into a salon for a trim and a colour and had a first proper consultation. She walked out with waist length medium golden brown glossy hair. After splitting from Damian she had cut her hair and kept it shorter, but never changed the colour.

'I was thinking we could make it more multidimensional. Soften it up by adding caramel and toffee shades as well as some blonde, face framing baby lights. Your natural colour is two shades lighter than this colour you've been wearing for as long as I've known you. I think it's a tad on the dark side for your colouring, something lighter will make you look...'

'Less gothic? Brighter? More conformative?' Evie filled in the gaps with words that she had heard so many times before. The difference was every time *lighter* had been brought up it had come with the word *blonde*, and Evie didn't want a full head of platinum hair, which was how she pictured blonde. The brown she had was lovely.

'All those, although I'd say summery, and less tarot card moon goddess.' Jae smiled, as though she knew summer was Evie's favourite season.

Evie took that statement and analysed it. Her hair was darker, she hid behind the shadows it created and the unapproachability it gave out. In her memories her mother had bleached her long hair. Evie had avoided doing anything to look like her. She mulled it over quickly and decided impulsively that it was time for her to deal with that trauma demon too. Changing her appearance could be a good thing. It was the old Evie that had allowed Yvonne to manipulate her into that hotel room advert. If she changed her hair, she would be a different Evie.

'I don't mind going lighter if you think it will suit me.' Evie had to force those words out. With a fast-beating heart she wanted to backtrack immediately. Evie held her mouth closed and told herself it was just hair. She could change it back if she didn't like it. The wildness inside her danced happily with the prospect of a change, of a new look, a willingness to let her inner self emerge.

'How much lighter?' Jae's eyes widened.

'Give me a couple of options to choose from. Let's not do safe ones, go for it.' Evie laughed, throwing caution to the wind and pushing the doubts in her head to the darkest parts she could find. She had to be over making herself smaller to fit other people.

Decisions made, Jae rushed into the salon to get the bowls, foils and colours she needed, mixing it all up in front of the camera. Whilst that processed in her hair in multiple layers of foils that made her look as though she was in a cartoon and had been struck by lightning, they put her nail extensions on. Her index fingernail became long and almond shaped, a dusky rose shade, her middle, ring and little fingers carried the nail shape but becoming increasingly lighter on each nail. Her thumbs were done in a delicate seashell pink. Evie had had enhancements before, it wasn't something she was overly keen on, but she wasn't turning down a pamper day and a hand massage. Pink would never have been her choice of colour, normally her nails were painted black. Once both hands were completed Jae checked her hair colour. The pair agreed to skip lunch in favour of a hot drink. Jae set up the camera over the bowl where she was going to wash and tone Evie's hair.

Afterwards Evie waited again with white towels covering her hair whilst Jae angled the cameras to get both the back of Evie's hair and her face in the mirror. Evie was so used to being on set that it didn't strike her as the slightest bit strange. Jae sat her down and removed the towel, Evie leaned heavily against the backrest and readied herself to catch a glimpse of her new hair. When wet, her hair still looked dark, Evie struggled to see any blonde after all the foils. Jae picked up a comb and a spray and began to untangle the knots. Her hair was dried again for the second time that day.

Evie began to see a softer version of herself appear in the lighter hair. It flattered her face and colouring, where once there was contrast, shadows and paler skin, she now had lightness and glowing skin. She liked it. Jae had been right about it suiting her. The timing felt right too, moving from what had become the Yvonne show to the new country show, their new houses being built, and the old farmhouse demolished, she was moving into a new life. An easier life. A lighter life without the burdens she had been carrying.

When Evie walked to the car after a back massage later that afternoon, she was more relaxed and content than she had felt that morning. Her shoulders had dropped from somewhere up around her chin to their normal place. She was even agreeable to requests for stopping off in the village for cake and fizzy drinks after collecting her children, something she rarely agreed to do in her desire to protect them from the same whispers and gossip that she had experienced. She took Max and Rey into Harriet's café, a change from the dimly lit, wooden panelled tea rooms they occasionally frequented. Max and Rey looked awed at the modern gothic décor. They chose a table at the back of the room, one with a black tablecloth and black vase holding a delicate pink flower.

Harriet came over with a smile and a notepad, 'Nice to see you again Evie, you look… you've had your hair done. It really suits you.'

'Thank you.' Evie smiled at Harriet, somewhat reassured.

'I like your hair.' Rey stared at Harriet's pink hair.

Harriet smiled, 'I do too. But it's a pain. Pink fades fast. I have to dye it once a fortnight. Have you decided what you're ordering?'

'A coke and chocolate fudge cake, please,' Max

declared.

'Could I have a lemonade and the raspberry pink yogurt cake with white chocolate? Mum makes yoghurt cake sometimes, but we've never had a pink one. What cocoa is the white chocolate?'

'Um, Rey likes her chocolate bitter rather than sweet. I have to buy the high cocoa percentage stuff for her,' Evie explained to Harriet, trying to convey that her daughter wasn't a precocious spoilt child, just a fussy eater.

'It's proper white chocolate, not baking chocolate but it's a sweet one, not a bitter one.' Harriet looked at Rey as she answered. Rey digested that knowledge then consented to try it anyway.

'Evie?'

'Can I get half a slice of tiramisu?'

'Sure. It goes well with Prosecco. Or an espresso martini? On the house.'

'I have to drive home.'

'It's a few yards down the street.' Harriet snorted. Evie smiled. The farm was literally a few yards along a small lane.

'Espresso martini with tiramisu then, but can I get a water with that too?'

'Yes. Mind if I join you?' Harriet asked. Evie shook her head.

'Are you the lady that gave mum a palm reading for the Halloween?' Rey asked. Evie had told her children about it in case they saw or heard anything about the one-off special. Harriet nodded.

She returned with a tray of cakes and drinks, sharing the other half of Evie's cake and an espresso martini for herself. Harriet sat down and the conversation was easy;

they talked about the children's school day, about Harriet's day, about Jae and Evie's day. Max told Harriet that they were going to watch a film he wanted to see. Rey talked about going to Guiseppe's for dinner and that Robbie was joining them too. Harriet let out a small, knowing smile but simply gave a nod, and asked the children how they felt about Robbie building their new home. Rey shrugged, she wasn't interested much in the build, she told Harriet she just wanted the new house with the big chandelier in the entrance lobby and the staircase that had a balcony and her new bedroom because it had a full-length corner window that her mum was going to hang a swinging seat from the ceiling for her so she could watch the woods and the woodland animals. Harriet told her that it sounded wonderful and she lived in a flat above the café.

'Harriet,' Rey asked.

'Yes sweetie?'

'How long have you lived in the village?'

'All my life. Except when I left for uni. I thought I wanted a big career and to travel but I got so homesick I dropped out after two terms. I missed the village, the people, the folklore and just everything about it. My dad was furious. I started cooking meals at home and making desserts. Then I moved onto baking bread. I took a course at college and got a job in a café in the city. I travelled there and back every day just like your mum does. When this place came up for rent seven months ago, I took a loan out and went for it. There's a lot of people who like the witch myths of our village, and a lot of tourists that come because of the witch myths so I tried to create something that celebrated the witches and my love of pink.' She looked over to the pretty pink kitchen part of the café.

'What is the local legend?' Rey asked.

'Hasn't your mum told you?' Harriet shot a confused look at Evie.

Evie admitted, 'I don't really know it. I caught parts. Nobody told me. They just whispered behind my back. Still do.' Evie shrugged.

Harriet gave her a surprised look, as though it should have been a bedtime story for her. She didn't make a comment but started to tell Rey and Max the story instead, 'OK, so a Viking family came over to live in Jorvik just after it was established.'

'York.' Rey nodded.

'One of the daughters was a powerful witch but because her sister was more powerful she wasn't given the respect she wanted and was married off to the landowner of this area. She was probably only twelve at the time. People grew to fear her, the rumour goes that she could create the death of people and animals if you crossed her. So, the villagers, the peasants, created an altar for her and made sure it always looked nice. That sort of grew into a local myth whereby every solstice we prick our fingers on a thorn and offer two drops of blood for the blessing of Yrsa. Her blessing bestows health and prosperity. It continues to this day. Except, in nineteen ten, some of the locals decided to be modern and declared that Yrsa was a myth, that they weren't going to be pricking their fingers for her. Overnight in the middle of the village cricket green three wooden logs appeared, sort of nestled upright together in a triangular pyramid shape.' Harriet used the forks to demonstrate on the table, 'and over this was the blood and the internal organs of an animal. Carved into the wood were the names of some of the people who had refused to participate in the spring equinox ritual. They died within the year. Although it was over a hundred years ago it's still scary enough that we participate in the ritual and invite tourists to do so. But here's the interesting thing, the logs came from your farm. And rumour is that your farm house was the original homestead of Yrsa. People thought that the family had links to Yrsa and that they had a part in the whole thing. So they just took off and disappeared. The farm was rented out until your grandparents took it over. Everyone knew that they weren't farmers and they were related to the landowners.'

'That was evident from their lack of interest in the farm,' Evie muttered.

'So why do we get witch hunters every Halloween on the farm?' Max asked.

'It's a mix of the Yrsa myth and the incident in nineteen ten. Because the logs were found to be from trees on your farm, gossips started to talk about a coven of witches up there assisting Yrsa.'

Even as Harriet spoke Evie remembered the letter from her parents to Atlas and wondered whether it was more than gossip. In her letter her mother had spoken of Genevieve's parents being involved in something too. They had mentioned Yrsa coming for her. Not Atlas though.

'You look a million miles away,' Harriet said.

Evie realised her fork was hovering over the cake. She put it down and finished her drink, 'I've never heard that version. You all still believe in Yrsa?'

It was Harriet's turn to shrug at that question, 'My Grandma does. I don't think my parents do.'

'Do you?' Evie asked Harriet.

Harriet paused and thought carefully before

175

answering, 'Do I believe that someone can live that long with blood sacrifices every equinox from a whole village? Yes. In theory. I practise witchcraft, I know that in its various forms it can be really powerful.' Harriet glanced over at Evie who was quiet.

Evie caught her look and offered a smile, 'I love how there's no small talk with you. You just dive straight in.'

'Please, look around, small talk is my job. If you're my friend you get the big stuff straight away.' She smiled. There was warmth in the wry smile.

Evie smiled back, 'We should do this again. I like straight talk and big stuff. I just have one more question, what does Robbie like to drink?'

Harriet smirked at that question, but gave her a straight, honest answer, along with the fact that she could buy it at the convenience store a few doors down. Evie liked her straightforward openness. Harriet told her to call by anytime, ending with, 'Once upon a time I wouldn't have opened my door to you, but if you need me, even if we're shut, just knock on my door.'

Chapter 16

A light drizzle had started by the time they arrived at the caravan, the type of rain that would steadily grow heavier as the night grew darker until it settled at a pace where it could last the whole night. Evie had half an hour to throw an outfit together and put a little make-up on. She was thankful her children were old enough to decide on their own clothes. In her caravan bedroom she lifted a new ankle length cream ribbed knit dress from a postal bag. Impulsively she had purchased the matching ankle length cardigan thinking it would go well with jeans or leggings, both bought well before her date with Robbie when she was trying to plan a smaller capsule wardrobe for colder months in the caravan.

Evie was in the middle of putting make-up on when Rey came in wearing two dresses, one after each other, took a look at Evie, walked out and came back in a third dress, a pink one. Her curls were pushed up in the messiest, biggest bun Evie had ever seen her do, 'Love the outfit Rey, how on earth did you do that bun?'

'Just twisted it around my big scrunchie.'

'Do you need a cardigan or a coat?'

'I'm going to wear my pink cardigan and take my fleece lined cape for the cinema because it's always cold in there, the pink and blue wool plaid one.'

'Do you know where they are?'

'I think so.'

'Go and get them. Max, how near ready are you?'

'I'm done. I'm just having a quick game with Oli.' Now that he had said it, Evie could hear the gaming noises coming from his room.

Evie popped into his bedroom. Max had gone for the nearest clothes he could find. She knew, because she had put those navy chinos away at the top of his drawer last night. He was mid game. His school uniform was a dark blob on the navy rug she had laid out on the floor in his room. She picked it up and threw it into his pop-up wash basket.

Evie walked into Rey's room and started to pick up the clothes her daughter had discarded. It didn't take long to hang them up. She threw Rey's school uniform into her ice blue laundry basket in the corner just as Rey shouted that Robbie had pulled up. Evie suddenly realised that she didn't have shoes on. She opened the door to the caravan whilst telling Rey to get her cardigan and cape and reminding Max to pick up a coat.

'Hi. Two seconds, I forgot to put any shoes on. Come in.'

Evie dashed into her room a few paces away from the door. She pulled out heeled polished city boots from the back of her wardrobe, and a clutch that she threw her lipstick, phone and purse into. She slipped a gold bracelet on and her nice watch, the one she saved for her cocktail drinking, city life. The one she had worn when Yvonne and Jess told her not to be seen with Robbie.

She turned around to see Robbie standing in her bedroom doorway, perfectly calm amidst the shouting from Rey that she couldn't find her cape and Max asking which coat he was supposed to pick up. Sound dulled to a quiet background noise at the look he was giving her. She suppressed a smile as excitement fluttered in her stomach at seeing him. He stood straight but relaxed, hands pushed into the front pockets of dark trousers, his dark shirt partially covered by an equally dark coat. She was impressed that he had put a tie on.

Evie couldn't judge the expression on his face until he said, 'How did I get lucky enough to take you out?'

'You asked.' She gave him a quick kiss as she deliberately leaned too close to him; the doorway was narrow and she needed to pass. He smelled of aftershave and clean laundry. Her kiss landed on warm, soft lips. She drifted past him on a waft of perfume, finding a coat for Max, and Rey's cape.

In the car on the way to the city Robbie glanced at her briefly before turning his eyes back to the road. Evie caught him sneaking another look. The third time she met his eyes. He smiled slightly and shook his head at being caught. There were a few seconds before he said, 'It's your hair. That's why you look different. It really suits you.'

'It was Jae's idea. I like it so far. I wasn't sure at the time though, it was a spur of the moment decision.'

'Sometimes they're the best ones.'

'In my case, possibly not. I know Garrett has filled you in.'

'Garrett says he's not even told me a third of the stories he has about you, or the worst ones,' Robbie teased.

Evie rolled her eyes, 'He will have. He forgets that he and Atlas and their group had a few rugby rivalries happening themselves.'

'He admitted those, including the time they took you and Tess along to glue the word *cheats* in glitter on a team trophy because glitter is hell to remove.'

'He told you they *took us*? He didn't say anything about breaking into a school or that they needed me to sign because Tess is partially deaf and didn't hear their whispers?'

He looked at her, surprised, 'You sign? I mean, I know you did it on your show for a guest, but I thought you just learnt the questions from someone beforehand, like, only those questions.'

'I'm rusty. We all learnt together in school. Our friend Tess lost her hearing when we were nine. We weren't isolating her from us just because of that, so when she learnt to sign with a special teacher who came in, Tess taught us. Eventually school clicked on and we all went to signing lessons twice a week. She's the one that taught me to be accepting about people more than anyone else. Some of the kids just didn't bother with her because it was slightly more inconvenient to communicate with her after meningitis. We'd get angry about that but if we could sign what they said then she was included much more.'

'I can see how you'd stick up for Jae now too, if you had to watch other kids dismiss your friend. You might hide it but I'm starting to see you're actually really soft on the inside.' He reached for her hand and gave it a squeeze.

Without that early experience with Tess, Evie wondered if she'd be the same person she was, or if she would have grown up like the other kids and been as dismissive of any inconveniences like them. Even before Tess's illness she knew what it was like to know people were whispering but not hear what they were saying, because the older villagers had whispered about her. Even at five and six she knew from the way they'd look at each other and nod to each other as she passed that they had talked about her. Every walk to and from school she had experienced that burden and weight, knowing that she lived in the witch house, on the witch farm, and wondering if they knew about her gifts too. It really wasn't that surprising she had responded to the overwhelm by turning wild and rebellious.

Robbie held the door and let the three of them walk in first. In the restaurant heads turned towards them as the whispers went around about who she was, it always did. Evie breezed Max and Rey past the onlookers with apparent casualness but underneath lay a protective fierceness. The comfortable warmth of the restaurant enveloped her like a hug, the Italian plastered walls exuded warmth, mixed with the rustic farmhouse décor, and crisp white tablecloths always made her think that they were eating in someone's house. Guiseppe had tried to bring his country's village here and she loved it.

Their usual table was by a window towards the back of the restaurant. A curtain on the wall behind them hid an unalarmed exit door, the kitchen doors were a few paces away. Guiseppe had always placed her there, far enough away from the kitchen for it not to be noisy, but close enough to two exits should she need to run. She had used the back door before, to enter and exit.

After the way Yvonne had gone after Robbie on her show Evie didn't want to sneak in through the back door unobtrusively and appear as though she was hiding him and their relationship, so she had used the main door. A server stopped by the table and asked for their coats.

Robbie took his jacket off and passed it over at the same time as Rey and Max. Evie tried not to let her eyes get as big as saucers or drop her jaw to the floor. She had only ever seen Robbie bulked up in winter work hoodies. His muscles filled the shirt. He turned, caught her looking at him and smiled in satisfaction. She raised her eyebrows and smiled back. In silent retaliation at the self-satisfied grin he gave her, Evie turned away to the open space beside her, her back to him, and slipped off her cardigan, revealing the deep cut out at the back of her jumper dress, passing her cardigan to the member of staff who held Rey's cardigan and Max's jacket.

She felt the warm, delicious roughness of his hand on her lower back as he leaned forward and whispered, 'That's an unfair advantage. I'm not going to be able to concentrate on the food or the film.'

Evie didn't think so. Unfair was how amazing his rough hands felt on her skin, if she'd known his hands felt that good, or that her body reacted to his touch like it did, she might have sneaked him in and out the farmhouse and the caravan. Now she had to live with the knowledge that she more than liked it.

'I think we're equal,' she whispered back.

'Evie!' an older man came out the kitchen in pristine chef whites with outstretched arms. Evie smiled and hugged Guiseppe, introducing Robbie to him. Guiseppe looked at him critically, up and down as though he were assessing a potential art purchase, not meeting somebody. He greeted Robbie the same way he had greeted Evie and the children, with a big hug and a warm welcome.

Afterwards he said to Robbie, 'I have seen you with Evie in the pictures on the internet. She is a good mother, therefore a good woman. Your hurt her, you will not get a table in my restaurant ever again,' he threatened, in an exaggerated accent.

Evie tried to add together how a good mother became equated with a good woman, and whether anyone had ever told her mother she was a bad mother and a bad woman. Would Ophelia have cared at all about someone's judgement? Evie didn't think so, her mother had carried the same haughtiness Yvonne possessed, a superiority ingrained through elite education. Despite both of them being less than mediocre at everything, they were both convinced of their own innate superiority to everyone else around them. Inwardly she kicked herself for not having seen the similarities earlier and gotten out of the contract with the studio.

'It's a pleasure to meet you. Evie speaks highly of you.' Robbie smiled at the man in front of him.

'Let's get drinks. Which one of you is driving?'

'I am.' Robbie didn't take his eyes off Guiseppe.

'Champagne for myself and Evie, bring the bottle, on the house.' Guiseppe spoke softly to a waiter who stood a few steps behind as if expecting the drinks order. He pulled out a seat for Evie, placing Robbie next to her. A server pulled out a seat for Rey opposite Robbie, next to Max. Guiseppe found an empty chair and sat himself at the table. Drinks arrived within seconds. Evie fell into a small talk with Guiseppe about work and his upcoming TV appearances, Robbie's thigh against hers, his hand on her leg as she sipped her champagne.

Guiseppe shared with Robbie that it was Evie's recommendations that got him initial TV chef appearances on her show, before he pushed himself through the door to become a household name. For those first few favours of pushing his name, then supporting him when he was a nervous wreck on his first handful of appearances, she would always have a table in his restaurant. He talked Robbie through the menu, advising on the best dishes, teased Evie for always ordering the same meal and asked the children about their sports and how their cooking skills were progressing. Once they had placed their orders, he left in a flurry of Italian words to oversee the cooking in his kitchen. A small lamp created a glow in the undressed windowsill. Outside city lights shone in rain puddles and raindrops trickled down the window.

After the film they arrived home in near darkness, aside from the warm lights coming from the windows of the far side of her caravan, the living area. Evie had turned everything off before they left. Robbie glanced at her. She gave a nod to confirm his thoughts. Atlas had popped in before he'd gone to bed and sorted out the lights and the heating for her. Despite being adults, his continued stress over her catching pneumonia was ingrained into his personality. Max staggered out of the car straight into the bathroom to clean his teeth, his eyes tired and pink. He had discussed the film with Robbie all the way home. Rey had fallen asleep at some point along the motorway. One minute she had been lively and talking, the next she was asleep. Evie opened the caravan door for Max and watched him into the bathroom, she gave a quick glance around the interior, a search for a lurking grey spectre before she turned around to go back to the car to get her daughter. Robbie already had the car door open and was gently unbuckling the sleeping Rey.

He lifted her out of the car, 'Where do you want her?'

he asked, walking towards her, pressing the lock button on the car fob at the same time.

'Let's put her in bed, if she wakes up in a bit, I'll clean her teeth.' Evie opened the door to Rey's room and lifted the duvet back. Robbie laid her down gently, then left the room.

When Evie came out of Max's room fifteen minutes later Robbie was sat on the caravan's white settee, his jacket laid neatly next to him. She opened the door to her room and stood just outside it, unzipping her boots and throwing them into the bedroom. She shrugged her cardigan off and poured herself a large rum and coke before she opened the white fronted fridge and lifted a beer out. His face lit up when he saw her intentions to spend some time together. She offered him the beer, breaking the tension in the silence. He took a look at it and looked up at her, surprised. She shrugged and teased, 'You didn't think you'd come to the witch house and not get your favourites?'

'How did you even know?'

'I could say that's a secret, but we stopped at Harriet's café earlier, so I asked her. She does a good espresso martini.' Evie sat next to him on the settee.

'I'm impressed. Not as impressed as I am with that dress though.'

'I'm glad you like it. It might be my new favourite Friday night dress,' she teased.

He raised an eyebrow but smiled, 'It's definitely a favourite of mine.'

'How did you like Guiseppe's?'

'Amazing. I've never had a celebrity chef come out the kitchen to have a pre-dinner drink with me before.' He twisted around so he faced her.

'It happens most times we go. But his food is amazing.'

'It is. So is that dress, and your new look.' He took a drink of beer and then placed his bottle on the wide windowsill littered with white quartz coasters and plants. He stood up and held out his hand to her.

After a hesitant second Evie reached out with doubt and took his hand, her eyes spoke how wary she was. He pulled her up. She set her drink down next to his and faced him, all the questions that she didn't dare ask written across her face, 'I've been thinking all night that your dress was made for a slow dance.' He wrapped his hand around hers and lifted it up and around his neck, putting his other arm on her back where a normal bra strap would have sat. Despite the dance position neither moved their feet.

'That's all you've been thinking?' she whispered, her spare hand slid up his arm at a slow pace. Her fingertips felt every muscle jump underneath his shirt when she touched him. He put his other hand on her lower back, gentle, no pressure from it, but the rough skin was enough to set every nerve tingling. Her thoughts in the cinema hadn't been clean at all. She held his eyes, not able to tear hers away.

'That's the PG version,' he whispered in her ear. A shiver went down her spine.

'I didn't have a PG version playing in my head in the cinema,' she stated, trailing her fingers down his back over his shirt.

He didn't reply but his calloused hand brushed gently across her lower back until his fingers slipped underneath her dress and over her bare hip and down, across her bum. Evie closed her eyes to concentrate on his hand leaving a delicious fiery trail from the roughness. He tightened his arms around her when she stepped forward to close the gap between them and rested her head on his shoulder.

'Can I ask you, why do you hate the Halloween teaser ad? You look gorgeous in it.' His voice was soft, not challenging her. His fingers continued to move, over her back, under her dress onto her hip, over her bum then back up at a slow pace.

Evie tried to concentrate. 'Really? You think that I look good in it? That's how you see it?'

'Yes.'

Evie took a moment to consider that perspective. The perspective that Yvonne might have been right to film it.

'She showed the world a deliberately objectified version of me, in underwear, knowing that I've argued against objectification in the past. I struggle to cope with people taking pictures. It wasn't about how I look as much as how likely that ad is to be perceived, if that makes sense. I wanted to remain professional. Behind the scenes can be quite tacky. We'll have rich men, sometimes women too, phone up the producers, because they know someone who knows someone, and offer insane amounts of money to whichever one of us they like. They'll say it's for a dinner, but we know what happens after the dinner with people like that. Jess knows not to even run those offers by me anymore.'

'You know someone will have taken a picture of us somewhere tonight?' Neither of them could have missed the few cameras that had been raised and pointed at them.

'I anticipated it would happen when I invited you to join us. Are you OK with that?' Evie waited to hear that he wasn't. Her hand tightened around his arm. It was a lot to learn to deal with for anyone. Max and Rey had grown up with knowing what her job was, but for Robbie to be thrust into it, unwillingly, could be too much to handle.

'I'm OK with it. You're in my arms, you smell amazing. Your new look is stunning. You're so beautiful. I've always preferred brunettes but I think you might have convinced me otherwise tonight.' He moved a warm hand off her back to twist a strand of hair in his fingers.

Evie raised her head from his shoulder and looked at him, she smiled, tilting her head to kiss him. He kissed her back. Her kiss was soft, tender and exploring. She pulled back after a while and looked at him, his eyes met hers, he understood what she didn't say, his hand circled around the back of her neck, his fingers spread up into her hair, then he kissed her again. This time she added depth and desire to it, and a rough edge that she kept hidden behind her polished veneer.

Part of her wondered if that was a side of her that he wanted to see, or whether she should play the city princess that he clearly thought she was. He seemed to be into the kiss so she persisted a few seconds longer, letting a little moan when he tightened his hand on her neck before he pulled away.

His eyes were serious when he looked at her, 'That was...' He seemed to struggle for words.

'Too much, I'm always too much.' She turned away. She was always too much. Atlas had told her all their lives she needed to pretend to be normal. She had to tone it down again.

Evie reached for her drink and picked it up, hiding her rejection behind a nonchalant sip, tasting the sweet after-taste of the rum on its harsh way down her throat. She started to shut down, to turn off her feelings. She let so few people in, that their rejection of her real self always slashed her insides as sharply as a surgeon's knife would cut her skin. Her friends had been the only people that embraced her for herself.

'It was not too much at all.' He reached the settee before she did and pulled her onto his lap.

'No?' confusion ran through her because he had been the one that stopped the kiss.

'That was a dream response. I never, ever in a million years, thought I'd have you kissing me like that.'

'I like you. Why wouldn't I kiss you like that?'

'Because you're Evie.' He looked at her like she was an illusion that would break.

She smiled at him and took another drink, basked in the admiration for a brief second before she said, 'I'm Evie. I want you to see me, not the person that I am on camera. I'm wild and careless, I love fiercely but not often, I'm happy in my own company and I would die if I didn't have the wide, open spaces of the farm to be free. I like the way your hands feel on my skin,' she added. She didn't say anything about her gift. That was a step too far. In response his hand ran up and down her back, his fingertips slipping just under the edge of her dress. She closed her eyes and murmured, 'Don't stop.'

She felt warm lips on hers again and melted into the kiss. Her back arched involuntarily. She was vaguely aware that one of her hands was on his biceps and another needed to put her drink down to take things further when a thundering knock on the door entered her head, 'Evie, nearby left crop field, now!' Atlas shouted into the caravan. The urgency and worry in his voice ripped her away from

Robbie and had her sprinting after her brother in bare feet towards the dark horizon.

Chapter 17

The rain had stopped for a brief respite. It was the first thing she noticed as she sped after her brother in the dark, her eyes quickly adjusting, the damp night air an unwelcome blanket against her skin. She tested the stretch of her dress as she ran and her bare feet squelched when they hit the ground regardless of whether it was building rubble, grit or soil. Over the years the pair of them had developed almost a shorthand language for the fields and land and Evie knew exactly where she was running. When she looked ahead, Evie saw a black clothed and hooded figure run off into the woods, light footed and certain.

They reached the field and slowed, not bothering to chase after the black figure that had already blended into the shadows of the woods. Atlas's breath came fast and shallow, disappointment on his face. As their breath slowed to a normal pace and their lungs regained air, they surveyed the mess in front of them.

'All these years you told me it wasn't you. I'm sorry,' Atlas apologised.

'How did you know it was happening?'

'I woke up and went for a glass of water, saw your light was still on and thought I'd check you and the kids were OK. I heard a scream in this direction, turned around and it looked like she emitted a black cloud from her mouth. That's when I knocked. I should have let the dogs out.

They'd have caught her.' He checked the tree line as though looking for the figure to emerge again.

'They're long gone by now.'

'No, she's there. Waiting for something. I can sense her. If she moves the tiniest bit I'll see her.'

'Leave it. We don't need you hurt.'

'I might have woken the kids up. I'm sorry.'

'Don't worry about Max and Rey. We're on half term for two weeks now anyway.'

'Why do these circles coincide with your dates. If it's not you then this thing, this person, has been following you for a long time.'

They both disappeared into the same stream of thoughts. The first time it had happened Evie had been eight years old and Michael had given her a kiss on the cheek and a bag of sweets at the farm gate on Valentine's Day whilst his parents waited in their Land Rover watching the whole thing. The next time, three years later, they'd been hanging out alone on the farm and Michael had attempted a real, adult kiss. When she was fourteen, she had kissed her date at the bottom of the lane and walked home alone. At fifteen, sixteen, and seventeen the dead, black, burnt circles in the fields became more and more frequent as she discovered drinking, partying and kissing boys. The circles had continued even when she had begun to fall out of nightclubs in a different city. Atlas used to call her after each one appeared. They had stopped when she'd gotten married. There hadn't been another one until tonight

Simultaneously they looked at each other, 'You had a date,' Atlas said. Evie nodded.

In front of them the ground was blackened in a perfect

circle. The nocturnal wildlife caught as innocents in the crossfire burned and charred. Evie bent down, placing her hand on the ground. Liquid oozed from her into the ground. She felt the soil beneath her stir and shuffle, 'I can fix this.'

'Fixing the others made you ill, Evie, we'll figure something else out.'

'I could be OK. I'm not bound anymore. We're not. We destroyed it all.' She referred to the altar they had destroyed in the old farmhouse. She stayed crouched, her bare feet and hand on the ground. She placed her other hand next to it. Atlas turned his head suddenly, his body growing even more tense. She followed his gaze. Robbie and her children walked up. Rey held her mother's sheepskin boots.

'I asked them to find something for your feet otherwise we'd have been here quicker,' Robbie said.

'Who did it Mum?' Max asked.

'A woman,' Atlas answered at the same time as Evie said, 'Just kids.' They looked at each other.

'It's a warning, isn't it?' Rey looked at the ground.

A little seven-year-old made it all make sense. Her mind flashed all the clues to her, unbidden. It linked up her entire life's events. Her childish terror of the Grey Spectre that still lingered as fear, despite her bravado in knowing that it was a real person. The symbols on the back of the photograph of her friends that had been, as far as she could determine, a spell to remove their friendship. The black circles at every date until she was married. The Grey Spectre had stopped when she was married to Damian. Damian had taken almost all she had, her sense of self, her confidence, her joy of life, her ability to make decisions.

Evie stood up, careful to hide her hands behind her back until she felt them cool down enough to be normal. Stillness hung in the air as they all remained silent. Evie went over to her children, mud oozing between her toes as she walked and put her arms around them, turning them round to walk back to the caravan.

Atlas broke the silence, 'You know, you two have beds made up in my caravan and your mum says its half term. How about we get a milky hot chocolate, watch some cartoons and then get some sleep?' Max was immediately up for the suggestion, but Rey looked warily over at her mum.

'I don't want to leave you, mum.' She passed Evie the boots.

'You don't have to, sweetheart.' Evie gave her a cuddle and slipped on the boots. Suddenly she was stood on clouds as warmth and comfort enveloped her feet and ankles. It made her even more aware of the throbbing cuts and bruises forming. She made a mental note to herself to not run over a building site or stony footpaths in bare feet again.

'But I don't want to miss out.' Her daughter shot a glance at Max and Atlas. Evie crouched in front of her, the rain started again, light infrequent drops.

'I know your Uncle Atlas makes the most amazing hot chocolate. Why don't you have one and then decide where you want to sleep afterwards? I need to wash the dirt off my feet anyway whilst you drink your hot chocolate.' Her daughter cheered up at the suggestion that the plans could be flexible and happily slipped her hand into her uncle's.

The walk back to the caravans was undertaken in silence in the darkness of the night. Evie felt a warm hand meet her own whose fingers intertwined themselves with hers. She didn't look at Robbie but held his hand tightly. She wasn't even aware that she needed that touch of comfort until she had it. It made her realise how she'd become used to dealing with everything by herself in silence and shadows. The dark air seemed to drop temperature with each step she took, until she was shivering before she reached the caravan. She gave her brother a look before they parted. He responded with a nod. She turned away, knowing that he had understood the silent request to wrap the children up in warm blankets and duvets.

Inside Evie downed her rum and coke, excused herself from Robbie with, 'The beers are in the fridge, I'll be a minute' and disappeared into the bathroom. She washed her feet in the sink and examined them with extreme detachment. There would be bruising, some was already coming out from the large stones she had run across. The small cuts would be fine with a bit of antiseptic cream. There was nothing that wouldn't be gone in a week. She needed to stop shivering, between the wet and the cold her body was tense, her jaw clenched and she was covered in goosebumps. When her feet were clean, she padded to her bedroom to put on some soft slippers and her thick winter dressing gown over her dress. Trying to look pretty for Robbie had not turned out well, he'd watched her run across the fields barefoot, like the wild thing she was. She had no hope of recovering from that. At best she could only expect a swiftly polite goodbye. No wonder her brother had warned about dating the builder before the houses were built.

Coming out into the living area she glanced up shyly.

Robbie leaned against a kitchen counter. He picked up her glass and offered it to her, 'I refilled it with a double shot. Thought you could probably use it.' Her surprise must have registered across her face because he asked, 'How are your feet?'

'They'll be OK in a week.' Even to her own ears, her voice was flat and expressionless as she instantly dismissed his concern.

She had retreated and was expectant of the forth-coming rejection from Robbie. She had revealed her true self, the wildness had surfaced, no normal person ran outside without shoes on. He looked at her, took a step forward and raised his hand to her hair. He twisted a strand through his fingers as he murmured, 'Don't do that. Don't dismiss yourself. Don't push me away. Let me worry about you.' He didn't make an excuse to leave, he stood right in front of her. Evie was thrown off balance. She stood silently whilst her brain tried to process that he wasn't leaving. It was unusual and she didn't quite know what to do next. She had always been able to predict how people would behave. She pushed them away and they left. This was new and her mind was blank. Evie was unable to respond. She stood still, holding a glass, mute. Rain began to fall again, pattering at the window in a soothing softness, cocooning her inside with Robbie who ushered her to the settee to sit down. He grinned broadly at her as he said, 'That was something to see. I'm impressed. Does it happen often?'

'Me running off somewhere? Yes.' She responded to his widening grin with a shy, wry smile, glancing from him to the floor then back to him. She shrugged and added, 'it's a farm. Unexpected things happen all the time. That was a part of my wild and careless side.'

'You love the farm?'

'Yes. Now. I didn't for the longest time. I couldn't wait to get away. I always felt that I didn't quite fit into the village like others did. I didn't understand why Atlas wanted to stay. But now, I do. We have so much of ourselves invested in this, not just money but our time, hours and hours that we can't get back, and so much of our future is built on those hours that we put into shaping it as our farm. And I realised that not fitting into the village is as much part of my presence here as the gossips in the village are.'

'Atlas told me that your dream had been to move somewhere warmer and sunnier. It came with a warning to make sure your house was perfect.'

'I couldn't leave now even if I still wanted to. Max is going to be a second-generation farmer. He loves the farm like my brother does. Rey wants to live somewhere cold and icy. She adores winter and wolves.' His hand trailed up and down her leg as she spoke. Evie began to notice the mud splashes on her dress from running.

'Can I ask you something?'

'Mmm, yes?' She was already cautious.

'I couldn't help overhearing the last bit of your conversation with your brother. What did he mean by fixing the others made you ill? And then you said you weren't bound anymore because you'd destroyed something?'

Evie drew in a sharp breath. She let it out slowly and took a drink. All the while Robbie was looking at her. Whatever she said here would change everything. She tried to find a normal thing to say, a rational explanation. Atlas was so much better at this, she had always let him talk to the adults as a child.

'I can fix it, meaning some compost and fertiliser and it'll recover. We're not bound by traditional ways of farming anymore because Atlas agreed when we went organic that we would rip up all the rule books.'

Evie swore he could see through her lies. He turned from her on the settee, placing both feet on the ground and leaned his forearms on his thighs, looking down at the carpet. After a minute he looked up at her without changing position, 'If you're not ready to say the truth, I'd rather you just said so. Don't lie to me. What happened out there wasn't kids, or a woman. I've seen enough fires to know that it wasn't a fire. Maybe I would have believed that if it was a different time of year.'

Evie pulled her knees up to her chest and wrapped her arms around them. She studied the man in front of her. She didn't see the way his shirt was tight around his arms and his chest, she didn't see the rugby thighs that she had a soft spot for, or his summer blue eyes. She saw his soul, a sweet kind gentle soul trying to offer her everything he had. She wished that her heart would soften, and she could have this, instead her body started to prepare to fight, as though a sabre tooth tiger stood in front of her instead, 'You really want this? You want me and all my secrets? You want Max and Rey?'

'Yes.'

'Can you wait until I'm ready to tell you?'

Chapter 18

The question hung in the air. Atlas took a sip of his coffee as he looked at her. The inside of his eyes narrowed. As he processed his thoughts a soft glow started to appear in his grey eyes. Evie raised a manicured finger and tapped her eye twice, to tell him silently. It should have made her happy to be able to return his lifelong warnings to appear normal. Instead, it ripped her heart apart that her sporty outdoor loving brother had to experience the same doubt, insecurity and warnings she'd endured her whole life about her gift. Since they had destroyed that altar hidden in the old library, he had struggled controlling whatever gift he'd been given.

'What did he say?'

'He wasn't happy. He's going to want an answer eventually.' She took a sip of her tea. She was in her brother's caravan and the rich wooden tones exuded the same warmth that her brother possessed. Robbie too. She didn't. She was reserved around the villagers, around people she didn't know, and that was often misread as aloofness and snobbery.

'I got this today. It was waiting at the milking shed. It means someone else was on our property last night. I'm going to look into getting some cameras and a security system.' Atlas slid a standard white envelope across the caravan dining table to her. Evie opened it and read the simple letter that claimed they could help Atlas with his emerging gift.

She looked at him, all the threats from the last few years fresh in her head, 'Don't think about doing it. It could even have been the same person as you saw last night.'

'You always said you couldn't be the only one, that there's others out there. I owe it to you and myself to learn what's happening to me. To keep the children safe.'

'You're not dangerous, Atlas. Unless I am.' Evie tried to reassure him.

Dangerous was what the villagers wanted to think of them, what the stories told them that they were. Evie had never thought that either of them were dangerous. Even before she covered up her gift, when she had been fascinated with the ability to grow new plant life, to encourage berries and fruits to form and ripen, and to produce an abundance of vegetables for them both, she had never considered that it was dangerous. Unusual, but never dangerous. It was only after the way the ivy had responded to her during the incident with the McGregor boys, how she had seen the ivy move in response to her panic and how she had used it to pin them down that she sadly realised her brother had, perhaps, a valid argument as to how others might see them.

'You grow things, Evie, you have nature at your fingertips. My eyes glow. I can see differently. Hear things, it's like I'm OK one minute then I can hear a mouse in the grass, or I go from seeing things in normal human vision to something weird.'

'Isn't that worth exploring? To see what you are capable of?' Evie meant alone, she didn't approve of seeking out a stranger and letting them learn about the farm witches.

'But it's not normal, we can't afford for me to be losing control of myself on the high street or in the pub, or at livestock sales,' Atlas countered.

Evie nodded slowly, partly in agreement, partly in understanding, partly just to agree even though she wanted him to be excited and explore what he could do. Silence fell as they both finished their mugs of tea, their standard ones for sale in the shops with the farm's pretty logo on and the words High Lēah. She looked at his worn hands around the mug. Atlas's mugs were a burnt earthen orange with a white logo. They also sold the mugs in red ochre, lemon yellow, and sage green. Evie had four of each colour set aside for their houses. They were changing the range in the summer to brighter, nineteen fifties pastel shades; the earth toned colours had been available for three years and sales were dwindling. Before that it had just been black and white options, and before that just white. Evie wanted to tell her brother not to explore the letter or find the person, but it would mean a conversation about the death threats she was receiving, and Evie did not want to talk about that.

Her phone pinged. Evie looked at it. A lump formed in her throat and she blinked back tears. She raised her head up towards the ceiling and breathed deeply in an attempt to squash the moths in her stomach that fluttered against their captivity. Her heart pounded with the heaviness of a sledgehammer. She couldn't hide the fact that her hands shook. Atlas took her phone from her hands and looked.

Robbie had sent a couple of links, the first showing photographs from the previous night. Taken from the woods, the photos circling on social media with the caption, *The myth of the white rose witches at the Hepburn Farm might be rooted in reality*, showed Evie bent down, hands on the ground in the darkness with Atlas stood over her. The photograph was taken from the edge of the woods. It was deliberately open to misinterpretation, intently looking as though it was Evie that was creating the black circle. Atlas was mid-sentence, gesturing, looking angry and as though he was shouting.

The other link had been sent with an apology from Robbie. It took the observer to pictures of Robbie and Yvonne in a house. Evie knew the house from her dreams. A fake cottage, built much more recently than the local cottages, it was a small house with a concreted lifeless, perpetually clean yard, and a small outbuilding attached to the high brick wall enclosing it. The brick wall itself was hidden by a hedge of yew trees. Evie and the farm were tagged in the post, with Yvonne joking, but not joking, that she was taking Robbie from Evie to build her extension as a priority over Evie's house. Her phone pinged again. Atlas passed it to her. Robbie had sent her a short text apology with a sentence saying that she was his priority, and he was only putting a quote together for Yvonne, but she had posted on social media. He wanted to be the one that let Evie know about the post online because Yvonne had booked the survey under a pseudonym. He also wanted to meet her in the café for breakfast the next morning.

'Say yes. If you don't want to see him, I will. I want the houses finished on time. Since you met Robbie everything has changed.'

'Do you think he's involved?'

'I wouldn't rule it out. Bit random meeting a builder in the woods just when we needed one. And you've told me that no man wants to take on someone who's a mum first and woman second. Yet he comes along and he's OK with it.'

Evie was silent. Her thoughts centred slowly on all the words her brother had just uttered. She hadn't seen Robbie's puppy since that day in the woods. He had turned up when she was looking for a builder, that information would have been easily accessible from the town's planning department. All the men who had asked her out over the years; at first Damian's so called footballer friends, then celebrities on the same circuit that she was on, producers and directors that wanted to promise her an escalated and meteoric rise to fame with deaf ears to her protests that she earned enough for her current lifestyle and was happy with it. Not one of those men wanted her for who she was, they had wanted her for who she could be in their eyes. Evie sighed. She could still feel Robbie's arms around her from last night. She knew how much she had wanted him to stay before Atlas had texted to say Rey was walking over and he was watching her from his caravan door.

Her brother looked at her and stood up, 'He could be genuine. I'll meet him with you tomorrow.' It was his deflated monotone and half-hearted attempt to conceal his suspicious that made her jaw clench and she tightened her body just as she had at six and seven years old when he had tried to sort some issue out at school for her.

'I'll sort it myself. I'm capable, Atlas.'

'Do you ever think that sometimes I offer to help because I know you're capable. You don't have to take on the world by yourself?'

'No. That's your role. It's always been you carrying us

against the world. Since we were children. Now I think it's your armour. You refuse to let anyone get close to you.'

'When did this turn on me?'

'Because I stupidly had a moment when I thought that Robbie was my person, and that he fitted in here.'

'Look around you at what's happening and the damage control that we have to do now. We've demolished the witch house and people still talk about strange things going on here because they do. Like last night. I knew from the look on Robbie's face that he didn't believe a single word and you've confirmed it. If it helps, I liked him for you. This is just another reminder we can't have what normal people have.'

In one shaded sentence her brother had taken their argument right back to the beginning of their conversation. Unspoken words hung between them that this was her fault. She had let someone onto their farm and into their lives in a way that left them vulnerable. Her head and heart were screaming at each other behind her outward anger. Her body told her not to push Robbie away. Unusually, her brain jumped to the feel of his calloused hands on her skin last night, the look on his face in the restaurant when she had taken the cardigan off. Her head knew her brother was right, but it didn't want to lose Robbie either.

Evie rose with a heaviness inside her on Sunday morning that made her sluggish and slow through milking, and then getting ready to meet Robbie for breakfast. The winter sun shone brightly through warm blue skies bringing forward reminders of summer. If Evie didn't know the Yorkshire weather better, she would assume some warmth came from the sun. Her bones told her that it was icy cold outside and the night would bring a frost severe enough to make Rey happy. Evie wrapped herself up in a silver-grey jumper and faded charcoal jeans, an outfit as grey as she felt. At the last minute she threw on a couple of green and silver bracelets and picked up her oversized sage velvet bag into which Max and Rey proceeded to place their gaming bits and other things that they absolutely needed for breakfast in the café despite the fact that she knew they would be mostly in the play area with the other children. They were both wrapped up in fleece lined tracksuits.

In the café Max and Rey seemed oblivious to the heavy cloud she was under, placing their orders quickly and running off to play even as she stood in front of the black painted wood and clear glass of the farm café door, clumsy and muddled with her keys whilst her mind focused on Robbie. A couple appeared behind her, clearly expecting her to let them in too. Evie shook her head and apologised. The plump man in his fifties arrogantly began lecturing her on customer service saying that they only wanted coffee. Smoothly, her manager turned up and defused the situation, helped by the early arrival of Robbie who strode up to the door and glared the couple into submission.

Evie watched through a large floor to ceiling café window as her children played with others on the equipment in the play area. Outside, people had seen her unlocking and were forming a queue to get into the café. One by one members of staff trickled in and the noise of various coffee machines filled the air. The heating came on and warmth began to slowly fill the building. Not that it would matter much in an hour when the doors were constantly being opened.

Evie placed Max and Rey's orders with the young waitress who was sent over before the doors were officially opened for the day. Sludge swirled around her stomach and she only wanted a sweet tea. She watched as the waitress left and another member of staff smoothly turned the key in the lock and opened the doors to invite people in. The man, one half of the couple first in the queue, glared at her but the manager swiftly carried his order over on a tray with complimentary biscuits packaged up in cellophane. Evie smiled inwardly at the silent *fuck off* gesture wrapped up in sugar.

'I want to tell you a couple of things,' Robbie started, bringing her attention back to him as she watched the café fill up. Evie turned to him, sad that this would be their last breakfast, she had lost the playfulness that she had recently gained around him. He looked at her, regret and resignation passed over his face. He shook his head, 'I'm starting to read you and those eyes are making me worried. You're ending it aren't you?'

Evie took a breath. She couldn't force a smile on her face, 'What did you want to tell me?'

'First, you're beautiful. Second, no matter what Yvonne does or says I will never sleep with her—'

'So she did try flirting with you?'

'Less flirting, more desperation, I think. Lots of innuendos, straight up asking me about whether we had slept together and making it known that she wouldn't be hesitant.'

'I've seen her destroy relationships of fifteen, twenty years. She takes what she wants. She'll flatter people and love bomb them until she has them.'

'I want you, Evie, but I can only make you feel secure in that by my actions not my words. I know it'll take time for you to trust me. For Max and Rey too.'

'I want you too. I'm just scared that you're going to get fed up before I'm ready to tell you want you want to know.'

In response his hands cupped her face. He answered her without words, his kiss long and slow before saying, 'I know what I saw last night. I know your home's reputation. I don't blame you for hiding.'

'Hi, Stranger, can I interrupt?' A coffee cup and a pair of sunglasses were expectantly placed on their table as a woman's clipped voice cut into their conversation. Evie looked up at the immaculate figure, from her polished flat boots, wine red trousers, black jumper, and a burgundy leather jacker that had an attached deep red jersey hood, then Evie recognised her. The pale olive skin, dark brown eyes accentuated with liquid eyeliner, dark brown hair pulled back into an immaculate low bun, red lips, her friend had the kind of style that was bred into Italian women.

Evie flew out of her seat, 'Gia! I thought you weren't coming back until Spring.' She encased her childhood friend in a firm hug, a hug that was reciprocated warmly.

Chapter 19

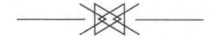

Gia and Evie sat down, talking faster than normal in an effort to catch up and cross the distance and time they had been apart. Gia shrugged off her leather jacket and laid it over her knees as they talked about her flight and her grandmother.

Robbie stood up, 'I can go, give you time to catch up.'

'No, please stay, don't let me push you away,' Gia spoke up.

Evie caught his hand and looked up at him. She didn't want him to leave, especially not with a half-finished conversation. She also didn't want to ask him to tag along if he wanted to leave. She froze up, only remembering after she had caught his hand that she had been about to call their burgeoning relationship off, and now she had acted on instinct, she had reached out to ask him to stay.

He looked down at her and smiled. Bending over he cupped her face again with his free hand and gave her a light kiss, 'I'll get us another coffee.'

Evie and Gia watched him walk away before Gia smiled at Evie, 'He looks as good in real life as he does in those pictures of the pair of you on the internet. I love your hair. When did you change it?'

'Last week. I think it was last week. Things have been a bit hectic lately. You've still not said why you're back early.'

'My book got cancelled. There's a small release in the East but the Midwest evangelists combined with the rise of the far right have scared the publishers and they're not willing to risk a huge promotion on a book centred around dark witchcraft, even though it's complete fiction. I've done the New Orleans promotion, Seattle, New York, and the East Coast. I'm homesick for English weather, English gardens, the cuteness of the village, so I booked an earlier flight.'

'I know you.' Evie put her head to one side when she looked at her friend.

Gia grinned, 'I may have a few ideas. I'm researching the history of magic in the isles and the waves of migration and invasion to see how they've changed the magical land-scape and incorporated themselves into folklore. Where better to be than our very own village with its own special deity?'

'Is there such a thing as black magic?' Evie's thoughts drifted to the altar Atlas had found in the old farmhouse.

'No. Magic is magic. Essentially, it's just another energy in the universe that's harnessed in different ways by different cultures. Honestly, I've met so many people and learnt their culture and sub-cultures around magic that I don't believe in black, white, or even grey anymore. There's intent, and that's a human trait, magic itself is a neutral force that people manipulate,' Gia answered her with serious eyes and a shrug.

'There's people out there you believe can use magic?' She had to check Gia's answer, hopeful that she wasn't alone in her gift.

'Of course. I've seen it.'

'Seen what? They'll bring our coffees over. I got Max

and Rey more juice.' Robbie set the bottles on the table and sat down, his hand going over the back of Evie's chair, his fingers playing with the loose hair at the nape of her neck. Evie couldn't ply Gia for more personal answers after Robbie's return without her personal interest being exposed.

Gia didn't need an introduction to her topic and continued to talk about magic, telling them about individuals she had met in America who could truly use magic. And those who only thought that they could. She told them about poverty-stricken shamans practising handed down knowledge; about witches, about voodoo and her experiences working with a young priest tracking down demons for the catholic church. Evie listened and chattered, all too aware of Robbie's warm fingers on her neck playing teasingly with strands of her hair. She couldn't concentrate on Gia's conversation as much as she would have liked to.

'They honestly believe in demons? I thought, I dunno, that it was just PR for those who believe they're possessed.' Robbie leaned forward a couple of centimetres to discuss demons with Gia.

Gia gave a nod, an expression flickered over her face that was gone in a millisecond before she confirmed that the priest she worked with did believe, and the two discussed the subject. Evie recognised the fear, and the urge to share before withdrawing. Gia had taken a sip of her coffee and her eyes took in the people around her in the café, as if reminding herself that she was in public.

Evie listened as Gia replied, 'I've seen them. I was sceptical about the whole possession thing. I worked with a priest off and on for the last four years. I'm more curious about how other people and indigenous cultures treat them. Organised religions are fairly easy to study and predict.' Gia had taken the personal self out of any experiences and remained a distant observer in the way she chose to recount her encounters.

Coffee turned to a light lunch in the café, then it was Gia and Evie's turn to crash Robbie's planned afternoon with his family in the pub, somewhat reluctantly on Evie's part who would have preferred to retreat to the caravan and spent the afternoon alone. Evie let herself be persuaded on the basis that she wanted to spend more time with her friend, and that she and Robbie had a conversation they needed to finish. She hadn't felt part of a group of adults, no matter how small, since she had fallen pregnant with Max. The warm fuzziness of belonging to a group instead of sat aloof by herself was energy for her soul.

People walked to and from her farm on the clay-coloured narrow country road and mud splashed grass verges in boots and wellingtons, weather appropriate clothes, all happily chatting between themselves and exchanging greetings as they passed others they knew. Evie shared to Robbie and Gia that she hadn't been in the pub since she had left school, prompting Gia to laugh and point out that it would be the first time she'd set foot in it at a legal age to be drinking. Gia proceeded to tease her about not dancing on the tables now that she was an adult. Evie smiled wickedly and told Gia that Friday karaoke didn't exist anymore. Gia expressed genuine shock and disappointment that their memorable Friday nights had stopped. They'd had legendary Friday nights in the local pub as teenagers at Friday night karaoke, although Evie's memories blurred into memories of sixth form, Friday night summer, English tea dresses, standing in the crowded courtyard in the cooler evening air after the humidity of the day as the sun dipped in the sky, out of tune singing carried on the air through the open pub doors, tendrils of them all laughing together.

That last summer, the Friday evenings during their exams were the final few times all seven met, each understanding that their unspoken escapes were on the verge of becoming real even as they tried to hold onto the last embers of their time together. They would dash inside when they heard the opening notes of a song they liked, because it didn't matter who was singing, if someone in the audience liked the song too, the audience joined in. That had been the true spirit of the legend behind the Friday nights, the camaraderie.

When she walked into the pub, Evie suddenly fell shy. She politely exchanged greetings with a few Oak Hall parents when walking past. Inside lay changes she hadn't even thought to expect. The pub had changed layouts, interiors, even the bar was in a different place. She hid behind Robbie when they approached his parents whilst Gia walked confidently into the pre-assembled family group next to Robbie and introduced herself, only to find that Robbie's mum and sister were fans of her books and her unexpected intrusion was warmly welcomed.

A few minutes later Max and Rey begged Evie to go to the park with a group of friends whose parents were already in the pub. Evie cast her eye over the crowd of children, some in football kits, some in muddied rugby kits, others in normal clothes. Evie hesitated, a grimace of worry passing over her face as she looked at the short distance to the small enclosed play park. She wanted to say yes. She wanted them to go and have fun, to have a normal afternoon with their friends.

The threat sent to the school flashed in her mind. Not knowing about the threat, Phoebe pointed out that they could see the park from the pub windows if she chose to let them go. Robbie asked Max and Rey who else was going, they reeled off eight names between them. Evie nodded a yes, not wanting to allow her anxiety to dictate their lives the way her parents' neglect had dictated hers.

When Max and Rey ran off out the door with their friends, Robbie put a hand on her thigh and whispered, 'I'll watch them too.'

Robbie walked them back up the lane in the darkening evening, after they had seen Gia and her grandmother home. Ahead of them loomed the last streetlamp, and Evie remembered the time Robbie had walked her home after work, the two of them surrounded by the cold of the night and kept warm by their attraction, still uncertain about being honest with each other. Just outside the halo of the streetlamp a pretty white and tabby cat crossed the narrow lane, stopping to glance at them halfway across, then haughtily disappearing fast into Evie's field to chase rabbits.

Evie's fingers were interwoven with Robbie's, their palms touching as she listened to the conversation between Robbie and Rey. The glow from the streetlamp disappeared behind them and soon they were enveloped in the gradual dusk.

Rey turned around to walk backwards as she asked, 'Will you come and spend Halloween night with us?'

Max turned around and agreed instantly, seemingly

knowing what his sister meant, 'Yes. I'd feel safer with you there too.'

'Hey, I make you safe, don't I?' Evie kept her tone light. She knew Halloween was a tough night, but she had tried hard to make them safe over the years, keeping them away from the ghosthunters and thrill seekers who clambered over their property in search of the witch ghosts.

'No offence, mum, but Robbie and Uncle Atlas can chase people away and you can stay with us. We don't like it when you and Uncle Atlas go out to deal with people in different places and we have to lock the door after you.'

'Fair point,' Evie conceded, without raising an argument.

She remembered how alone she had used to feel in the old farmhouse, especially on Halloween waiting for Atlas to return. The nights when people had knocked on the kitchen windows and asked to be let in. She turned to Robbie, her expression openly backing her children's request with a wicked glint behind her eyes. He gave a slow smile, and a nod, but looked at Max and Rey when he replied, 'If you want me there, I will be there.'

Her caravan had the lights on, even from a distance Evie could see Atlas had been in to turn on the lights and the heating ready for them to be home. For the three of them, it was completely normal. The lights signalled their way home.

'Does your brother always leave everything on at night?'

'Yes. It's a complicated story, but he does it because he knows what it's like to go home to a cold dark place. We remember running from light switch to light switch growing up, or he would go into the darkness to turn on the next light and once he had, I would turn off the light behind him and run to him. Now he goes out of his way to make sure that we don't endure that again, that Max and Rey don't have that lifestyle.' She left it unsaid that Atlas did it to help protect her against illnesses from the constant cold and damp. There was nothing romantic or attractive about being ill. She disliked it with an intensity that rocked her whole body, it meant that she was incapable of looking after her children without help, she was incapable of helping on the farm, and back in the days when her gift was the only thing that fed them, she had needed to be out on the farm growing food. The helpless invalid was not a role for her, it caused her body to tense in anxiety the whole time and her worry mounted over not having any food, the circle inside her head went round and round on those days when she was in bed.

'We had that experience during the renovations. It's not fun. You'll be able to control the heating and the lights from your phone once the houses are built.'

'There are certain things that I really love about this century and that is one of them.'

Inside the caravan it didn't take Max and Rey long to flake out. Evie put the small side lamps on in the sitting area and turned the harsh overhead lights off, and passed the television remote to Robbie.

She made two cups of tea, did a final check that her children were asleep and sat next to Robbie on the settee. He was flicking through channels on the television, finally settling on a replay of an eighties quiz show.

'Gia's conversation was interesting. All those people she's met for research into magic.'

'Yeah,' Evie murmured quietly, not wanting to get into

a conversation which meant that she might slip up and end up talking about Friday night.

'What's wrong? You two have made loads of plans.'

'Gia and I are fine. She's one of my best friends.' Her back stiffened in the effort to be normal.

'So?' he prompted.

'Did you have a good time? Your family wasn't miffed that we interrupted your get together?' Evie changed the topic.

'My family loved you and the kids. They loved Gia too. That's not what we're discussing. I'm guessing you don't want to talk because it will raise questions about Friday night. That's really why you were ready to cool things this morning.' He put his arm over the back of the settee and rested his hand on her shoulder.

'It might have been.' She wrapped both hands around her cup.

'So, let's keep ignoring the elephant in the room until you're comfortable with it.' He squeezed her shoulder. There was no sarcasm in his tone, just a straightforward suggestion and an acknowledgement that she had asked him for time, then he suggested that they see who got the most answers right.

Evie turned to look at him, she noticed his straight nose, Liam had a prominent bump from a broken nose. Robbie's skin still held a slight tan. He was sat with an arm thrown over the back of the settee holding onto her shoulder lightly, a cup of tea in one hand after a day of steadily drinking beers, she'd had as many rum and cokes with Gia as he'd had beers. He looked at her when her shoulder left his hand.

'Where's your puppy?'

'My puppy?' He looked confused at her question.

'Your dog. The cute little black puppy you had when I met you.'

'Brontë? She's my parent's puppy. They had gone away for their wedding anniversary and we all took turns looking after her. I'd love a dog but I don't have a lifestyle for one.' Evie took a few seconds to process that information, recalling conversations in the pub when his mother had talked about Brontë. She'd assumed Brontë was a baby, maybe a grandchild. But replaying those conversations with Brontë as a puppy suddenly made more sense.

Evie turned back to the TV. Robbie looked at her then settled in, his hand on her shoulder again, his fingertips drew circles across her jumper. He slid his hand backward until it was on the nape of her neck.

'I love that.' She closed her eyes to block out everything except the curve of his fingers around her skin, the warmth that sank straight through her skin and soothed her muscles.

'I can actually see you thinking.'

She felt the amused smile on his face through her closed eyes. 'I overthink a lot.'

'Can I distract you?'

'Anytime, all the time, every time,' she murmured opening her eyes.

He chuckled, 'That's good because I can barely think straight these days. If I'm not with you I'm thinking about you. If I see you and you're not within touching distance, it's hell. This is nice. I like this. Today was good.'

Evie agreed with him by giving a nod. She didn't need to do more than that. The entire time they had been in the pub he had found subtle ways to touch her. His leg next to hers, his hand on her thigh, his arm over her chair touching her back, her shoulder, or her neck.

'It was good.' She swapped hands holding her cup of tea and placed her hand high on Robbie's leg, curving her fingers around the rugby player's thigh.

'You want a dog?' she asked. She had no plans for a puppy. Max wanted one, a farm dog of his own like his uncle's.

'I like the idea of one, a well-trained one that will sit in my truck whilst I work and guard the tools in it, one that I can go for long walks with. I'd never been in the woods before I had Brontë that day and I liked the walk. But like I said, my lifestyle isn't conducive to having a dog.'

'Max wants a farm dog. My brother sends his away to be trained. He could do it himself but,' she cut herself off, *But he has this gift with animals, and we have to appear normal so he sends his dogs away for training*, had been on the tip of her tongue. She ended with, 'but I'm thinking I'd like a cat. Max and Rey would get a pet, but a cat would give us more independence, and they'd have the whole farm to roam. I can't stand the idea of a dog, the slobber and the training, their absolute neediness to be with you, their reliance on you, ten plus years of picking up their mess... I mean, children are toilet trained in a couple of years or so, they develop voices to speak when they're hungry or thirsty, they're capable of having cute conversations and you can take them almost anywhere.' Evie suddenly sat up straight, stiff as a board, every muscle tense as she realised that they had different opinions. To her surprise Robbie laughed, a full belly laugh, amusement twinkled in his eyes.

'That's only the second time I've heard you voice an opinion that isn't filtered with politeness. You're like a politician sometimes, trying to please everyone. I always put it down to how Damian treated you, and your job, but, have opinions Evie. It's OK. We won't get a dog.'

He was still stroking his thumb up and down the back of her neck. Her back curved and relaxed into the feeling. She leaned over and kissed him, meaning it to be nothing more than a quick kiss. When her lips left his he applied pressure with the hand that was on her neck to continue the kiss.

She balanced her cup of tea carefully as she leaned forward. Her brain told her that if she didn't pull back she would easily cross the bridge into being wild and reckless. Evie continued, her breathing changing as her body craved more. Robbie broke off to put his cup down. Evie followed the gesture with her own. As they resumed kissing Evie straddled him. His hands slid under the hem of her jumper and her lace bra did nothing to hide her response when his thumbs brushed over her nipples. He pulled the jumper up and over her head. A slight chill brushed over her skin but she was too flushed to care. Her jumper landed on the settee. Warm hands cupped her breasts in their white lace bra before he reached around to unfasten it, rough hands slid over her ribs tantalisingly slow, round to her back.

'Sorry about my hands,' he muttered.

'They feel amazing, don't go getting soft hands,' she whispered.

Robbie looked at her before he pushed his fingers under the straps and slowly slid them down her arms. He was clearly expecting her to say no, to push him away. She took her bra and put it on her jumper carelessly. Her hands found their way into his hair when he took each nipple in his mouth in turn. She pulled back, and got up, he looked up at her, 'These need to come off,' she said.

Standing up, Evie unfastened her jeans before turning away, cheekily teasing by pulling her jeans down slowly on the way to her bedroom, showing of her white lace shorts. She felt the movement, a gentle rocking of the caravan floor as Robbie instantly followed her. Evie only knew that his own hoody was off before he got into her bedroom from seeing it thrown onto a pillow, followed quickly by a well washed T-shirt that wafted a clean laundry fragrance towards her when it flew past onto the same pillow. She turned around, her jeans unfastened but still up. He reached for her and pulled her to him. She had a second to see his broad chest with tattoos down one side of his body, half a sleeve, defined stomach, muscles that she'd only felt through a shirt before he kissed her like she was his air. Unlike his other kisses, this was raw and deep as he wrapped his arms around her and pushed her up against him. Evie closed her eyes and tilted her head upwards to meet his lips. Her hands splayed out across his back exerting their own pressure.

Eventually he broke off, peppering kisses on her lips, 'We need to close the door,' he whispered.

One of his hands landed on hers, keeping her within touching distance as he pushed the white door shut gently. From behind her, his lips landed on her neck, involuntarily her head moved to the side and goosebumps broke out over her body at the delicious sensation. A hand cupped her breast, his fingers roughly playing with her nipple. His other hand left a burning path down her ribs, across her stomach and into her knickers. She couldn't stifle her moan this time as her breathing grew shallower and faster. With her eyes closed she could concentrate on the sensations he was drawing out of her. Every muscle started to tighten, 'Faster,' she breathed. He did and she lasted seconds before she shuddered against him, her hands going over both of his to still him whilst she absorbed the moment. She still wasn't satisfied. She needed more, telling him so by exerting pressure on his hands to start again.

With an edge of roughness that she found incredibly sexy after her reinitiation of sex, he bent her over the bed, pushed her jeans and pants down. She felt him teasingly position himself. Evie tried to move backwards, to feel him but his hands held her in place, one on a hip and one between her shoulder blades. The pressure he used was enough to tell her that he needed her there.

'Give me a minute,' he muttered hoarsely. She didn't. Pushing back as much as she could she felt a little of him inside her, then with a moan he took the hint and pushed himself fully in. His hand held her hip tight as he buried himself inside her, she moved with him easily, taking what she wanted.

She had no idea what she was feeling but it was everything, euphorically high, alive, full, she couldn't even name it. One of her own hands went to her clitoris. It was only a few strokes and she came again, her muscles contracting around him. He swore. She felt him pull out almost fully, then thrust back in hard enough to elicit a little gasp from her. A few more thrusts and he came, pushing into her so fully she felt as though he was an extension of her. He stayed there a while, catching his breath, then pulled out slowly, 'You OK?' he asked.

'I don't think I can stand up,' she used her arms to

push herself up slowly. He chuckled and pulled her up, wrapping his arms around her from behind, but gentler, calmer.

'I had planned all these smooth, seduction techniques,' he murmured into her ear. Evie laughed softly. There had been nothing smooth and seductive about that raw sex.

'I prefer it this way. Seduction is overrated. It suggests a reluctant partner. Mutual lust is far better and more honest,' she replied. He stroked his fingers down her arm and placed a kiss on her shoulder.

'You really do keep surprising me. That was so fucking sexy, the way you knew what you wanted, and you weren't shy with it.'

'Why don't you stay?' She turned in his arms and looked at him for his first reaction. Evie held her breath.

He thought, and said carefully, 'I'll give you a chance to take that back, you've been drinking all afternoon. You've already made it clear that Max and Rey come first in your life.'

'They will still be my priority. It's Halloween tomorrow, it's only a night in advance.' She wouldn't ask again, her eyes darkened as he looked at her, assessing her, she waited for the rejection.

Chapter 20

Sounds from the kitchen roused her from sleep, cutlery clattering, the kettle boiling. Evie rolled over and reached out. Robbie had left her bed. She closed her eyes to relive the night. She remembered the way he had pulled her to him so they could sleep, how his body had curved around hers as though they were made to fit like jigsaw pieces. A gentle sway of the caravan told her he was walking around.

He brought her a cup of tea to her side of the bed. He whispered to her as he placed it down, then woke her by running his hands over her body. Evie refused to open her eyes, intent on enjoying his hands on her bare skin longer, she stretched out so that he had access to all of her. She heard him chuckle as he took the hint.

'Good morning, beautiful.' He kissed her neck, her collarbone, then her breasts. Evie still didn't open her eyes. She let out a contented sigh, sinking deeper into the white bedsheets and the clouds of sleep that still wrapped themselves around her with whispers of hope and nice dreams, thinking of the morning she would wake in her own house.

'Tell me it's not morning already,' she murmured, revelling in the attention of his hands.

'It is I'm afraid. I'd much rather it be Sunday again and I could spend the day in bed with you, make cookies and chocolate fairy cakes with the kids and eat them all during a movie afternoon marathon. Work might be just outside the door, but my team will start to arrive soon.'

It hit her that she had to be at work herself soon, in the toxic studio with Yvonne and Jess. Evie sat up, propping her pillow up behind her and lifted her cup of tea from the bedside table where he had placed it. He walked around the bed and sat on it next to her. They had their drinks in companionable silence, Robbie looked at his phone and typed replies to emails. Evie ignored hers, her eyes roved around the cramped white room that was already starting to irritate her. She was already full of dread about going to work, it sat like a weight in her stomach. She didn't want to take a look at the emails on her phone to see if anyone had contacted her. She pondered over what he had said and then asked, 'You bake?'

'Not really. I'm not bake off ready if that's what you're thinking. I noticed recipe books in your kitchen. I can follow a recipe. I'm more into making small pieces of furniture or restoring old furniture.'

He opened the camera on his phone and showed her some pieces, resin side tables resembling geodes or with flowers trapped forever in a display. Immediately her thoughts turned to Dutch still life paintings that she had studied in school but hadn't appreciated their dark moodiness back then. She could see it working on a resin table in her house to contrast with the lightness, or in her brother's house where the colours would fit perfectly. Robbie had a picture of a restored dressing table with a woman sat at it. He told her the woman was his youngest sister Paige, the one still living at home who was training to be a midwife. She had always wanted a large dressing table with drawers at both sides and space for a chair where she could sit and do her make-up and hair. He had taken an old worn piece of furniture and restored it for her.

'When do you find the time to do this between work and working on your houses?' she wondered.

'There's time. There's days when I'll be waiting for plaster to dry or I'm waiting on a delivery of replacement tools before I can go any further and I'll take myself off into the garage.'

'This is amazing. I mean, its sexy that you can build things anyway, but to be creative too.' Evie was in awe. V.V had painted and drawn. Gia wrote. Tess had painted well too, but next to V.V she hadn't shone until she attended art school, Kat had crocheted, she had always come out with hats for them or matching scarves and hand warmers.

'Thank you.'

'I wish I had a hobby.'

'You read.'

'I do.'

'What do you like doing the most, if you didn't have to consider the farm or the children?'

'Growing things. Plants. Gardening. My next thing is to open a garden centre and I'd like to start doing more show-case stuff, maybe enter Chelsea eventually, always focusing on native plants for insect populations. I'll start with the new courtyard and my garden and build up.'

'So you made your hobby your career? Being an Eco Consultant?'

'I guess. I love doing those projects and putting wild-life friendly gardens together. I've just worked with a council in another district to plan a borough wide wildlife corridor. Their in-house ecologists hadn't done a bad job but it all needed linking up and I identified how they could do that and go for a few awards once they've implemented the plans.' She realised what he had said. She had made her hobby her career.

'Are you going to juggle that landscaping competition gardening career alongside everything else?'

'No, something has to give. I'm just not sure what,' Evie sighed.

'Do you have plans for the courtyard and garden?' Robbie put his phone down and paid attention to her.

Evie smiled, she grew animated when she talked about her plans, 'So many. I want an outdoor kitchen on the perimeter where the slope down to the café and shops starts so that it obstructs our view of them. I'll plant trees and shrubs behind it on the slope to hide the courtyard and make it private for us. I'm going to terrace the slope with the tallest trees at the bottom to really make us feel like we're further away and higher up than we are. The court-yard will be filled with herbs in raised beds where the private patios end and the courtyard starts, so we can have fresh herbs all year round.' She told him that she wanted to interspace the paving slabs with Mexican daisies, thyme, feverfew and camomile.

'Why Mexican daisies and not more herbs?' he interrupted her with a question.

'There's no big reason. Daisies and daisy-like flowers are my favourites. And I'll have a couple of olive trees by the cabins. There will be aspen trees with a formal lawn blocking off the beginning of the current drive because we're not using it anymore. Where our caravans are now we'll have a sort of curving, meandering path through year-round gardens with cut flowers growing and benches to sit. The dried plants will give an amazing structure in winter so when it gets frosty, Rey will love it.'

'Rey likes the frost?'

'Rey likes everything about winter in Northern Europe. I took them to Lapland last winter and Rey was adamant that she wasn't coming home. We stayed in the bubble domes to see the Northern Lights, then the Carpathian Mountains to see her beloved wolves in the wild.'

'So Rey likes winter things?'

'Yes. Howling winds, snowstorms, frost, and wolves.'

'What about Max?'

'He loves the farm, animals, and the stars, and his little motorbike. He'll indulge me and enjoy watersports on holiday but he's happiest at home, whatever the season.'

'What about you? What's your favourite season?'

'When we get a heatwave. That's my favourite season. Sometimes its June, sometimes its September. Just sitting in the sun, being warm and OK, with a drink and a book. What about you?'

He thought about it, she could see his face calculating an answer, then he replied, 'Spring and Autumn. I love being outside working then. When the sun is warm but not scorching and there's still enough of a chill in the air to keep cool. I'm not so keen on the weeks where it rains constantly. Which reminds me, I spoke to the architect last week, she's going to call you for a couple of things.'

He would have continued but Evie interrupted him. Worry already creased her forehead, 'What things? What's wrong?'

'Nothing is wrong. Everything is fine. We're talking to each other. She checks our progress and we talk about materials for the next stage. But I mentioned putting progress pictures on our website and she loves these houses as much as you do and wanted permission to do the same. She also wants to do a site visit but wants to check with you. I can meet her if you're busy.'

'Is that all?' Evie's back relaxed against the pillow once again. She let out a long breath. Muttering, more to herself than Robbie she said, 'That's OK. I can cope with that.'

'I think you can cope with anything. But you shouldn't have to. What's with you and Atlas being so worried and tense if you think there's a problem? You've set up a thriving business, surely there's not much you can't take in your stride?'

Evie paused. She stared into her cup of tea trying to formulate the words for something she had no idea how to explain to Robbie. What were the words that a grown woman used to explain a constant state of fear and anxiety? She tried anyway.

This time when she spoke there was nothing animated about her, she turned back into the reserved, private woman she presented to everyone, 'Atlas and I know that people think we're privileged. We were gifted a farm, and I realise that even in its run down state it was more than other people start with. We had our private school tuition paid, possibly because our parents couldn't outright neglect us, but on the other hand, we were getting our own food or going hungry at three and seven years old, we were digging out the fields and treating the weeds by six and ten to grow crops. We were fairly accomplished cooks at seven and eleven with our own herb garden, stealing butter from shops, and we knew how to make potatoes and vegetables into a decent meal. We only had bread at school until we started the farmers' markets and we had money in our hands for store cupboard staples. Even getting ill was a challenge because the doctors expected to see our parents bring us in. Atlas took me for antibiotics so many times our doctor just stopped asking where our parents were and it was normal. I couldn't be myself in school because Atlas warned me to tone it down so there weren't any calls home. No one could discover that our parents weren't parenting, or that we were feeding ourselves. We knew we'd be taken away and we'd lose the farm. Above every-thing we needed to stay on the farm. Our stress comes from that. I know we're older now and it doesn't matter but it's so ingrained that it's hard to stop.'

'It's called survival mode. Your parents didn't feed you?' He looked as though he couldn't comprehend that.

'They just forgot. It started in the evenings, then it was breakfast too. Then they slowly started to forget other things like waking us up for school, washing clothes, so we took over raising ourselves. On the plus side, we stayed out as late as we wanted, we decided when we ate, we developed the farm how we wanted to. I know that their relationship was unhealthy, they were obsessed with each other to the point where they would get jealous if one of them spent time with Atlas and me. Food wasn't one of their priorities. But children need food.'

'Is that why you've got such big hidden pantries?' He referred to the plans for the houses.

'Yes. We like to have spares of spares. So, if we open the spare bag of sugar, we know we're OK. Please don't tell anyone. I'm hoping that the new houses are a fresh start, with the last part of our childhood gone we might be better and relax about our issues more.'

'Hey, I wouldn't talk about you. But things about your houses are making sense. Two ovens, two fridges, storage space, two hobs, it's so if something breaks you're not left with nothing right? It must have been hard.' He reached out for her hand.

'I didn't think anything of it. But I know that I would never let Max and Rey live like I did.' Noises of vehicles and people talking in loud voices distracted both of them. Robbie swore and put his cup down, 'Sorry. I meant to be out of the caravan and on site before they turned up.'

'Finish your cup of tea. I'm not ashamed. I was trying to protect Max and Rey, not your work team. The last thing I wanted was a series of men coming in and out of their lives. I'm not perfect but I'm also sure that would be more damaging to them.'

Robbie got up from the bed and walked around to her side. He put his arms either side of her, so close she could feel the muscles tense as he rested his weight on his hands. He leaned forward and kissed her hard, pushing her head back against the headboard, he kept her there whilst he whispered, 'There won't be a series of men for Max and Rey or you. There's me and there will only be me.' Robbie gave her another kiss before he got up and left. When the solid cage of his body moved away, he took the protective-ness against real life with him too.

Evie stopped him when he got to the door, 'Keep an eye out for people. They turn up as soon as the café opens. Today could be a health and safety hazard for you. If it gets bad with people looking around the witch house just call it off and send everyone home.'

Left alone inside the white room with its cold, impersonal surfaces Evie started to get ready for the day. Without really thinking about her outfit, her thoughts elsewhere when she chose her clothes, she dressed in jeans and a light blue shirt, cream ballet flats and a chunky off-white cardigan. Still reflecting on her childhood and how it affected her behaviours as an adult she moved out to the kitchen area to start breakfast, popping her head into each child's room. Neither was awake so she made herself another cup of tea and sent her brother a text; he was supposed to be coming by after milking and looking after her children.

When Atlas failed to show she opened the door and wandered out. Red-grey clouds heavy with rain contrasted against paler puffs above the neon coated workmen in bulky, lined outdoor hoodies and worn bottoms. Evie fixated her eyes on the milking barn, the new structure standing out against the old, crumbling barns dotted across their land.

She wrote a note and left it on the kitchen surface under two empty clean glasses from the dishwasher to tell her children where she was. When she stepped out again, a frown on her face, she had swapped her cream flats for green wellingtons. She locked the door and pocketed the key, knowing that Max and Rey could open the door from the inside. Robbie jogged over as she marched to the milking barn, 'Is everything OK?'

'Atlas should be here by now. I'm going to check.'

'Do you want me to come with you?' he offered.

'Do I look that worried?' she tried to force smile.

He nodded.

Evie hesitated. She would prefer to be in the caravan with her children and ask Robbie to check on her brother. But the animals could be dangerous even to seasoned farmers. She shook her head as her eyes went to her caravan, 'Can you watch the caravan door whilst you work?

Max and Rey are still asleep. I've left a note and I don't intend to be long, I just want to check my brother is OK. I can't ask you to go and do that, every year cows crush at least one experienced farmer to death. I don't know what to expect if milking hasn't gone smoothly. I'm pretty certain he's just found an injured animal and got distracted, he does that.'

Robbie nodded and told her he'd watch the caravan for her.

Evie continued her march to the barn through grass wet with pearls of water, mud patches, and an increasing smell of animals the nearer she got. Once there she saw the cows in their stalls, but only the regular member of staff who helped Atlas. A teenage boy was assisting him. Evie walked over, 'Jim, is Atlas about?'

Jim, who had worked on the McGregor farm before Evie had poached him, shook his head, 'He didn't turn up this morning. I rang our Billy to get here and help out. I'm running a bit behind schedule.'

'That's fine, don't try and complete everything if my brother isn't around. Just get the priorities done. Billy, do you want to send me an invoice for double time? I'll pay you for being good enough to come in and help out without notice?' She looked at the teenage boy who gawked at her, whether because of who she was or the fact that she'd just offered to pay him double time, she wasn't sure.

'You don't need to pay him double,' Jim interjected.

'I do. He turned up to help out after a phone call. I bloody hate it when work rings me at the last minute to turn up to something unscheduled. Billy doesn't have a contract with us, so compensating him appropriately is the least I can do. Just, please be careful if he's inexperienced.

I don't want any accidents.'

'It's unusual for Atlas. He's here no matter what. I've never seen him with as much as a cold in all the years I've worked here.'

'I know,' she agreed, patting the rump of her favourite cow, Flora, on her way out.

Flora, a beautiful fawn coloured cow, stood rigid, her eyes following the movement of Evie's footsteps as she listened.

In a dark room lit by candles a woman smirked. She picked up a key that sat next to a plate of gingerbread snap biscuits on a central wooden table. The key was thrown into a cage with a large fearsome black wolf, it hit its body and fell to the floor.

'See if you can get out.' She threw her ginger biscuit in after the key, hitting the wolf on its head. It shrank backwards into the wall, its eyes watching her every move. She picked up a phone and another biscuit and ascended the stone steps to the outside world.

Chapter 21

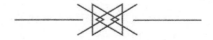

A storm raged inside Evie, between her heart and her head, on the way back to the caravan. Her heart was telling her that something was seriously wrong, and she needed to protect her children whilst looking for a brother who had never been absent at all in his life. On the other side of her internal argument her head pointed out that she had a commitment to show up for and she had to stick to her word and be present for work because it was her work that paid the school fees and funded their lifestyle.

She had Atlas's caravan in her sights as she walked hastily back. Uneven grass mounds rose up from nowhere underneath her feet the more she lost herself in her head, causing her gait to flow up and down. Her internal arguments tossed her around as though she was a small boat lost in their storm. She banged on her brother's door hard, then tried the handle. The door opened. His phone was at a forty-five-degree angle on the granite kitchen worktop by the door, the place where he put it when he walked inside with it in his hand. One wellington stood inside the door, she couldn't see the other. Evie pushed her way into the cosy Christmas atmosphere of the wooden décor, 'Atlas?' she called. When no answer came she tried fruitlessly again. She checked every room. He had clean jeans, a long-sleeved T-shirt and a brushed cotton shirt laid out on the bed, a pair of thick ski socks neatly laid on top of a beanie. Two cellophane gift baskets of Halloween chocolates sat on his dresser, her children's names iced onto a chocolate bar inside each gift. He had been planning to turn up. Evie left the caravan, her heart and stomach trailing behind her.

Robbie jogged over to her, concern plastered across his face. Evie shook her head before he even asked. She clenched her fists, her emotions overflowing, panic rushing through her at her speeding chain of thoughts and she could feel a burning starting in her palms. Robbie pulled her to him and wrapped his arms around her. Evie took a deep breath and let it out. Whenever Robbie's arms were around her, she felt that things would turn out alright. That was a gift in itself.

'I can watch Max and Rey, or call my mum. She's off today. She'll be happy to help.'

'I should call in sick.'

'If it were any other job I'd agree. I don't like Yvonne, but she told me if I didn't do her extension, she would blacklist you and you'd never work again. I should have said sooner, will she do that if you call in sick?'

'Technically she can't. But I've already had to juggle the country show and Yvonne's demands when they've clashed so it wouldn't surprise me if they already think that I'm difficult to work with. But I can't leave Max and Rey with—' She almost said strangers but held back, not wanting to offend Robbie.

'I know they don't know my mum or me as well as they know Atlas, but they will be looked after. My mum managed five of us. Two would be a doddle for a few hours. Do you have any idea where Atlas is?' he asked.

Evie shook her head, a lump forming in her throat. She

blinked back tears when she said, 'He's left his phone so I can't call him. He's got clean clothes laid out on his bed and Halloween gift baskets full of chocolate for Max and Rey. Something happened between him getting up and not turning up to milking time.'

'I'm going to call my mum and we're going to drive Max and Rey to her house. She'll make them breakfast and lunch and a million snacks, and they'll be safer there than here if something's happened. Then I'll take Atlas's phone to someone I know, ex-military. He runs a security company now and if he can't get into your brother's phone to look through it, he'll know who can. We'll find him. I can ask Garratt if—'

'No. I don't want people to know Atlas is missing. He'll be mortified.' She was going to say something else, but she stopped as a sudden thought swept over her. She needed to check for another black circle. She had spent all the previous day with Robbie. She had let him stay the night. If there was another black circle somehow it would be linked to Atlas's disappearance. Someone was watching every move she made. Evie ran from Robbie asking him to watch the caravan.

Taking Atlas's quad out of the barn Evie raced it up the peaks, creating her own wind that blew her hair back, messing up the perfect curls into a wild windswept arrangement. Evie parked up the quad on an elevation and mingled with the sheep that grazed on the grass between jutting out rocks. The grey clouds were so low that on any other day she would have joyously reached up to try and touch them. Looking over the crop fields, her fields, she didn't see anything. She cast her eyes over towards the McGregors' fields and orchards, then her brother's animal pastures. She saw it. A perfect black circle encompassing half the field and two cows at the centre, blackened, dead, worse than dead. Her heart trembled, followed by her body, Jim and his teenaged son were approaching the dead cows. Not thinking, she acted on instinct as she raced down to meet them on the quad.

The pair were already bent down examining the blackened cows when she turned off the ignition and ran over. Jim straightened up. Evie could heal the land, but the animals, the reporting and the investigations, and the officials involved, she couldn't comprehend how to explain it all. As if reading her mind Jim said, 'We'll bury them. No need to get the officials up here. They won't understand.'

Evie looked at him, confused, 'They won't understand what?'

'Yrsa. You pissed her off again. I'd warrant she's got your brother this time.'

'You believe in Yrsa?'

'I've seen her plenty. She walks around in the night. She visited the McGregors and threatened to curse them if they didn't sell to you. Colin McGregor told me she wanted to see things return to how they used to be, all the land belonging to her.'

'But—' was all Evie could manage.

'You think the sale was for you? They disliked you and your brother. Called you witches and halflings and cursed. I never had such a problem with you. You both work hard, you don't lord it over people and you just offered my lad a fair deal for coming in without notice. He'll be putting that towards his laptop savings. He's got a gift for computers, school tells me.'

'But—' Evie tried to take in what he had said. She

237

started to speak but when her lips began to form the word *but* again she stopped. She filtered through the massive amount of information that she had just received and squared her shoulders. Looking straight into Jim's blue eyes with her grey ones she asked, 'What does she look like?'

'Brown hair, thick, lots of braids, but when she went to see the McGregors she went as your friend.'

'My friend?' Immediately Evie picture Gia.

'Yvonne.'

'Yvonne?' Evie asked. Incredulity rippled through her. Jim was either taking the piss with a straight face, or he believed every word.

'Your brother didn't believe either. I tried to tell him that you shouldn't be working with her. That was whilst you were buying the farm though, after Colin McGregor told me. I would have told you, but I don't see you as much. I'm here to help with the animals, you do the crops, we rarely cross paths.'

Mud splattered from the fast quad ride, with wild hair, Evie walked back into the farmyard to find Max and Rey sitting on the caravan steps laughing at something Liam had said, mugs of something in their hands. A shiny, pale silver car and multicoloured motorbike sat next to each other near all the other worker's cars. Robbie was arguing with two men in dark casual clothes, one holding a camera, another a coffee cup. She waved at her children and walked over to Robbie.

'Evie,' one of the men said. Evie looked at him in silence.

'We just want a few hours at the ruins of the old farm-house. To see if we can contact anyone.'

'No.' Evie shook her head.

'Told you. Leave or I call the police.' Robbie crossed his arms. The men tried to argue, their protests falling on deaf ears as Robbie's team stepped in and crowded them off the site and Evie's land, without laying a hand on either of the men.

Robbie turned to Evie, 'Any luck in whatever you rushed off to do?'

'A little. Tell me where Yvonne lives?' Evie couldn't begin to fathom where to start, or how to tell her sexy builder of the strangeness that had just unfolded. He told her without hesitation. As far as she knew, Yvonne lived in the city in a penthouse style flat. That was what she told everyone. Instead, Robbie listed a house on the other side of the woods.

'When are we going?' Robbie asked.

Evie shook her head, 'It's not your mess.'

'That's not what I asked. I'd prefer if you let me go alone.'

'I'll go, at some point.' Her mind was jumping around a clock face. She had to get to work, then after work she had Max and Rey. She had to be ready for more ghost hunters, there would be no time to go.

'Mum wants to take the kids home, if that's OK. There's the security of CCTV on the premises. We have a pool table and Brontë is there, they'll have fun. My sister is off today too. They'll be warm and looked after until you finish work. We'll sort this mess out afterwards.'

'I—' Evie wanted to protest. It was her responsibility to handle it all, alone. Then she stopped. She had absolutely nothing to protest about. There was nowhere else for Max and Rey to go. She wouldn't, and had never, asked anyone for help, aside from her brother, after Damian's refusal to return home. She had to be at work, these people were being kind, even as maternal instincts rose her brain quashed them down with reasons why she couldn't refuse. She ended with a small, 'OK.'

Evie knew that she would be far too late for make-up and wardrobe, so she quickly chose to change into pink trousers and a white fine knit top, keeping her make-up simple with eyeliner, mascara, and a berry lipstick. She avoided Robbie as she jumped into her car and sped off. He made her feel safe, and she wasn't.

4500 BCE

The woman submerged him in the marshes. He was stuck to the clay bed, chest deep in water alongside her as she plucked a fish from the tidal waters. She sliced the fish from its throat, along its belly, all the way to the tail, muttering something in her language. Next to her, his wife held their newest son in her arms. The woman emptied the fish's insides over his son. She studied the pattern they made. Then raised the knife above his son.

His shout and struggled step towards the women became lost as an arrow hit the witch in the shoulder, causing her to stagger backwards and drop the knife. He turned to look around. She was on the path. Her eldest daughter next to her was holding the bow, another arrow drawn, ready. She called out to the other woman in their language. The woman bowed her head and didn't reply. He got the impression she held some higher position.

'Nobody kills babies.' She spoke in his language, disappointment and disgust written across her face.

'That wasn't discussed,' his wife interrupted.

'Learn to ask the right questions, Anders, son of Eric. Not hear what you want. Listen to what is not said. I told you the price was too high.' She turned away.

'You're not going to kill us? We're here. Defenceless.' His words made her turn back.

241

'I saw my death in your eyes the first time we met, Anders. You will be present for it. There is a long journey for you first. Your spirit inside you needs its path travelled.'

'What about the curse?'

'The true curse is what she has given to your baby with your permission. The ability to see that which you fight against. You talk of monsters, but you don't see them. Now your baby son and his descendants will.'

Chapter 22

Evie arrived too late at work for anything other than a quick powder brushover. Jess approached her, marching through the set that parted for her, staff moving out of her way. Evie noted that the set was distinctly Halloween themed for the day, and instead of their table and stools they had an orange settee, faux fireplace with LED candles, autumnal garlands, and bunches of orange flowers decorated every available surface.

She turned to face Jess who was unusually dressed in jeans and a band T-shirt, she'd had a haircut and looked less the middle-aged executive and now a very hip producer. Evie complimented her look. Close up, she saw the panic in Jess's eyes, 'Yvonne hasn't turned up. I didn't think you were going to make it. Elsy's here and that's it. I've got an up-and-coming presenter called Leyla coming in, she was the nearest available person but English is her second language, she'll be another half hour. It's our Halloween special and everyone has deserted us.'

'Why?'

'Yvonne's told everyone not to come in. Elsy has the story.'

'I didn't want you to have to carry the show alone, which was her plan. She wants to see you fall from grace today. Its revenge for the way you stood up to her in front of everyone.' Elsy came up behind them.

'We've got thirty seconds. Places,' Jess snapped, rushing away.

Evie and Elsy started the show. Without Yvonne present, the oppressive atmosphere lifted. Elsy's outgoing, infectious enthusiasm for life carried through to Evie who laughed and joked with her over their experiences of filming the Halloween special. The pre-recorded, edited segments from Elsy's fruitless ghost hunting, Evie's sceptical night with the ghost hunters in the church graveyard, her tarot card and palm readings were shown. Leyla arrived and added her own ghost stories from her parent's Turkish culture.

The set seemed warmer, their normal tea was replaced with weak white wine spritzers in prosecco glasses, topped up with lemonade from the bottle once they had reached the halfway mark of the show. Jess checked with Leyla about the alcohol who smiled and admitted she did drink, but only lightly. The rapport between the three of them quickly established itself and in the breaks they laughed about the mistakes they had just made whilst Jess briefed them at a hundred miles an hour on what was coming up next. The autocues kept the pace of the show, a credit to those writing them on the spot. At the end of their allocated hour, interspaced with last minute guests, including her own farm café chef, who Evie called in the break to come in and offer different but easy toast toppings aimed at families after trick or treating. Evie's favourite was the roasted red peppers from a jar, thrown onto toast with some feta cheese and sliced chillies before being put back under the grill. Elsy preferred the scrambled eggs and spinach with cream, joking that there wasn't an avocado in sight. Leyla confidently announced that she would choose the ricotta, figs and honey option every time. Her chef rushed off immediately afterwards, to get back to the farm.

Once the show was over, the high adrenaline, fast paced atmosphere suddenly stopped, and Jess rushed over to the three of them, full of praise. Clapping broke out, which they joined in. Jess's eyes were watery, 'I feel like crying. That was amazing. That was a promise of what we could be. I think, moving forward, I'm definitely changing the show. Yvonne has gone. You three were so wonderful together.'

Leaving work, Evie picked up her phone with intentions to check on Max and Rey. Instead of her having to make the first contact, Phoebe had sent her pictures throughout the day. Max and Rey playing with the puppy she had first seen Robbie with. Max and Rey with Robbie and Liam learning how to play pool. Max and Rey seated at the table with Robbie and Liam with a huge ploughman's spread in front of them, the television on with her show. Evie smiled at her children being so warmly welcomed whilst she was having a crisis. A text from Robbie told her that amongst Atlas's last messages had been a threat from an unknown, untraceable number but very similar to the threats he had seen aimed at her, *Your sister will die for the greatness of Yrsa.*

Evie's thoughts drifted back to her strange conversation with Jim as she drove back on autopilot, stopping at a drive through, whose outer building walls were painted maroon, to order a coffee before she was out of the city. Sun broke through the burgeoning rain clouds at intervals, darting out between tall buildings. Evie found herself longing to have a leisurely walk through the city one more time, to mindlessly meander in and out of shops, nothing more on her mind than buying bits for her children and herself.

When she pulled up at the farm it was eerily quiet, everyone had left. In its place was a chaotic mess of a building site partially hidden by tall metal fences held together with solid clamps, signs telling people to stay out. She glanced around, failed to see any ghost hunters and went into her caravan. Evie changed from cream ballet flats to boots and picked up a coat. She planned to walk from the farm to the old schoolhouse, Robbie's family home. The air would be good to clear her head, it was a tangled yarn of worries and she couldn't see a way to be alone long enough to find her brother.

The late afternoon was the type of damp she hated, where it etched itself under her skin and into her bones, the promise of rain hung in the air with a specific scent of damp soil and imminent rainfall. Evie pulled up the hood on her long woollen trench coat in preparation. Dismal daylight helped the air feel even more charged as she drew close to the first of the buildings; small cute stone-built cottages that would soon give way to the village high street. Some had pumpkins outside their front doors, real ones, clay ones, plastic ones, a couple of gardens had gone the very American way of decorating. The first had three witches around a cauldron. Another had gravestones and outdoor lights. A few of the cottages had lamps on. Some had televisions on, creating flickering colours in the windows. In another garden a woman was nimbly unfastening pegs and slipping them into her apron pocket, bringing her washing in off the line. She shouted to a younger woman two gardens down, who was pulling clean clothes off her own washing line. The younger woman didn't have an apron on, just jeans and a baggy jumper. She left her pegs on the line. Evie used to love these cottage gardens where life happened in the front because they didn't have a back garden. It had given her a view into what normal might look like.

She walked down the high street as big globules fell slowly from the sky, infrequently at first, one hit her hood and she felt its weight. The busy half term throng of the tourist influx was still strong, attracted by the myths but encouraged to stay by the Halloween decorations in each shop. Evie had thought about paying a visit to Harriet, but it was likely that she would be as busy as her own café was. Evie went anyway, an inner urgency pushing her forward. By the time she reached Harriet's the infrequent drops had turned into a full rainstorm. When she opened the door to Harriet's café, conversations buzzed in the air much like her own café. It was half full. The sounds of a coffee machine grinding beans overrode all the conversations and hurt her ears. Harriet was packing up a box of pumpkin faced fairy cakes for a customer in an orange jumper and pale blue jeans, horse boots on her feet and a country coat over her arm, her glossy brown hair pulled back in a pony-tail and car keys jangling from her hand. Evie guessed that she was one of the new invasion of middle class residents.

'Can I get a cream éclair boxed up for my husband, better make that two,' she said to Harriet, checking a hand-written note on yellow paper in her hand. She pointed to each item on the list, muttering to herself, 'Got, got, got, got, meat for dinner, I need to go to the farm next, rosemary and thyme in duck fat for roasties – the farm, garlic butter – the farm, nice bread.'

Harriet looked at a hooded Evie as she rang the total into the till. Evie pushed her hood down; she had forgotten that it was up. Harriet's face brightened with a smile when she could see Evie. She let her customer pay then turned to Evie, 'I hear your afternoon teas are all booked up for the entire half term.'

'Are we?' Evie was surprised to hear it, but not astonished. They had a new chef. She was straight from training in London, hired in July and started in September. She had been born and raised on a farm in New Zealand. Evie wouldn't be going over the monthly figures until Friday.

'You don't check?'

'I go over the numbers once a month. I'm not a chef, or very good in hospitality. Crops and plants are my thing.' She offered a half apologetic smile for having professionals run her café whilst Harriet was doing it all herself.

'Yeah, I forgot you ran a farm as well as the café.' Harriet shook her head.

'Can I grab a flat white and talk to you?'

'Sure. Bex, can you cover for me after this order?' Harriet asked a woman stood behind her replenishing mugs and cups with a tray straight from the dishwasher.

They walked over to a spare table by the window for two and sat down. Harriet carried a black tray with two black coffee cups on. Evie was spared from starting a conversation by Harriet diving straight in, 'Is Atlas OK?'

'OK?'

'He normally drops by the post office on a Monday. And there's rumours from the farm.' The last sentence had been added casually, to try and hide the pale pink blush that swept across Harriet's face.

'You know my brother's post office visits?' Evie tried

not to smile, the situation reminded her of being in school when every one of her friends had liked her brother at some point.

'He's kind of hard to miss when he walks down the street.' Harriet defended noticing Atlas.

'He is,' Evie conceded, picturing her tall brother, made strong from labouring on the farm, the man bun always in place because cutting his hair required time away from his beloved farm.

'Is he OK? Because the rumour is that he didn't turn up to milking and Yrsa has taken him.'

'How does this stuff travel so quickly?'

'Jim phoned his son to go in and help, who cancelled his plans with his friends. His friend Sam told his mum who came to the post office and told Janice who works there, and once Janice knew she told Mrs Everly who brought Yrsa into it saying you two have long disrespected her and she's out for revenge. So now everyone knows that one of the farm witches has been kidnapped by Yrsa, the original witch, because you've pissed her off too much.' Harriet said it all without taking a breath.

'I love how you tell me exactly what's happening.' Evie smiled.

'So?'

'Atlas is… somewhere that he hasn't communicated with me.' Evie stumbled over her words, trying to phrase the sentence in such a way as to not diminish her brother or confirm the gossip.

'So you don't know where he is.'

'Not exactly. He's left his phone so I can't call him to find out.'

'Not exactly?' Harriet probed.

'Jim said something to me. He thinks Yrsa is disguised as Yvonne. Robbie tells me Yvonne has a cottage literally just outside my farm's boundary.'

'She wasn't at work today, was she? Mrs Mangham from the cottages comes in everyday after your show for a cup of tea and to chat about it. She was telling me that it seemed strange because Yvonne's been hyping Halloween up for a couple of weeks now.'

'Does it all sound really strange and fiction-y?'

Evie wanted Harriet to put her straight and tell her that there was no reasonable likelihood of a presenter in her late thirties or early forties being a mythic local deity over a thousand years old.

Instead, Harriet shook her head, 'Not at all. The local historical society put some pictures up today. Hightly Hall has gone up for sale and they've had a donation of old photographs. They're in pieces about the old hall being sold. Even in its derelict state its already gotten interest.'

'Hightly Hall is for sale?' It was news to Evie. It bordered her property, it had its own farm and had the same amount of open land again as gardens, plus its own woodlands. The deer park alone would be a wonderful addition to the farm.

Harriet was on her phone, 'Don't get distracted, look.' She showed Evie the pictures that the Historical Society had put up on their website about Hightly Hall from its last heyday.

There was a picture of a young woman in a dress that finished just above her ankles, boots, gloves, and a hat. She was posed on the lawn in front of the house, it was blurry around her, the image wasn't sharp. A close up showed the same photography problems, the image was blurred but her eyes shone sharply, cutting through the lens with their icy glare. It wasn't the features so much as the level of ice and hate in the eyes that made Evie think of Yvonne. Her parents had told her Yrsa's last known incarnation was Lady Ursula something hyphenated something of Hightly Hall. Evie looked at the photographs again. The blurriness meant something. It tugged at her, she felt that she should know what she didn't know.

Harriet spoke up, 'It's the eyes. She could be anyone but the eyes don't change, the level of contempt and haughtiness doesn't change. Yvonne has those eyes, even if she wears blue contacts.'

'She wears contacts?' It had never crossed Evie's mind that Yvonne's bright blue eyes weren't natural, not with the blonde hair.

'You really need to get into the village and catch up on information more often. She buys them a month at a time from the opticians. How did Jim find out?'

'The McGregors told him.' Evie wasn't going to offer more until Harriet propped her elbow on the table and rested her head on her hand. She didn't speak but sat with her eyes on Evie, unwavering, and waited for more. Evie elaborated, 'He told me Yvonne had been to visit them about selling the farm to me and said that it was about time all the land was back in her ownership.'

'Wow. That's a story I'd love to hear. It's a pity they moved away in their retirement. Although they couldn't really show their faces here. Not after what their sons did.'

'You too?' Evie asked softly.

'You as well?' Harriet's eyes widened in sympathy. Evie gave a nod. Harriet pulled a sour face and added, 'They were pretty horrible people themselves. What are you planning to do to get you brother back?'

'Back? He's a grown man.'

'If Yrsa's got him it doesn't matter if he's three or thirty-three.'

'Thirty-four,' she corrected, when she remembered another August had passed.

Harriet shrugged, 'It still doesn't matter. Someone needs to rescue him from Yrsa. I'm up for helping but I'm not Yrsa's level of witch.'

'Helping? Like barging into a cottage with a rescue party?' Evie asked, liking the idea of outnumbering Yvonne.

'Helping by getting my coven to switch the blood worship from her to someone else we have faith in. Someone that can defeat her.'

Evie gave the smallest of nods and took a drink of her coffee from the black cup, noticing the cute, speckled design in blue around the edge of the matching saucer. She conceded Harriet's point. It really was a game of chess. It didn't matter what piece she was anymore, she was playing alone like all the other pieces, taking the only steps she could take according to the board. Everyone around her seemed insistent on telling her that a thousand-year-old witch had her brother.

'OK. I'll go and get my brother.'

'When? The ritual is due tonight. We don't make a big thing out of doing it but we will, if you're going to get your brother.'

'I don't know when, I have Max and Rey. Its Halloween, we get trespassers, I'm not leaving them.'

'It might be too late tomorrow. Lady Ursula left Hightly Hall November first nineteen forty when she realised that the war wasn't going to be over quickly. She threw one last party and left. Now that she's surfaced again as Yvonne you could be running out of time.'

Evie put those words together along with the events of the past season, after years of threats, things were changing. She had taken charge of her life and Yvonne hadn't liked it, but worse than that, today had backfired on Yvonne. The organised boycott of the hyped Halloween Special had been to see Evie fall flat on her face in front of their entire audience and diminish her as a person and a presenter. Instead, everyone had pulled together to deliver one of their best shows in years. The energy had been transformed without Yvonne.

Evie pulled up her hood when she left the café and arrived at Phoebe's house within ten minutes. She stopped and took a moment to appreciate the homeliness of the covered porch over the door that hadn't been there when it was a school. The porch was deep and wide, with a tiled roof, lights and scattered benches and small side tables. She didn't even have to knock on the dark blue door, it was thrown open by Robbie who greeted her with one of his amazing smiles and a kiss. A smell of home hit her, of home cooking, and love; even though love didn't have a smell if she was being technical. In this house it did.

The noisy old floor that she remembered had been replaced. It was tiled now, white and navy, covered by a navy runner. A grouped arrangement of orange velvet pumpkins, fake Chinese lantern plants, and orange candles in tall slim black metal candle holders greeted her in front of warm blue walls. Max and Rey rushed past Robbie to hug her and drag her inside, talking about the pool table and their day. Robbie helped her out of her coat, placing a subtle but potent kiss on her neck that left her with goosebumps.

Phoebe pressed a cold wine into her hand and ushered her to a pale fabric chair when they walked into the open plan room from the cosy entrance. For the next hour Evie couldn't speak about Atlas or Yvonne as Max and Rey talked about their day and showed her their pool skills. Phoebe asked her about work, Liam chatted to all of them but especially reminding Rey to hold her cue firmer, that she couldn't kill it, and telling Max that sometimes a gentler approach would get a result.

The oven timer cut through the laidback chatter with a shrill, continuous beep. It made Evie jump in her anxious state. Phoebe insisted that everyone stayed to eat. Evie watched as Robert walked into the house as the table was set, kissing his wife and handing sweets to Max and Rey with a grandfatherly wink. Robbie slipped into a chair next to her, his thigh deliberately next to her own. Evie realised she was perched on the very edge of the seat.

Over a roast beef dinner, Evie gained a glimpse of what it was like having siblings, parents, and family dinners in a loud, rambunctious home where the loudest to speak had attention, siblings conversed with practised ease in raised voices, no one was mad at being interrupted and laughter broke out a lot. She could see why Max and Rey had enjoyed their day here. Phoebe and Robert were relaxed hosts and clearly enjoyed the company of their own children plus Max and Rey. When Max answered Paige's question about costumes and trick or treating with the truth that they stayed in during Halloween because of trespassers looking for the witch ghosts, a sympathetic Phoebe immediately offered to let them sleep over, saying that they could hand out chocolate to trick or treaters and experience a normal Halloween night. The youngest of the family, trainee midwife Paige joined in the enthusiasm by adding that she had some fake blood and could do a slashed neck on them with pale faces. Max and Rey were up for the gruesome joy of their first fearless Halloween and begged their mother to let them sleep over. Evie gave a slow, reluctant nod. It would give her extra time to find her brother. She could pass on a night of sleep to find him.

Robbie drove her back to the farm to pack the children's things for the night. Evie looked out of her window whilst he drove, not wanting to talk. Thoughts and emotions swirled around in her brain. She was tired of being logical about everything. A tennis ball lump formed in the back of her throat and tears welled up in her eyes, falling down her face, matching the raindrops running down the window in wet pathways. Robbie parked up as near to her caravan as he could get. She didn't even notice until he put his hand on her arm.

'Hey.' He brushed some hair from her face. Evie wiped her tears away.

'I'm fine.' She fumbled for the key to the caravan.

'Talk to me?' he asked. Evie shook her head.

Everything in her brain had been put into a blender and mixed together until she couldn't think enough to separate the ingredients. In the waiting silence of the car, whose only sound was the pattering of rain she admitted, 'I didn't just pack up and leave Damian, despite what the papers said at the time. I had pneumonia and I couldn't breathe. I called and texted him to come home so many times and he just ignored me. I had to call an ambulance. They said they'd put Max and Rey into respite care through the social workers because they couldn't stay in hospital with me, so I called Atlas to get them. My brother drove for hours in one night, at a text, to come and collect my children. That's when I left Damian. Things were already rocky, he wanted me to be this partying doll that he brought out for his friends to look at. I came back to the farm afterwards with armfuls of antibiotics and painkillers and other stuff I can't even remember. And I promised Max and Rey they'd never spend another night away from me again until they were ready, and now they're ready but I'm not, it actually hurts inside that they're not going to be here with me tonight.' Tears rolled down her face.

Robbie pulled her into a hug, despite the awkwardness of the handbrake between them. He wrapped his arms around her and she cried into his shirt. He placed a kiss on the top of her head and murmured, 'You're really brave. You're not ready for this but you're letting them do it because they want to. You're getting death threats, but you still allowed them freedom to run around with their friends yesterday in the park because they needed that outlet.'

'I'm a mess.' She pulled back, wiping her eyes.

'You're beautiful. We'll take Max and Rey's stuff to my mum's house, then we'll get Liam and go to Yvonne's to get Atlas. Evie?'

'Yes?'

'You can be a mess anytime. I'll always be here. You don't have to do it by yourself anymore.'

Chapter 23

Evie packed her children's bags amidst floods of tears that refused to stop. She wanted her children with her. She went through the motions of what they needed; pyjamas, their favourite toys, an extremely squashed grey and white wolf soft toy for Rey. She held it up to smell it. It had recently been washed so only smelt of clean laundry. A floppy corduroy cow in caramel for Max. It smelt of his night sweat, an almost sweet scent of child sweat that would, quickly enough if her experience of having a brother was true, turn into a horrible teenage boy smell. Their electric toothbrushes, a charger just in case. Pyjamas. Clothes. She dumped the bags on the caravan floor as Robbie passed her a rum and coke.

In the distance Evie heard chanting. A group of voices. Flickering candle flames danced before her eyes in semi darkness. She blinked to get rid of them because she knew the caravan lights were on. From far away the drink fell from her hand, she heard the glass shatter. The caravan floor rocked when Robbie moved towards her. She saw him stop, putting out his hands to feel something, unable to get closer to her. In two places at once Evie could see clearly but was unable to participate.

She was still in the caravan, remnants of the rum and coke on the floor around her. She was in the middle of a circle drawn in chalk on the floor of Harriet's café. She was in both places but then, neither, she floated in space, amongst the stars and heard whispers from those that had gone before her, from the gods and goddesses, from her ancestors:

I used to roam the earth
I used to be powerful
Catch the mammoth
That herb treats wounds, this one poisons
I will not marry
Control yourself, do you want everyone to know
what you can do?
She captures our souls for our powers
Evie not Yrsa, Evie not Yrsa, Evie not Yrsa, Evie
not Yrsa, Evie not Yrsa

Evie was back in Harriet's café, enclosed in the magic circle. Trapped within its confines she couldn't move beyond it and none could set foot in it, only observe and feel. Men and women filtered into a line, wandered around the circle and dropped their blood on the floor just inside the circle. Harriet saw Evie in her physical form inside the circle. Her eyes widened with shock as Evie looked directly at her, but then she smiled too, as if under a spell, and she shouted to the room: 'Carry on. It won't work if it's not finished. Evie not Yrsa. Evie not Yrsa.'

Evie reached out, her palm up, the solemn energy in the air struck her as odd. She turned her palm anticlockwise until her fingers faced the floor. Blood droplets rose from the floor and drifted towards Evie inside the circle. The few plants in Harriet's café began to grow at an unnatural speed. She controlled the blood, circling it around her, changing the atmosphere from solemn to happy and joyous. From the stars came the whispers of the universe that they were creating the base for a new immortal. Joy and excitement on a scale she had never known flew through her in waves.

In the caravan she saw Robbie as he stilled and watched as the plants grew taller, new leaves unfolded, and a green ink danced around Evie's hands. She saw him and she wanted to speak but behind him his ancestors gathered. Tall, bearded men, strong women, all Scandinavian, some clearly Vikings, others from different time periods. Without even talking over the chanting, she noticed their strength, and their loyalty to family. A man with runic markings drawn onto his face made two stars fall from nowhere and merge. His message was clear. Evie met his eyes and saw Robbie's own summer blue eyes in the man's worn, drawn on face. But behind those were older ones, angrier ones, they pushed their way forward, disapproval on faces, not at Robbie, but at what she was.

Inside Harriet's café the last of the line finished walking around the chalked circle she was enclosed in. Harriet turned to someone in a pulled down hood whose face was obscured behind a mask and a veil. Her eyes lifted and followed Evie's form. She gave a nod. Evie felt the blood absorb into her open hand. She looked down. Her heart starting to beat faster when she saw the floor some inches away from her feet. She closed her eyes and willed herself down.

Her feet crashed down onto the caravan floor, into the mess of the fallen rum and coke. The stars and Harriet's café disappeared. Robbie's ancestors did too. She looked down, then at her hands, then in horror at the plants in the caravan. She covered her eyes with the palms of her hands,

'Atlas is going to fucking kill me for this.'

'For dropping a rum and coke?' an amused voice asked. She lifted her hands away from her face and hoped that was all Robbie had seen. His face told her otherwise.

'You...' She didn't know what to say.

'I saw it all, but let's get this cleaned up before it gets sticky.' He busied himself picking up the pieces of glass.

Evie opened the cupboard under the sink to get out cleaning materials and a cloth, 'I'm so sorry.'

'No need to apologise. It was pretty awesome watching stars inside the caravan. What happened?'

Taking in a deep breath, Evie concentrated on mopping up the dark liquid in front of her, her arms shaking with fear. Picturing Robbie's ancestors, their approval and their loyalty, gave her the strength to admit the truth to him. She blocked out the hateful ones.

'Harriet had an idea of switching the blood offering ritual to me instead of Yrsa on the stipulation that I kill Yrsa. That's what you saw.' She hadn't expected it to work. The veiled woman had been the key to it all working the way it did. The circle had been drawn by an experienced practitioner, a serious practitioner.

'You do the same stuff as Harriet?'

'I don't really know what Harriet does but my gift doesn't require anything to make it work. What you just saw was...' Evie wasn't sure how to describe it, or the veiled woman's presence which had been key to it all, 'experienced practitioners working together,' she concluded lamely.

'No spells, rituals, special holidays?'

'No.'

'Can you show me?'

260

'Sure. It'll be the most boring thing you've seen today after that show.'

The prospect of showing him didn't make her any less scared than she would have been previously. Evie was backed into a corner and couldn't think of anything to say to bullshit her way out, not after what Robbie had just witnessed. Standing up, Evie surveyed the mess she had made. She rinsed the cloth out first, cold water hit her burning hands and cooled them down. A tinkle of glass told her Robbie had emptied the glass into the bin. She threw an apple to him and told him to cut it up and get the seeds out. Meanwhile she reached into a tiny cupboard that had the central heating controls in and pulled out a hoover. Robbie cut the apple up whilst she hoovered the tiny, leftover shards of glass.

When she switched off the hoover, she asked him to pass her two seeds. In bemused silence he placed them on her palm. Evie held them inside her cupped hands. Her hands began to warm up and forge their own fire. When she felt the leaves touch her skin she opened her palms, hovering one hand above the tiny, growing trees. Robbie's eyes grew wide.

'That's real. That's not the ritualistic shit with candles and spells and counting coincidence as manifestation.'

'It's real,' she confirmed.

'Can you do it on anything?'

'Almost any plant. Nothing animal related. I grow things. That's why I like gardening.'

'Show me again.' He passed her another seed. Evie did. He took the tiny tree from her offered hand and examined it.

'You grow things?'

'Yes.'

'Is that how you provided food for yourself when your parents didn't?'

'Vegetables, fruits, and salad produce, yes.'

'Raw stuff. You said you stole butter?'

'Yes. We used butter for the potatoes. They're kind of bland without seasoning.'

'It's all starting to make more sense. You said you needed wide open spaces on the farm, is that so no one sees you?'

'Yes. I have an intrinsic drive to grow things. If I ignore it for too long it starts to seep out of its own accord.'

'What can Atlas do?'

'Atlas? Nothing. Neither can Max or Rey. It's just me. I've always done this, since before I could walk.' She quickly pushed the rest of her family away, knowing that she could be revealed at any moment and wanting them safe.

Robbie held up his hands. His relaxed posture didn't make her feel completely safe. Thoughts ran through her head that he was going to tell someone, reveal her secret despite the silent promise of loyalty that his ancestors had made to her. Her assertions that it was just her fell on deaf ears, 'When we have children, would they be able to do anything?'

'When?' she challenged. He smirked and crossed his arms, muscles bulging, leaning against the kitchen units.

'I want more than two. You said back in the café you hoped for a big family. So, when we have more children, will they be able to do anything?'

'It's random. I can't say yes and I can't say no. But you really can't tell anyone. I don't want to end up in a laboratory somewhere being tested on. I don't want my babies sold to another country to be lab rats devoid of cuddles, love, siblings, and friends.'

'I promise. I won't tell. I know why you couldn't tell me on Friday.'

'I wouldn't be telling you now if you hadn't witnessed that. It's not something normal.'

'It doesn't stop you from being amazing.' He said the words with a gentleness, his gaze steady and his arms unfolded. He placed his hands on the worktops behind him that he was leaning against, opening up his body. Evie wanted to wrap her arms around him and be enclosed in one of his hugs. Instead she forced herself to remember what had happened and why her children were sleeping out.

'Let's go and take the bags.' She turned away so he couldn't see her panic.

Evie bent down to pick up the bags. She was pulling back. Pushing him away. She recognised it but learning to trust someone with her darkest secret felt impossible. She turned her back on Robbie to refuse the help that he would offer. The bags weren't heavy. He locked the caravan door and slipped the key into his jeans pocket. When she was putting the bags in the boot, he held open the passenger door for her, even in the rain. He drove them back to his parents' house in a silence that drove a chasm between them.

Walking away from Max and Rey after a few minutes, even though she was leaving them in the warm cosiness of a real home, hit her hard. It was the type of home they had never known but she had wanted to provide for them. When faced with the reality of a home built on love, Evie knew she could never achieve this level of cosiness by herself, because it wasn't the cost of the things in the house, or the way they were styled, it was the underlying warmth that resonated unseen but impactfully felt around everything in the house. She couldn't create that. With Max and Rey otherwise occupied alongside Paige handing out sweets to the latest round of trick or treaters Robbie ushered his parents close and explained about the threats Evie was getting, and the one that had been sent to school. Evie looked at him, he shrugged.

'Atlas and I talk. We both want to protect you and the children.'

'We'll take good care of Max and Rey,' Phoebe said. A surge of gratefulness flew through Evie towards this maternal woman promising to look after her children whilst she flew out into a cold, rainy night to find her brother. It still didn't sit right that she was leaving her children. Robbie opened the door to let her out.

Chapter 24

The veiled woman was bent down on the porch, putting something inside Liam's motorbike helmet he'd left outside on the bench. When the door opened, she looked up startled and stood up quickly, the helmet tumbling a few centimetres from her hand to the bench. She backed off the porch, stepping down gracefully and moving away towards the shadows in the garden. Evie moved fast, running after her and grabbing her arm.

Rain bounced off the woman, her side illuminated by a black streetlamp a few metres away. No one looked their way as trick or treaters gathered towards the other end of the street. Her black hood was up, her long wool coat similar to Evie's paler, mocha version. Evie spun the veiled woman around to face her. Through the lilac chiffon, Evie recognised the face. It was older, a few lines starting to appear around her eyes and the sides of her mouth.

'Kat?'

'Not your Kat.' The figure shook her head and started to move her body sideways, in preparation to leave.

'You were in Harriet's café.' Her tone was accusatory, a question, a statement, and laced with undertones. Evie didn't loosen her grip on the arm even as *Not her Kat* tried to move away.

'I had to.' She turned around to face Evie full on.

There was something about this Kat that wasn't her

Kat. The self-confidence, the way she took up space in the air around her, her tilted chin and proud stance, but more than all that, it was knowledge that shone from her eyes. It reminded Evie of the time she had been in the stars a short time ago.

'No, you didn't,' she protested. Her voice sounded weak to her own ears. Her mind flashed to the circle, to the moments where she was both in the caravan and in Harriet's café, and she knew in her heart that the Kat in front of her had taken control of the transfer of power from Yrsa to Evie.

'The first time was a mess! You took no responsibility for anything happening, you just drifted along reacting to everything, being scared that someone would figure out what you can do. Harriet's spell didn't work. You only injured Yrsa and temporarily stripped her powers. Yrsa comes back and kills every single descendant, we can't find her despite trying. You've spent the last ten years trying to find her after we found out she's alive. She comes back to you fifteen years today and kills you in the courtyard in front of all of us. She kills Atlas and then your children. Afterwards she will go after every natural witch in the world so no one can ever challenge her again.'

'Harriet's spell did work.' Evie defended her new friend.

'This time. Gia sketched a magic circle for me to draw as she lay dying in the courtyard. Harriet's what we call a disciple of our ways. You left her alone to do a major spell with no magic to speak of and no guidance. Disciples are important but to use magic they need guidance and knowledge. Neither of which you helped her with!'

'Gia's dead?'

'We're all dying. Fourteen people plus children. In your courtyard. You can change that. You have to kill her this time. Take responsibility. Stop being scared of who you really are.'

'How did you... how did you come here?'

'I can slip between time and dreams. This is the first time I've tried to change the future, or my past as it stands, other than some uni stuff. Make it my last, Evie. Be the woman that's my friend, be the teenage version of you, just anything except this conformed shell of scaredness.' Kat's hand gesture of disgust told Evie exactly what she thought of her at that moment.

'I've already failed at this once?'

'We've all just paid the price for that.'

'Max and Rey?'

'They're dead. Change it.' The words were issued without any sympathy. *Not her Kat* slipped away from her. One second Evie was holding the arm of her black coat, the next she was gone, like a ghost she had vanished into thin air.

Evie wanted to scream. She wanted to let out the longest scream of frustration and anger that was bubbling away inside her. Self-control made her just stand still. Then she remembered what *Not her Kat* had said about her being a conforming shell, about being scared to be herself. Gritting her teeth and clenching her fists she let the anger run through her.

'I'll be your fucking Evie if that's what you want. I'll burn her ass to the ground.' Behind her she heard a car click open. She turned around. Robbie was stood by the driver's side. Their eyes met.

He gave a small shake of his head, 'One day we need

to have a proper conversation. This might go down as the weirdest yet most authentic Halloween I've ever had. Until we all die in fifteen years.'

'She never said who was there. Except Gia.'

'Fourteen adults plus children, not to mention the other descendants that get obliterated too. Remind me how many best friends you have?'

'Six.'

'Seven including you. Seven and seven plus ones?'

'Fourteen plus children.' Realisation dawned on her.

'I have so many questions,' another voice interrupted.

Both their heads spun towards Liam, who held a piece of paper in his hand and his motorbike helmet in the other. Lit by the porch lights behind him, wearing a leather jacket and work boots, he looked every inch an avenging angel. He tucked the piece of paper into his jeans pocket.

'What does it say?' Robbie asked.

Liam shot him a look that only a sibling would get away with, 'I've got to save your ass and go with you. You're going to Yvonne's, right?'

'Yes.'

'No.' Evie said loudly.

There was a pause in the air. Even the rain appeared to hover mid fall. The world stilled and fell quiet. Both men looked at her. Evie rethought her hasty plan. Yvonne would have the upper hand if they went to her house. But she had managed to overpower the McGregor boys by the fallen down dry stone wall that bridged their land and hers. It was, and had been, an ivy-covered wall, home to all sorts of native animals.

'That was our plan. Kat said I failed. So, we change the plan. We'll get Atlas later. I'm certain he's in her wine cellar. I think she showed me her plan ages ago in order to get me there. It's a cellar, there's nothing there, which means I can't do anything in that sterile place. I'm going to get her up on the top field where the sycamore row is. I have an advantage outdoors.' She hoped Robbie understood the very clear yet unspoken message she had given. Sycamore row was on one of their higher fields, away from the village without having to traipse the stony peaks of higher ground in the dark.

'How?' Robbie asked.

A wicked smile spread across Evie's face, 'Social media.'

Evie took a snap of herself in the rain in portrait light. She blurred the background, added a caption, hashtags, and posted it. She watched it load across several platforms instantly:

Not a night I want to be out checking fields,
thanks for freaking me out with the Halloween
Special, can't get the thoughts out of my head
now. Sycamore row field and then back home to
dry off. #farminglife #countryside
@lunchtimelivingshow @officialElsy @itsLeyla

Robbie grinned, 'That will work. She's obsessed with social media. Casual enough to anyone else that you're just freaked out.'

'I'll watch for her leaving her house then I'll try and find Atlas. I'll join you as soon as I can. You didn't tag Yvonne in it though.' Liam pointed out the obvious flaw in her plan.

'She knows I hate her. It's too suspicious if I tag her. She'll see it,' said Evie with the same faked confidence she had used when she had met Robbie in the woods that day.

Chapter 25

Robbie's warm hand kept her grounded as they walked along the hedging on the field boundary up to the row of five sycamores. The rain was being blown at an angle onto their backs. Evie began to wonder who had planted the five sycamores, why five, and when.

Up to now they had walked in silence to the field; the rain and the darkness their companions. It was enough negotiating the uneven ground in the darkness. Ahead of them, the sycamore trees loomed closer with each step, and as the prospect of facing Yrsa materialised, their pace jointly slowed. Each step they took nearer to the almost bare trees in the dark and the rain was tortuously slow, yet too fast at the same time.

They were almost under the trees when Robbie said, 'Time travelling witches notwithstanding, if what she said is right, how will this time be different?'

'When you meet Kat, we're going to have to pretend that never happened. Because to her, it hasn't. It doesn't happen until fifteen years in the future,' she said, still play-ing the meeting over and over in her own head. Kat's warning to *step up*, and her own response of *I've already failed at this once?* rolled around her head soft, then loud, soft again, then loud, reverberating around her brain.

Robbie pulled them to a standstill, his hands went around her upper arms. 'I'm not losing you. Not now, not in fifteen years. How do we make this time different?'

'I change my way of thinking. I have to stop hiding who I am. I guess I become what the villagers say I am. When I was little, all I wanted was to be the princess in the fairy tales, but the reality is that my story is the villain's one.'

'Look, when you were on the front page of news-papers as a teenager, I thought you were beautiful. A bit wild, but nobody looked better leaving a club than you did. When you started to appear on TV, I thought you were far too sophisticated for me. But the woman in front of me is the one I love, the one who reads books, gardens and takes care of her family, and doesn't want a dog. You're beautiful, sophisticated, intelligent, and caring. You're not the villain. There's been a hate campaign against you for so long about leaving Damian that I can't believe you still get up every day. You're amazing. You didn't retaliate, you've stood strong through all the years of threats on your life, on your children, through Yvonne trying to control you. You don't need to change.'

'I never said I had to change. Kat only said to stop being scared of who I was. The two don't have to be separated. You liked who I was last night, and I think, now that I know it's all linked together, Yvonne turning me into a city girl was less about control over my image and more about taking me away from nature.' She leaned forward to kiss him, using the kiss as a way to avoid her fear and not have to carry on the conversation.

That move backfired on her the moment Robbie's hands went around her neck, inside her hood, his thumbs resting on her jaw in a way that made her melt inside. He held her as he deepened the kiss, eliciting a small, involun-tary moan from somewhere within her. She pushed her hands into his jacket pocket and tugged him forwards, until she could feel his body against hers, a solid rock to hold her up whilst she fought for her life, for Max and Rey's lives. She kissed him so she didn't have to tell him that she loved him.

He pulled back and placed a soft kiss in the middle of her forehead, 'I can't lose you.'

'Oh, thrilling,' a voice laced with sarcasm spoke at the side of them.

They broke apart. Yvonne stood there, or a version of Yvonne. Brown hair in multiple braids, icy cold grey eyes, her silver sequin evening dress was completely inappropriate for the weather. Robbie's hands left Evie's neck, in a flash they were around Yvonne's. Her face turned red. She raised an arm and placed her hand directly over Robbie's heart. Evie thought it was a weak protest, until she saw Robbie's expression change. Blood drained from his face, his hands fell from Yvonne's rain-soaked neck, he turned grey, his knees buckled. He clutched his heart and fell down on the wet grass.

Yvonne laughed as colour returned to his face, 'It's taken me years to perfect that curse. Everyone else I tried it on died. You get forty-eight hours away from her before you die. I would have loved to see this play out for another fifty years, but unfortunately for you both I have a need for her gift.'

Evie stepped between Robbie and Yvonne, but Robbie rose up and pushed her away.

Yvonne looked at him, then at Evie, then her hand before turning a hard stare onto Robbie, 'Vandir. You're Vandir. They were slaughtered like squealing pigs.'

'You didn't get us all,' Robbie clutched his chest. He

273

struggled to stand.

Evie watched raindrops run along Yvonne's bare arms. She stood tall and proud. Kat's words echoed in her head. Her own words followed. *Step up, I've already failed at this once?* over and over as she eyed Yvonne silently.

Yvonne sneered at them both. Evie just stared back at her. Inside her bunched up fists the burning started, her anger funnelling and uncurling in her palms. The roots of the sycamore trees responded to the droplets spilling. They stirred beneath the earth and began to stretch. They were sleepy and slow, but waking up, pushing earth out of their way to reach her. An idea began to form in Evie's head.

Rain filled the silence until Yvonne spoke, 'I'm almost sorry you have to die. It's been a long time since someone stood their ground around me.'

'Why do I have to die?'

'You're part of *him*, your gifts come from his lineage.' The male word was spat out of Yvonne's mouth with distaste.

'Him?'

'The man I had to marry.'

'Humour me with how my gift is so important to a thousand-year-old witch?'

'My somewhat great granddaughter, or great great granddaughter studied under me. She adored me. Until she made a jar and unbeknownst to me, she wove my hair into the clay and inscribed the inside with a spell I couldn't see. Then she smashed it and scattered it into the sea around this island. I can use your gift to get the seaweed to bring the pieces to the shore. When all the pieces are in my possession I will travel. I cannot leave this island with the spell casting a circle around it. A power as strong as yours, and hers, doesn't happen every generation.'

'All that effort for a holiday?' Evie littered her voice with amusement, keeping it light.

'You don't understand the power you have, to walk the world unharmed by any. To kill, to manipulate, to control. This world is going to be mine.'

'Can we just rewind this to the beginning. Why kill your own children?'

'When we came to this country my father married me off for power. I begged him to choose anyone else. I'd marry any man for him but the one that had beaten his wife to death. His sons were older than I was, the youngest fourteen. Neither I, nor my children would have land or status. He had power though, more than I ever knew was possible. His sisters were even more powerful. Our children were instructed in their native ways but not I. I was to teach him, his sons, and his sisters our language and our ways so they could dine among us in dignity. Every time he grew frustrated with his learning he lashed out with his fists against my bones. Leif suffered from his violence too. My sweet shy boy who loved animals wasn't the fierce killer that man wanted him to be. He already had one son like Leif from his previous wife. I begged him to treat Leif with the respect he treated his other son, but he said he didn't need two the same. Leif taught me what his father taught him, in secret. I killed him out of mercy, and in killing my son I started the rumours that I was powerful, and to be feared, I became what they talked about instead of that family. Then I set about killing him and his children until everything he had became mine. I endured his fists, and with every single punch, every broken bone he nurtured a hatred of him and his kin inside me like a fire.'

'What was Leif's gift?'

'He could project his consciousness into animals. It has proved the most useful. I heard every conversation you had in the old farmhouse.'

'That's how Damian knew everything I said?' It started to make sense.

'That's how Damian knew everything. I started sleeping with him before you were even married. I was the one he was with when you were riding in an ambulance to the hospital.'

'Why, I mean...' Evie faltered. She had so many questions.

'Do you think it was his idea to have a baby? He didn't want to be tied down. I needed you to stay close. I couldn't have you leaving for warmer shores like you had planned to. He told me you were already applying for jobs in Europe. I told him to mess with your birth control and ditch the condoms. And then when you were thinking about leaving with a baby because it was all falling apart, I told him to get you pregnant again. It's harder to leave with two.'

A hand wrapped around Evie's upper arm. Robbie's hand. Reaching out to support her as though he knew that those words would hurt. Evie had almost as much time as she needed. She anticipated what Yvonne would do. A black circle. The same as she had been doing on their farm. Atlas had seen the smoke come out of her mouth. He had told her that was how the Grey Spectre created the circle.

Beneath her feet Evie silently manipulated the roots of the sycamore trees. She could feel the rumble as soil was pushed aside, and how the roots twisted as they edged towards her deep underground. She needed a few more seconds until they reached Yvonne. Evie could make them move faster if she brought them above the soil but she wanted surprise on her side. She put her burning hand over Robbie's and turned her head to look at him. Her eyes moved to the boundary then back to him, imploring him to move further away. He followed her eyes. From beneath her own hand, he lifted his and rose her hand to his mouth, placed a kiss on the back of her hand and started to back away.

Her heart broke for Max and Rey who saw their friends with fathers but never had their own, and deep down she had hoped that maybe Damian might ask for half a day here and there, for their sake more than hers. Her life plans had been ruined, not by her carelessness as she had thought, but by a calculated move from an enemy with an accomplice. Evie digested the bomb that had been thrown at her. She held her head high, but she couldn't help asking Yvonne, 'Was it your idea for him to date me?'

'No. He was actually quite besotted with you. Even in my bed he'd talk about you.'

'You used him and his contacts to get on screen.'

'Yes. After I saw your meteoric rise, I knew they would never leave you alone. You were the darling of the media wannabes; young, beautiful and posh. I brought you onboard to keep you close. You had so much potential to fly, and you limited yourself because I told you to.'

'The threats, the social media posts...'

'That was me.'

'That was a mistake.'

'Really? I had you scared. Until recently.' Yvonne's eyes narrowed, the same way as Atlas's did.

Evie watched Yvonne's fingers point to the ground. Black smoke drifted from them with intention. Yvonne was casting a circle as she talked, keeping her occupied. Evie wished she'd studied the books Genevieve had sent her. Life had gotten in the way. They were still in the back of her cupboard.

'You did. Until you pushed too far. Are you so used to seeing people's spirits break you miss the signs that fear is no longer a reaction?' Evie stalled.

'They usually break well before you did. You were near, at one point.'

'Before you sent the threat to school.'

'Why did you stop being scared?'

'You showed that you started losing control of me when you tried to up your harassment game.'

'I'll work on that for Rey.'

'Rey doesn't have a gift.'

'Oh, she does, my darling. An amazing one. She possesses the ability of languages. I heard stories from him, about the first of you having that gift. She can learn any language she wants easily, but her words make people do what she wants. Like you, I almost missed it, except that day she caught me in your bedroom and told me to go away. I felt myself compelled to obey her and that was when I knew her extraordinary gift.'

'What about my brother?' Fear coursed through Evie and froze the roots below the soil as she wondered if Yvonne had already killed Atlas.

'The ability to transform into animals? I already have that, and I don't need it. Why be potential prey when I can simply project consciousness into one and listen in on conversations. If you die in animal form, you die. Your brother isn't the first to have that gift. Yours however, hasn't appeared since I first saw it in *his* sister, and it's even stronger in you than it was *in her*.' The way Yvonne sneered those last two words, her mouth curling distastefully as she added emphasis made it clear whose sister she meant.

Her life fell into place. Her parents' reference to the cat and mouse game Yrsa was playing. A life spent terrorised by the Grey Spectre. It was all a revenge game to Yvonne. The smoke had almost encircled her now. Evie realised she only had a little time to stop Yvonne, she had tried to stall by talking. Evie started to rise the sycamore roots to the surface. Slowly. Controlled. Surprise was her only advantage. Yvonne opened her mouth. A puff of smoke came out. Evie made the tree roots rise up and wrap themselves around Yvonne. Yvonne looked down at the roots. Then smirked and opened her mouth.

Black smoke emerged from her mouth. It rose up a centimetre then flooded outwards, its radius encompassing the circle Yvonne had cast. Evie ignored it and told the roots to carry on, rising up and covering Yvonne. The black smoke hit the tree roots and they stopped rising, turning black and shrivelled. Evie tried to force the roots up from under the ground. Inside her own body she could feel the shrivelled roots as they died faster than she could push them up to bind Yvonne. Black smoke hurtled towards her from Yvonne's mouth. It crashed into her and left her lungs on fire as she struggled to get air into them.

All the dead animals she had seen inside the circles over the years flashed through her head in images. This must have been how they had died. How they had suffered. The fire inside her lungs hurt. Her lungs had no air, yet they were painfully full, so full of something else that she couldn't get air into them. She bent over to try and catch a breath in ragged, ratchet breaths, each gasp more strangled than the previous one.

Evie began to see shimmering gold threads leading from Yvonne. She raised her head to look. She saw souls. All the souls Yvonne had collected over the years. Souls tethered to her for their gifts, subject to do Yvonne's bidding for eternity. Yvonne was calling on the same spell now, words were leaving her mouth instead of the black smoke. Evie tried to breathe. She tried to stand up despite the charred burning in her lungs, a piercing pain stitched a path through her heart.

Her hands held a different type of fire, she tried to switch her attention. The delicious heat inside her palms was different. Evie struggled to think of more ways to fight Yvonne. She had been better at this the first time around. Kat should never have come back to warn her. Dying in fifteen years seemed preferable, even avoidable if she had forewarning to plan for it, her last-minute change of plan had backfired.

The fire in her palms dampened and the heat began to dissipate. Another white-hot pain seared across her heart. Even without being told what it was, she knew. Her soul was being ripped from her. Her brows furrowed, her instincts overrode her ability to think. Her palms started their fire again and she placed them on the ground. Their warmth spread through her, giving her legs strength and circling upwards. Air found its way into her lungs, the charred burning slowly eased to a comfortable point, her throat worked again, allowing air to pass through.

Yvonne looked surprised. It was a miniscule flash across her face before the icy hatred descended. That split second was all the ammunition that Evie needed to continue. She defied years of self-control and built-up restraint and let her gift loose. She let the wildness return to her spirit. Grass green ink surrounded her hands and bounced around. Droplets fell into the ground as she slowly rose. Blackened grass grew green under her feet. The tree roots came alive again and continued winding their way around Yvonne to bind her.

Yrsa fully emerged from Yvonne. Her brown hair rapidly grew streaks of white in it. Her cheeks lost their fullness and sank. Evie was looking at a living skeleton. Yrsa began to struggle against the tree roots. She had thought she'd won. Evie smiled as she watched the roots reach Yrsa's fingers.

'I had Harriet switch the spell from you to me,' she shouted to Yrsa.

Fear, hate, and contempt filled her black eyes as she shouted, 'You know nothing! She's not even a true witch. It's impossible.'

Evie didn't take the time to register those words until later. When the roots had enough of Yrsa to hold her in place, Evie stopped concentrating on them. Instead, she aimed her green ink to dance and jump along the ground and up the roots before it spun directly into Yrsa's mouth. Another scream started to emerge, the green ink mixing with the smoke. Evie forced more into Yrsa's mouth, pouring it down her throat and inside her. She twisted it around her heart, tightening it so that the heart stopped beating. Painfully slowly, Yrsa began to age, her skin shrivelling, drying, loosening and wrinkling before turning grey. Her eyes, once so full of hatred, fell empty. Muscles and ligaments fell from her bones as it decayed. Her bones turned to ash and floated to the ground.

The sycamore tree roots formed a trunk in the shape of a woman, bare branches arched into the air in one direction only, towards Evie, as though emulating the last breath Yrsa had taken that hadn't quite reached her. The sycamore tree roots changed into rowan in an inexplicable move. Evie stood and looked, even after it was all over and her gift stopped, her palms returned to normal, she stood and watched. Waiting for the return of Yvonne.

It was when she accepted that Yvonne wasn't going to return, that she wasn't going to burst from the tree at any moment that she took a few steps forward. Resting her hand against the newly formed bark on the trunk she tried to feel for any presence of Yvonne. The tree was silent. There was nothing. In the distance, behind the trees a black shadow moved towards her. Evie jumped. It padded towards her, as cautious of her as she was of it.

The black shadow emerged as a wolf. Her heart pounded faster as she wished her brother could be with her to deal with this moment. Animals always behaved around him. It stopped a few metres from her. Closer, the amber eyes with flecks of grey were instantly recognisable. The reality of her day sank in as she whispered, 'Atlas?'

Chapter 26

The wolf lifted his head, its tail between his legs. It snarled. Evie jumped backwards, her heart in her mouth. Her stomach threatened to retch in fear. She edged away from the black fur until she bumped into Robbie and Liam behind her. She hadn't even realised that Liam had found them. As if acknowledging that he had scared her, Atlas took two paw steps away from her, still watching her intently.

'It took me a few minutes to realise it was Atlas. She'd thrown the key to the cage inside with him, he used his paw to push it to me. I told him your plan. He raced here and crept up around the back of her, ready to rip her to pieces. But you had the situation under control.' Liam caught her up on what she had missed in brief sentences.

'It didn't feel like I had it under control,' Evie admitted.

'I propose that we wrap this up, turn Atlas back, then go and drink a shitload of beer whilst everyone explains to me what happened and when witches became real,' Liam answered.

Robbie reached out and put a hand on the small of her back. Evie needed that gesture. She felt her bones relax a fraction and her shoulders dropped. His hand moved slowly up her back at that reaction to him, resting between her shoulder blades.

'I keep expecting her to burst out.'

'She's gone. We watched her age and crumble. Her skull fell to pieces.'

'I wish I had that confidence.'

'It's going to haunt my nightmares for a good few months.'

'Evie, how do we turn Atlas back?' The first words Robbie spoke brought her attention back to the immediate present. Evie raised her eyes to the wolf once again.

The fear in the wolf's eyes mirrored her own. Her brother was scared that he couldn't be changed back. That he was trapped in that form forever. Evie bent down and gestured for him to come forwards. It took a couple of minutes of small, hesitant steps before he reached her.

She whispered to him the only myths around shapeshifting wolves that she knew, 'The Faoladh is a shapeshifter that shifts into a wolf. But they are protectors. They are known to look after children and be kind. That's you Atlas. You look after us. You're a protector not a monster.'

Atlas looked at her when she finished speaking. The amber in his eyes changing back to grey. He laid down on the ground. Fur dropped and mounted in piles, washed off his skin by the rain. His snout shortened, then retreated. His paws turned into hands and feet.

Evie met his grateful eyes and smiled, 'Nice to see you again.'

'I needed to hear that,' he admitted. She gave him a nod and stood up, turning away she unfastened her coat and passed it behind her back to him.

'I don't need to see my brother naked.'

He took the coat from her and adjusted it, using the sleeves to tie it around himself, apron style. They walked back to the caravans in heavy silence, all lost in their own thoughts. Evie kept turning her head to look back, checking that the rowan tree still stood. She was still expecting Yrsa to emerge from it. She checked until it was out of sight, and then her thoughts sat uncomfortably in her stomach with the worry that she hadn't been successful.

Liam and Atlas took quick showers in Atlas's caravan to warm up. Evie made Robbie go in hers first. She turned on the heating and sat looking through the window with a rum and coke and worry on her mind, until Robbie emerged. Then she asked him to speak to his parents and check on her children. He took the rum and coke from her hand and pointed to the shower. She listened dully as he talked to his parents, picking up the beautiful queen from the chess set, the side that Atlas played, rolling the piece around in her fingers as she studied it whilst listening to the conversation that her children were fast asleep in bed and the house was locked up.

'The Halloween pyjamas you wore last time are on the bed for you.' She tried not to look at him, turning her back against his almost nakedness. She put the piece back, her eyes moved to her side of the chess board. All those years ago her brother had known what side she was on, the side of monsters, chaos and evil.

'I had you down for the princess in this fairy tale—' Robbie started.

Evie turned around and gave him a withering look that made him stop speaking. She would have liked to have been the person he saw her as. But she wasn't. 'I'm going to wash the mud off.'

'Evie—'

'You don't have to stay. I'm fine.'

'You're—'

'Cold. I'm just cold. I'd rather be left alone, thanks.'

The scathing hot water ran over her without warming her up. She went through the motions of showering without interest in her routine. She played the image of Yrsa's skin turning grey, then falling off her and her bones crumbling as the roots enclosed her into the new tree trunk, except, inside her head, this time the doubts played on her mind and inside the soil, Yrsa reformed. But behind that, she replayed the horror in Yrsa's eyes when she had looked at Robbie and said *Vidar*, and she knew that Robbie wouldn't leave because he would want to explain that to her.

Evie was in her bedroom, frozen into place, her brain stuck between wearing actual clothes or putting on fleecy loungewear, defence or warmth, when Atlas and Liam came back. Atlas pounded on her locked bedroom door twice, telling her to put some pyjamas on so that they could all talk, that no one expected to see her in her normal clothes after what they had all just been through. Through the thin walls she heard the metallic clink of bottles being opened and a subdued toast being made. Evie chose a pair of soft pink silk pyjamas teamed with an oversized hoody she kept to wear over layers on cold days on the farm. Make-up free, the mirror told her that her skin glowed and her eyes were bright. She padded out in grey sheepskin slippers. Robbie had refilled her rum and coke. He was only wearing the pyjama bottoms. Her eyes wandered as they took in his muscles, tattoos, the broad chest and she silently wondered if she would ever feel any of it under her fingertips again. She had a gut instinct that their light flirty easy relationship would never return after the events of the night.

He looked at her, full of silent questions of his own as he held out her drink. Evie took it from him, her fingers hesitatingly meeting his as she accepted the drink.

He offered a slight smile, relief crossing over his face, 'I was worried your walls would go up and we'd be back to the beginning. I was prepared to start all over again if I had to. I meant what I said, I can't lose you.'

Evie pushed her coldness and anger down for a minute. They were her weapons and she needed to store them for future use. Robbie's parents had her children. She still didn't know if the family were another threat to her.

'I'm sorry. About the curse. Did it hurt when she did it?'

'What curse?' Liam spoke up.

Evie and Robbie ignored him for a minute, 'Only as much as she hurt you,' Robbie said

'I couldn't breathe, that was the most intense pain I've ever felt in my life.'

'Yeah, it fucking hurt,' Robbie admitted.

'Again, what curse? What happened to my brother?' Liam's voice cut into their world.

'What's a Vandir?' Evie asked.

From the corner of her eye she didn't miss Liam's face darken. She waited. Strained silence hung in the caravan for an eternity, until Liam snapped at Robbie, 'How the fuck did she find out?'

'Yrsa knew, she cursed me and somehow she knew.' Robbie answered his brother but didn't take his eyes off her face.

Evie's stomach sank, whatever a Vandir was, it was not good for her. 'I'm going to get my children, I don't know what you are but I'm making sure my children are safe.' Evie snatched up a set of car keys from the kitchen top and moved away, towards the door of the caravan. Robbie grabbed her arm at the same time Liam jumped up from his seat too. Sensing the fight Atlas rose to his full height and blocked Liam from reaching her.

Evie looked down at Robbie's hand on her arm. Her blood froze in her body, anger simmered too close to the surface for her to control her gift, her jaw clenched to try and regain control as she slowly rose her eyes to him. Suddenly the kind eyes, the relaxed, laidback man was replaced by someone much harder, the summer blue eyes froze to ice. He was tensed, his muscles rigid.

'Max and Rey are safe. My parents won't touch them. I promise you that they're tucked up in clean beds in a safe home and they'll wake up to a fantastic breakfast spread in the morning. I won't let anyone hurt you by hurting them.'

'Get your hand off me.'

'Can we talk this out before the war starts?' The strain in his jaw only heightened her sense of danger. She looked over at her brother. He locked eyes with her. They were currently even, two against two. They could rescue her children after dealing with the brothers.

'It's always brothers.' Evie jerked her arm out of his grasp, 'first the McGregors, now you.' That comment only served to make Robbie angrier as he growled, 'We're nothing like the McGregors. If we were going to hurt you, don't you think we'd have taken the opportunity a few minutes ago? One on one? Or attacked Atlas two against one when you were still in the bedroom?'

Evie didn't answer him. The anger and tension simmered in the air of the caravan. No one moved, not even to breathe. Evie locked eyes with Robbie, neither of them was backing down. Robbie swallowed, she watched his throat bob as he pushed down anger. She knew that gesture, she'd forced herself to push her anger down far too many times. Evie vowed not to this time.

'Sit down please, let me explain, Evie,' Robbie asked.

Evie didn't recognise the man in front of her. This was the man who had put his hands around Yvonne's neck without thinking. This was who Yvonne had seen. There was a coldness, a force about him that she had missed. She wondered how she could have missed it. Had Harriet seen this side of him?

'I'm staying right by the door.' She had her hand on the handle ready to escape.

'Can we start with the fucking curse?' Liam spat.

Robbie didn't take his cold blue eyes from Evie, 'I can't be away from Evie for more than forty-eight hours or I'll die. I'm fine with that. I love her.'

'I know you love her, I didn't ask that, you idiot. I asked if you were going to die or not.' Liam's tone softened.

'I guess the answer is up to Evie.' His voice was low and soft, directed at her so that if they hadn't been in an enclosed space no one else would have heard. Although Evie had been there to see the whole scene unfold, it wasn't until she was stood in front of Robbie and heard his voice confirm it was her decision whether he lived or not that the truth really started to sink in.

Liam was the first to take a step backwards, away from Atlas. He gave her brother a conciliatory single nod, then he picked up another two beers, opened them, passed one to Atlas and sat back down. Atlas accepted the beer, not taking his eyes from Liam, still ready for a fight. He slowly moved further into the whiteness of the caravan to sit next to Liam on the settee, still acting as a buffer between her and the brother. Robbie took a few steps backwards into her caravan too, picking up her drink and offering it to her. Evie took the glass and downed the drink. Robbie reached out to reclaim her glass and silently refilled it with a much larger drink for her. Evie watched every movement, in a state of tensed anxiety. He passed her the drink and she took a step backwards as she did. Frustration and regret flitted across his face before it was quickly blank. The brown beer bottle was picked up and Robbie joined the other men in the living area. He stood at the far end of the caravan in front of the curved window. Evie stepped gingerly to the entrance to the dining and sitting room in her caravan. She refused to sit down.

She stared hard at Robbie, until her silence forced out his words, 'The name Vandir is an old ancient name, long forgotten, possibly used as a precursor to Tyr. There was once an Order of Vandir, charged with ridding witches and magic from lands that the Vikings wanted to invade. They had their own system of magic and beings, they didn't have the need for others.'

'Once upon a time you would have killed me?' Evie asked Robbie, she still hadn't taken her eyes off him. He shook his head.

Liam picked up the narrative in his normal voice, 'Like all ancient secret orders it's shrouded in mystery but we do know that even by the time Christianity hit the world, the Order was already ancient and had all but disappeared. By that time it had experienced its own problems over the years; internal arguments, changes of direction, becoming political, people like my brother falling in love with the so-called enemy,' Liam's voice was gentler now. He had reverted to his normal relaxed friendly tone.

Robbie pointed to a tattoo, an axe with detailed runic symbols, 'This is the mark of Vandir. But mum and dad are the heroes of this story. They broke away from Vandir teachings as soon as they were married, and raised us to believe that every witch, fae and other being deserves to live as much as we do. So long as there's no mass curses, plagues, end of world events, we don't have the right to interfere unless the threat to hurt someone takes a choice away from the person being hurt. Your fight with Yrsa tonight was one of equals, but if it hadn't been, we would have needed a different plan.'

'But there's others with different views. That's why villagers still talk, because so long as they can get the sheep on their side, they'll keep the stories and the divisions going. Their end game is the justification of any action taken against you, whether that's petitioning against your new houses, or against the building of the farm shops, or spreading rumours about the witch house. You should pay attention to the details, the ones that you missed, because the same group of names appears over and over again.'

It was the last sentence that made Evie look at Liam instead of Robbie. Then she looked at Atlas. Her brother's eyes met hers, they both knew there had been strong resistance to any plans on the farm, but they had dismissed the protests as people not liking change, they hadn't thought to go over the names and identify people.

Atlas took a drink of beer before he asked the brothers, 'Did you research us before approaching Evie?'

'No. After. Even though we'd heard rumours of the farm and the witches we were focused on other things, then Gia popped up and I was worried for you, her name is quite well known amongst the handful of self-proclaimed remaining Vandir for openly practising. In New Orleans its mostly live and let live, but even so, I had to make sure she wasn't a threat to you.' Robbie hadn't taken his eyes off Evie.

'You've researched Gia?' Atlas almost spat out his mouthful of beer. Evie's brow furrowed as confusion filled her about the depth of his anger. Robbie gave a single nod.

'Have you researched all my friends?' she asked. She felt Atlas's eyes on her, surprise evident in his expression. He knew that tone even though he hadn't heard it for years. She turned her head and looked at him. He cast a worried face to Robbie even as he shifted forward to the edge of his seat and put the bottle down slowly on the floor, ready to get between the two of them.

'No.'

The way it was said made Evie finish the sentence for him, 'Not yet.'

At her words Robbie at least had enough shame to look at the floor of the caravan.

Evie wanted out, out of the caravan, the relationship, the shame of believing that she had something with Robbie. There were so many holes in the story she had been fed that she only half believed it. Her next question was direct, even as her heart beat faster and her breathing grew shallower in panic, her legs started to shake she asked, 'If the mark of Vandir is a tattoo, why did you get it? Why not just do what your parents did and adopt the live and let live approach?'

'Vandir as it stands, has deviated from its origins. The tattoo is just a mark. I don't know how it started, the stories

292

we're fed is that a witch once cursed a group of Vandir. The curse became a bloodline. It's no different from you being born with the ability to be able to grow plants in your hand. A tattoo won't change or alter that ability. Bloodline Vandir see things normal people don't. Inherited Vandir, another sort of faction, are just misogynistic power-hungry conspiracy crazy people that I want to keep you away from.'

'Did it let you see who I was?'

'No. What we see are shadows and odd things that are just not quite right. You passed as normal because you're a decent person, Evie. The farmhouse on the other hand, that wasn't right. There were definitely things about that house that were off. We both knew we couldn't walk away from that job and leave you all in there to face it yourself. Yrsa had made it that way with the circle underneath. When I showed it to you, you clearly didn't recognise what it meant.'

'I was ready to interrogate you, Robbie thought you deserved a chance,' Liam added.

'When we tore that place apart, Liam and I were looking for anything that matched the uneasy feel of the place. It didn't have to be done as carefully as we did, but if we missed the cause, you might have had a shitshow happening here with Max and Rey around.'

'So you get to decide who lives and who dies according to your morals?'

'No.'

'We've never killed anyone. We've never had a decision that hard. Things, yes, people, no.' Liam spoke up, his face as serious as his tone.

Robbie spoke next, 'Those houses I told you about?

The ones that we lived in? They had things in them, bad things. We dealt with those.'

'We're not talking about actual people anymore?'

'No.'

'I don't believe in any of the other stuff.'

'I know. I will do my best to ensure you never come across any of it. Ever,' Robbie told her.

Evie shook her head, 'I don't need protecting.'

'It's less about protecting and more about letting you be the person you want to be. I love watching you laugh and enjoy yourself. You barely know how to relax, you grew up in a fucking nightmare, having someone walk your house at night. You've had someone threatening to end your life. You don't need to add this shit. I'll handle it for us.' He looked at her with hope. Evie still hadn't forgiven him.

'This whole time, you could have said something,' she accused.

He shrugged, 'Likewise. It's not the easiest, most everyday subject to bring up in conversation. I tried that night when you ran out barefoot in the rain, and again after we'd spent the day with Gia, I thought you might open up, but you shut both conversations down fast.'

'Did you ever think, or know, what I was?'

'Not until last night. My focus was on the house and the things in there.'

'His focus was on looking after you and the kids and making sure nothing got to you.' Liam looked at her with an expression of intent, as though he could project how much his brother liked her from across the room.

'How do I know you mean all those words? That you're not playing my sister?' Atlas's voice was calm.

Robbie looked at him, before looking back at Evie, 'I guess time. Like I said in the café, only my actions will prove how I feel, words are easy.'

'This Vandir cult, who's in yours?'

'My family and Shane. We work together and we keep it private.'

Evie felt the surface of her anger being scratched off like sandpaper would rub a surface. It was still there, but tiny grains were being rubbed away. Her eyes fixed on Robbie whilst her brain turned over every word he had spoken.

'I can see you overthinking, it's taking all I've got not to walk over and hold you and tell you it's going to be alright.'

Evie shook her head and took a step back at his offer. She didn't need his arms around her. 'Why come here? You said that it was your dad's ambition. But why?'

'It's as simple as dad saw a few postcards of Yorkshire as a child. He fell in love with the English villages and countryside and said he'd come here one day. Believe me, we all had doubts about coming here or staying here. We all missed home at different points.' It was Liam that answered her.

'I can speak for myself.' Robbie looked at Liam, amused. Liam shrugged. It was clear he was protective over his older brother. Evie suspected it was returned equally.

'Are you going to let him die?' Liam asked Evie.

'Of course not. I'm just not sure about whether I'm safe, whether my children are safe if he's around.'

'Of course he's going to keep you safe. Right now, he needs you more than you need him. If I know my brother, he's at least fifteen steps ahead of you in being safe, in his head he's already got Shane fitting a security system to your new house.'

'Security?' She looked at Robbie, alarm already running through her body and thoughts of being imprisoned in her own home.

'Thanks Liam.' Robbie's tone dripped with sarcasm. He looked at Evie when he answered, 'The houses aren't built yet, we're still building them. There's plenty of time to talk about installing security for you. Even just to check on deliveries when Max and Rey are teenagers and home by themselves. At some point they're going to start to ask to stay home alone again, and you'll have to trust yourself that they're going to be OK.'

'He's got a point. We didn't plan for it to go wrong,' Atlas spoke.

Evie took a step to the dining booth and perched on the end of the seated booth like a bird ready to take flight. She looked at the three men, then at her hands. She considered that her nails still looked perfect, after everything they had been through. All the fear was tearing her insides, but no one would ever see it.

Before she looked up Robbie was crouched next to her, 'If anything ever happens on the farm again, wouldn't you rather have a team to protect the children? You don't have to do it all alone. Let us in Evie, let me be there for you.'

Evie heard the gentle voice, when she looked, she saw her Robbie again. Summer blue eyes in a tanned face, she reached out with her left hand and trailed her fingers from his shoulder to his collar bone. He didn't take his eyes off her, he didn't flinch or show fear, she looked for anger or hatred, but she didn't see any. Evie gave a slow nod. The caravan seemed to sigh with relief. Atlas pulled out a phone and pressed a few buttons. Evie could hear a ringing tone. She looked at her brother, confused.

'I'm bloody starving. What's everyone's pizza order?' Atlas asked.

Chapter 27

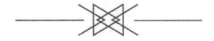

Late the next afternoon whilst Robbie was still working, the four of them took their own off-road bikes up to the field with the row of sycamore trees. Atlas wanted to check that the tree was still there as much as she needed to. To know somehow that Yrsa was permanently trapped. The rowan tree stood, its branches still arched as a final breath headed towards where Evie had stood. Then they rode home with the winter light fading behind them, heading towards the building site, their caravans, a chicken and rice one pot meal in the oven in Evie's caravan for them all.

When they were putting the bikes away in the barn, as Max and Rey raced towards the caravan with her key, Atlas asked her, 'What do we say when it's noticed that Yvonne is missing?'

'The truth? That my threats have stopped too. That my work is a better place. That I didn't like her profession-ally and we didn't see each other outside of work.'

It took a week before Yvonne's absence was mentioned in the studio. Evie acted as though she hadn't overheard Jess discussing it on the phone with HR. She had no idea who informed the police Yvonne was missing. The first she heard of police involvement was from Gia, over a coffee in the farm café. The optician's shop had been questioned, they'd told the police that Yvonne had failed to collect her contact lenses. That the police had called into

Yvonne's house and found it open and empty, everything still in its place, including her phone, as though she had popped out and never returned.

Jess was the one who blew it up into a big deal. Evie suspected that the police might have let it remain as a missing person until Jess told them that she knew Yvonne would never leave her phone anywhere because she was addicted to social media. Rumours began to run around the studio. Evie kept her head down. She had a few brief questions from the police, but everyone told the same story, Yvonne had made work hell, and no one was friends with her outside of work. No one in the studio missed her.

It came as a surprise when she answered her caravan door to find a uniformed officer and Oliver there. The dislike in Oliver's eyes made her uneasy, Evie ran her brain over their last few encounters, trying to remember what she had done to him. They introduced themselves, flashed ID, and Evie reluctantly invited them inside out of courtesy, checking her phone before she sat down. Robbie and Liam had gone away for a friend's stag weekend. He was due back in the next few hours, pushing the forty-eight hours that Yrsa had told them they had. In his last text he had been fine, they were in the car, hungover but on their way back, stopping off at a motorway service station for drinks and burgers.

'Are your children here? Robbie?'

'Max is at a go-karting party, Harry's mum will drop him back. Rey is at Sophia's for the afternoon to play. Robbie is with Liam at a stag night.'

'So it's just you? Great, it's just a few questions.' Oliver sat down at her dining table and pulled out some paperwork.

'When did you join the police, Oliver?' Evie sat down opposite him. The uniformed police officer looked between them.

'I joined their graduate detective scheme after university.'

'You realise it's not really protocol if you two know each other?' the uniformed officer interjected.

Oliver dismissed the statement with arrogance, 'We know of each other, we don't know each other. We attended the same school, we didn't move in the same friendship group. Evie was always with a super select group of cool kids. I was a nerd.'

'That's not how I remember it. You put your hand up to answer questions and saved me when the history teacher picked on me. You sat next to me in sociology and you'd point to the answer in the textbook when I was asked a question. We didn't do A Levels together, you did humanities, right?'

'Yes, History, Sociology and English. You took all three Sciences and Spanish and became the teachers' favourite with those choices. My dad loved you.'

'Your dad?'

'He was the Head at the time.'

'Mr Metcalf was your dad? I never knew. You had a different surname.'

'I lived with my mum in the shop you stole butter from. You were wrapped up in yourself. You and your friends, all of you.'

'I might have been. We might have been,' Evie agreed with a nod. They had been so busy hiding their own secrets and each other's that noticing too much about the other students was difficult.

Oliver looked at the papers in front of him and Evie took a sip of her tea. Despite the conversation his frosty demeanour hadn't changed. Evie didn't talk, the quicker the questions were over the faster she could get the pair out of her caravan and get on with her day. The look of confusion on the uniformed officer's face was replaced with a mask of professionalism.

Oliver started, 'When was the last time you saw Yvonne?'

'The last time? I think it was the meeting someone posted online. Where I quit.'

'But you're still there?'

'Temporarily at the moment. Without a contract. We're in talks.'

'We've been told that you said it's you or Yvonne.'

'That's not true. I specifically said I don't want to work with Yvonne anymore but if the show still wanted us both I would agree to a workaround. She can keep her executive producer and presenter roles and work separate days to the days the studio wants me in. I'm willing to be reasonable.'

'On the day you said you quit, Yvonne said she owned you. Tell us about that?'

'I was naïve when I let the show give me a contract and I agreed that they could control my image. Back then all I wanted was to work and come home, so when they proposed this idea of presenting me as a city person I agreed. To an extent the studio did own my image, they'd created a whole persona for me and expected me to keep it up. Maybe Yvonne phrased it poorly, but she wasn't wrong either. When someone took a picture of me walking back up to the farm the day Robbie came to survey the house Jess and Yvonne went apeshit at me because it didn't fit the image that they wanted me to have. Tensions just escalated after that.'

Evie forced herself to sound reasonable. She was already on record as not liking Yvonne. Oliver clearly held a grudge against her for something. Her instincts were telling her to be careful and very safe. She took another sip of her tea and looked down. She was in jeans and a jumper, presentable but not pretentious. She had slippers on. She'd had her nails redone with Jae, a black tipped French this time. Evie reassured herself that she looked approachable and normal.

Oliver spoke again, 'We were going through Yvonne's phone and we found the original images of you on it, the photos that were uploaded to the internet. Of you and Robbie. Were you aware that she was the person posting your life online?'

'No. I didn't even know she lived in the village. I don't want my children online, those photos with them definitely crossed a line. But, like I said, she owned my image. As an executive producer she probably made a decision to boost ratings. I'd like to know why she didn't approach me and talk about it first.'

'Would Yvonne reach out to you if she was in trouble?'

'I don't think so. Our last fight was put on the internet. We weren't really on friendly terms.'

'Do you think that bothered her?'

'Yvonne? No. I think she liked the drama she caused.'

'You posted on social media on Halloween. You're not a regular poster on social media.'

'I wasn't really allowed to do much social media without the show's approval. They controlled my image.

We had a really good show that day. I was happy again, and a little spooked walking up to the field. It was a spur of the moment thing.'

'What did you do afterwards?'

'Came home, had a shower, spent the night with Robbie, Liam and Atlas. We had some drinks, ordered pizza,' she shrugged.

'There's talk that your brother went missing that day.'

'Atlas caught a sickness bug the previous day, twenty-four hours of vomiting. He was a bit weak that night but fine.'

The caravan door flew open. Liam was holding Robbie up, half pulling, half dragging him into the caravan. He stopped in shock when he saw the police officer and Oliver. He gave a nod to Oliver and pulled Robbie through to Evie's bedroom. Evie followed him. Without even asking, her face implored them to tell her what had happened. Liam released Robbie onto the bed. Robbie struggled to open his shirt. The skin over his heart was bruised and thick black veins had begun to stretch outwards.

'She said forty-eight hours.' Liam stared at Evie as though she had the answers.

A knock on the door was followed by the uniformed officer's voice, 'Is everything OK in there?'

Liam opened the door and slipped out, closing it behind him. Evie could hear as his voice reassured the pair, filled with lies quickly designed to hurry their exit, 'He's got the sickness bug. And he's hungover as fuck. Do you need Evie or are you done?'

'We're done with Evie for now. Where were you on Halloween?' She heard Oliver's cold voice cut through the wall.

'Here. We had a few drinks and played cards, got pizza.'

'With just Evie?'

'No, my brother and her brother.'

'Thank you. Can you ask Evie to come out.'

Evie came out, closing the door behind her. Oliver stared at her, scrutinising her, as though he knew she was lying and he needed just one tiny slip to prove she had killed Yvonne.

Instead the uniformed police office spoke, 'We found stacks of these in Yvonne's house. Do you recognise it?' she handed Evie a small black envelope, the thickness of the card brought on a racing heart and a panic.

Evie nodded. The words sank into her head, 'In Yvonne's house? She was the one threatening me?'

'Have you had any more threats since her disappearance?'

'Actually, no, I haven't.' Evie met the uniformed officer's eyes and handed the card back. She hoped that she sounded innocent when she asked, 'Why would she do that to me?'

'We don't have that answer.'

'We'll be in touch. Don't disappear.' Oliver told her as they left.

Evie closed the door after them and went into the bedroom. She sat on the bed next to Robbie, touched Robbie's black veined skin tentatively, looking for a reaction from him as to whether it hurt or not.

He placed his hand over hers and kept it there, 'It only hurts inside.' His voice was gravelly and low.

'Can you fix it?' Liam came back into the bedroom.

Evie shook her head, 'I don't know. She said he'd die

if he spent forty-eight hours away from me. It hasn't been forty-eight hours.'

'Forty-four, I put a countdown on my phone, just in case. Maybe just being here is enough.' Robbie rasped.

'She said she'd like to watch how it played out. That must mean there's a way to recover.' Liam spoke, his eyes accusing her of hiding the answers.

'I'm so sorry I dragged you into this.' Evie leaned forward and gave him a tender kiss. She looked back down when she pulled back, trying to think of a way to heal Robbie.

'Try again.' Robbie reached for her. Her lips met his in a kiss. His hand swept up to her hair. He kissed her back. She pulled away after a few seconds. The bruising was fading. Robbie was breathing easier.

Liam edged forward for a look. 'Lucky bastard, that's a cure. What did Oliver want?'

'He was questioning me. I get the impression he's trying to tie me to Yvonne's disappearance. I don't know what I've done to make him hate me.'

'He changed at university. We used to train together at the rugby club. He got into religion in a big way. Not in an intelligent way either. You've got to be careful, Robbie could die if Oliver finds anything.'

'He won't find anything.' Evie widened her eyes in warning at Liam for even bringing up that night.

'I'll see you both at mum's tomorrow for dinner. Tell Atlas I'll beat him at pool.' He left with goodbyes. Satisfied she wasn't going to hurt him further Evie leaned over and gave him another long kiss.

When they finally pulled away, Robbie smiled, 'If I'm going to be cursed, I like this one. Cured by kisses, can't be away from you, I can live with this.'

'We've got a few minutes until I have to collect Rey.'

Chapter 28

Through the woodland canopy autumn leaves flew downwards in a wild wind, warm grey clouds above were starting to gather. She could still see blue patches in the sky. She scrambled down the bank into a ditch that ran close to the entire length of the public footpath and placed her hand at intervals.

Green liquid warmed her hand, pushing its way into the soil, fixing the problems that had been created generations before. Droplets spilled as she walked and small green shoots of plants pushed their way up as though it was a warm spring day. Ahead of her Max and Rey played. Robbie walked alongside on the footpath. When the banks where as high as her head and the ditch ended, she heard an amused voice, 'Are you supposed to be in the ditch?'

'Yes.' She looked up at Robbie's handsome face. She wondered why he'd bothered to dress in new clothes for a walk in the woods, the gilet open, his new hoody and jeans not yet muddy.

'Do you need a hand?'

'I could use a hand.' She smirked, letting her thoughts go to less innocent places.

He laughed and shook his head, 'The more I get to know you the more I realise that you really do keep yourself hidden until you trust people. Is it done?' He reached out an arm and pulled her up from the ditch so that she fell into his chest. Evie stayed there. She looked up at him. He held her tightly, one arm around her waist, the other cupping her jaw. He kissed her.

Evie smiled and returned his kisses playfully, 'It is. No paperwork, no form filling, did anyone see?' She looked around, checking that they were still alone.

'I wanted to do that the first time.' He still didn't let her go. Evie smiled back, she raised her hands to his stubbly jaw and kissed him again.

When she pulled away, mindful of Max and Rey, she checked their plans with him, 'Are we still OK for lunch at the café then we'll sit the worst of the storm out this evening in the caravan?' Around them the wind was lifting up leaves and old worn branches creaked with the threat of falling.

Robbie nodded, 'I've joined the matching pyjamas bandwagon.'

'You could have had pink ones like Rey and me,' Evie teased.

'Actually, there's something else I'd like you to be wearing with those pyjamas.' He loosened his grip on her.

Evie's mind flashed through her underwear, trying to predict which ones were his favourites, she'd learnt that he had a soft spot for white lace. She did not expect him to drop down to one knee amongst the leaves, the dirt and the wind. He pulled out a small black box from his pocket. Max and Rey ran over and stood either side of him, grinning.

A gust of wind took his words so all she heard was, 'Will you be my wife?' He opened the box to reveal an emerald ring, diamonds either side of it, the cut and style giving a hint to vintage, but new and modern.

'We helped to choose it. The emerald is the Northern lights and the diamonds are stars,' Max told her.

'As my promise that I know it's not just you, it's Max and Rey too.' Robbie added.

'You knew and you kept the secret?' Evie wondered how they'd managed to keep a secret from her when she thought that they told her everything.

Rey looked at the ground, 'I might have accidentally told you a few times then told you to forget it.' She was playing with her gifts now that they knew what they were. Evie didn't like that, Rey was still young but if she could compel her mum to forget now, the possibilities for a potentially wild teen were endless.

'I checked with them, I gave them a chance to tell me that they weren't alright with it.'

After the curse, Robbie and Evie had been honest with Max and Rey about both their relationship and the reasons behind it going faster than planned. It eased Max and Rey into Robbie being around more gradually. It was only Evie who was surprised by how well Max and Rey had taken to Robbie's presence in their lives. She reasoned that it was due to the fact that Robbie was laidback, as happy to bake with them as he was to teach them how to restore furniture, or fix their bikes, or play board games with them. Atlas told her she was blind, that even the children could see she was a better person with Robbie around, she relaxed more, laughed more, and added spontaneity back into her life.

'I'm kind of dying here.' Robbie drew her attention back to the ring. Evie realised she was stood, staring, overthinking.

'Yes.' Evie smiled, pushing aside the warning voices in

her head that were getting quieter and quieter as the weeks passed. Robbie was open with her, about every-thing, about the house his father had just acquired with some entity in, about the fact that her architect had been approached about a renovation TV show and suggested Robbie as a co-presenter because he knew buildings and was good with people. Evie had told Robbie that his relaxed way of discussing buildings, finances and situations would go across well on the programme.

Robbie took the ring from the box and slid it onto her finger. It fitted perfectly. He stood up with a smile, catching her hand as they continued to walk behind Max and Rey he said, 'I knew from the moment I met you I was going to propose to you in that spot.'

Evie looked at the ground as they walked, greys and browns merged into each step they took. The wind whipped her hair around. Her hand tightened on Robbie's as she admitted, 'I was thinking about asking you in a few months up near the sycamore row. That's where you saw who I really was.'

'I saw who you really were that first day, Evie, when I realised the gossip about you being stuck up and snobby was wrong. You were reserved, not without reason, but you were talkative enough, and happy, and you didn't give a fuck what the villagers were saying. I liked you then and I've loved you more with everything I've learnt about you. I love that you have a sexy mischievous side that no one else sees. I love that you only care for a very few people but you'd put your life on the line and set the world on fire to keep them safe. I can't protect you as well as you can protect them, but I want to be there for you.'

They stopped at a ridge and looked down, into the

distance, where Yvonne's cottage stood. Police tape danced in the wildness of the wind, torn and battered. Evie had stayed away. Robbie reported that occasionally there was a police car there.

'What happens to it now?' she wondered.

'My best guess is the bank will take it back, unless she owns it outright and the police find a relative.'

'That's not an outcome we want. I don't want the next Yvonne moving in.'

'You are the next, Evie. Remember Harriet's spell?'

'The blood ritual doesn't have to continue anymore. It's not something that I want. I'm happy to die. Obviously when I'm old.'

Max and Rey shouted them.

Evie and Robbie moved past the ridge, turning towards the fields. They came out of the woods and saw the five sycamores ahead in the distance. Evie's hand gripped Robbie's as it always did when they walked to check that the little rowan tree still stood in its place. The womanly shaped tree hid perfectly at the angle they approached from, the bare bark merged seamlessly with a sycamore behind it. Evie always held her breath the last few paces when the trunks split to reveal the landscape separating the two trees.

She relaxed when she saw it was all as they had last left it. Her grip on Robbie loosened as it always did, and he squeezed her hand in response, a quick squeeze, no words had to pass between them for him to understand the anxiety and trepidation that overtook her at the thoughts of having to confront Yrsa again. Once they reached the sycamore row, they turned again and headed down the fields to the caravans and the farm café, repeating the walk

Robbie and Evie had taken on Halloween. The wind blew in their faces and through their hair, nobody spoke again until they were seated in the farm café.

Thirty years after that first meeting, Anders, son of Eric, strode to the forest clearing. He built a small fire, cursing the drizzle that thwarted his attempts. Once it was hot enough, he set up a rabbit roasting over it. Without looking up he called out, 'I have my sword but I'll not hurt you today. Come and sit with me.'

She edged forward, wrapped in winter clothes, graceful and as smooth in her movements as the small wildcats that roamed the land. He watched from the corner of his eye. After all these years, she was still as cautious as the wild animals around her. He had thought her grown when they had first met but now he understood she had been but a child. Now she was grown. Lines had begun to etch her face that made her, somehow, look kinder and wilder at the same time. She had lost the hair colour that changed with the seasons allowing her to blend into the forest, but she gained another beauty in age. She drew closer to the fire in silence, tall and proud.

'You've led a good life, Anders. Now your name lives on in the sons of Anders.'

'And your beauty lives on in your daughters, although I still don't know your name. Please, sit.'

'In your language it translates into summer's evening. In our language it relates to a specific moment in a summer's evening when the sun reaches the horizon. It means warmth, orange, glow, summer and evening.'

'How did you learn our language?'

'I like languages. Yours, ours, others, the birds, the wind, everything speaks.'

He folded one hand over a closed fist, his elbows on his knees and gave a nod to show that he had heard. 'In all my journeys and battles I've thought of you often.'

'I know. I can slip into people's dreams. I kept track of you. Even when you went across the seas. Our fates were interwoven a long time ago.'

'Sometimes I think the blood we spilled is meaning-less, that your way might be the right way. You hold no anger, no relentless desire to kill or maim despite what we were told.' A rack of coughing hit him.

'It seems we are destined to die at the same hour, Anders.'

'You have seen this?'

'Yes. A long time ago when you trapped me on the cliff. For you, time carried on. For me, the world stood frozen when I looked into your eyes and our lives with all their possibilities unfolded. There was one constant. An enemy would end as a friend. Our lives would end at the same time, no matter when that was. I have told my daughters and their husbands where to find us. I have instructed them in your customs. Your soul will go to your great hall.'

'Where does your soul go, summer's eve?'

'I am of the trees. I belong right here where we are. But others go where they belong, the sky, the rivers, the sand, the sea, the moors, the rocks, we all have a place with the ancestors.'

'It would be an honour to die in your company. Good conversation and a beautiful woman. I could not ask for

313

more on my last night. I think my future son will be happy with your future daughter, summer's eve.'

'I hope so. The women in my family are a wild handful. I don't know why I presumed that being a mother of daughters would be easy.'

He laughed at that, loud and long, followed by another bout of coughing. Unlike the time she had nursed his sword injury and fever when she had treated him with softness, she kept her distance now. She treated him as an equal. A friend.

'When will it happen?'

'Not for thousands of years, until they have both forgotten their origins, when they meet as people, not enemies, not as Vandir and a witch, as you call us.'

White Rose Witches

Watch out for the next book from Georgie St-Claire in the White Rose Witches saga.

In the rolling green hills of Yorkshire sits a quaint, picturesque stone village where the white rose witches are both their own heroes and their own worst enemies.

The group of women were once close knit childhood friends. As adults they are scattered over the world. Evie broke the spell intended to separate them from each other, now, one by one, they're free to find their way home. Not all might stay, nor all survive the trials they face.

It is possible that by trying to control the future with one spell, Yrsa inadvertently changed the future of all the friends.

Follow them into their powers as adult women on their journey to find a place called home:

Gia ~ Tess ~ Liberty ~ Kat ~ Nina ~ Genevieve and Isolde

Georgie St-Claire was born in Yorkshire. At age three she contracted meningitis and lost a large portion of her hearing. Her earliest memories include loving being alone, getting into trouble for not hearing teachers' instructions, and relishing quiet reading time.

Georgie wrote her first story at age six. She found it clearing out her parents' house. She clearly had no understanding of punctuation; every sentence ran into the next with 'and then' for a whole page of A4.

She loves reading, weird films, dark folklore and myths but refuses to watch horror films about how bad humans can treat other human beings.

Her schooling was in Doncaster, before attending Coventry University. Georgie is intrigued by different magical practises, psychology, social anthropology and pre-history. She loves art, especially abstract cityscapes.

She spent a few years as a volunteer reading mentor in a primary school supporting children to read in her spare time and is currently a secondary school governor, vice chair (chair's nomination choice and not a comfortable place to be with hearing issues), Safeguarding and Careers Lead governor. She has two perfectly hearing secondary school aged children and is trying to learn BSL.

Georgie can be found on Facebook, Instagram, and TikTok. She runs 'Teaser Tuesdays' releasing short extracts, 'Research Thursdays' sharing notes and research, and 'Scenic Sundays' to build a picture of Yorkshire.

BAD PRESS iNK
publishers of niche, alternative and cult fiction

Visit

www.BADPRESS.iNK

for details of all our books, and sign up to
be notified of future releases and offers

Also from BAD PRESS iNK

Bella is defective. You need to take her back.
Everyone tells her she is normal. Everyone is lying.
Eugenics, chimeras and the fierceness of a mother's
love in a terrifying near future.
All three books in The Take Her Back Trilogy.

Two love affairs and two summers, 75 years apart.

Cantankerous Tilly is determined to grow old disgracefully.

Shy Ava is finding out looking after the elderly was never meant to be like this!

Future Imperfect – the new eco-thriller from
BAD PRESS.iNK

Climate catastrophe isn't in the future... it's now.

Climate refugees aren't other people... they're you.

Printed in Great Britain
by Amazon